BLIND JUSTICE

An Innocent Bystander

Tania Park

National Library of Australia Cataloguing-in-Publication entry
Creator: Park, Tania, author.
Title: Blind Justice : an innocent bystander / TaniaPark;
Laila Savolainen, illustrator.
ISBN: 9780994284747 (Paperback)
ISBN: 9780994284754 (Ebook)
Subjects: Suspense fiction.
Detective and mystery stories.
Dewey Number: A823.4

Printed & Channel Distribution
Lightning Source | Ingram (USA/UK/EUROPE/AUS)

Also by Tania Park

Mistaken

'*He never got around to telling me why he wanted me dead.*'

Bella Perez had just landed a more lucrative position in a larger company. The twenty-seven year old widow was content with her life as an accountant. When her new boss whacked her across the head and dropped her over a cliff, her life changed in an instant. She became a naïve pawn caught in a very dangerous game.

Retribution

Living with a new identity in a different state on the other side of the country, Amy Masters is stunned and terrified when her ex-husband turns up at her place of work. After almost killing her, he is supposed to be still in jail.

Amy spends the next week of her life in hiding as she makes plans to escape the clutches of Rico and his family crime gang once again. It is a week when details she never dreamed about, are revealed

Chapter One

Death.
     The aroma was in the air. Too soon to be a stench it was more like a heavy sensation. A sibilant hiss of frustration escaped as his gut wrenched then twisted tight at the unpleasant but familiar scent: too familiar. As he stepped over the threshold, Ben Somers unzipped his sodden raincoat, slipped both arms out of the sleeves then shook off as much water as he could before entering any further. Before moving closer to the man who stood waiting for him he ran his fingers through his hair to rid it of any drops.

'What happened, John?'

'A man, the owner, was shot. First indications are that he may have surprised someone breaking in but it's hard to tell.'

'Wife? Family?' Ben asked as he glanced around the room taking in the opulence of the furnishings. Rich people. He sighed. Such easy targets. But wealthy people tended to have homes alarmed. He searched for sensors, saw none and shook his head. Stupid.

'Only the wife,' John interrupted his line of thought. 'She was upstairs asleep when she heard the shots. At first she didn't know what the noise was then she found her husband in a pool of blood. Death would have been instant.'

Ben raised his eyes then always seeking the smallest inconsistency, glanced down at the sleek gold watch on his wrist. 'It's a bit early to be in bed isn't it?'

'Jetlag. Been overseas. Only arrived home early this morning.' Sergeant John Markham, his second in command and best friend, tracked his eyes over Ben's clothes and hooked up one brow. 'You're a bit overdressed for this aren't you?'

Glancing down at the sharp creases in his well-cut trousers, his favourite pale blue shirt with a darker tie and expensive leather jacket, Ben winced. His outfit showed more wealth than a detective usually earned but he liked to look smart when off duty and with a reasonable inherited wealth, which brought him excellent returns from wise investments, he could afford it. But he was on his way out to dinner when he'd been called. Again.

'Yeah, you know I'm supposed to be off duty. I have a dinner date and I'm already late. Damn phone rang halfway to the restaurant.' He grimaced. 'Looks like I'll have to ring the hotel. Trish doesn't keep her mobile switched on in public places.' An inconvenience for him since he usually needed to call her at the most awkward of times – like now.

Knowing full well this delay would not be appreciated, Ben huffed on a long sigh as he slid his mobile phone from the inside pocket of his jacket. In recent weeks Trish had made her thoughts about his irregular hours very clear so he figured another messed up date wasn't going to go down at all well. From the outset of their meeting Trish had known about his job, the kind of hours it entailed and that he could be called in to work at any time. Things had been fine for about six months, but of late she seemed to be less understanding. He couldn't really blame her considering, lately, he had been called in after hours more and more often. Quite a few dates had been cut short or cancelled at very short notice.

Turning away for a modicum of privacy Ben called headquarters and asked his desk sergeant to find the number of the hotel where he was supposed to already be dining. Message given he nodded to John who led the way through the tastefully decorated house until they reached a study.

A cursory glance showed two walls lined with glass-panelled bookshelves; the books in neat lines according to subject and size. A heavy antique desk stood in the middle of the room with another more modern desk abutted at right angles. The second desk supported an extensive range of computer and electronic equipment, while the magnificent oak desk held only two stacks of trays along the back. Nothing else adorned the surface, showing the beautiful patina of the centuries-old wood under a thin layer of dust which supported the owner's absence.

Ben dropped his eyes to the floor where an old striped flannel sheet covered the bloodied body just a few metres inside the room. Not the standard police cover so someone inside must have provided it. The wife? Why would she take the time to retrieve a sheet if she was traumatised? His eyes slid skywards. Please don't let this be a family spat gone wrong?

Even the sheet couldn't hide the extensive dark red stain. For a brief moment he didn't hear the scuffles of Forensic officers already scouring for evidence as his thoughts centred on the victim.

'Poor bugger must have bled to death,' he muttered.

A volley of regular flashes shot his attention back. After acknowledging the police photographer, he knelt on one knee by the sheet. As he lifted a corner his stomach knotted tight at the sight of the bullet-ridden body. Ah hell. He stared at the deceased with regret and pity for the uncalled-for slaughter – for slaughter it was, the chest looking like the hole-riddled bullseye on a well used dart board. His innards tightened, as did fists that wanted to punch the perpetrator into a pulp. But calm was needed so he could do his job and find the animal that did this. No matter how many times he encountered death, it always cut deep.

'Nasty business, John, what do we know?'

A pair of black leather lace-ups requiring a good polish came into view. John. Shoe-shining was not one of his strengths. In fact Ben doubted John's shoes ever received a lick of polish from the time they were bought until they were binned.

'Not a great deal yet,' John said as he squatted next to Ben. 'Victim is Mr Tony Bates. Runs his own import business with his wife, Kathy. They were away on a buying trip. Been away five weeks. Came home a week early so no-one knew they were back. They were hoping to have a week of peace and quiet. It'll be quiet for him now.'

Twisting his head sideways, Ben shot John a frown. The comment was a tad sick and uncalled for.

John flinched. 'Sorry. Five bullets to the chest: .38 by the look of things. We're searching for a sixth bullet. Mrs Bates is upstairs in the bedroom. There's a female officer with her. She can't give us any reason for Mr Bates being a target. Says the business is legit. We'll need to investigate. The fact that they were supposed to still be away leads me to think this could be a random burglary gone wrong. The house could have been cased for days to ascertain if anyone was home.'

'You could be right but then why break in when it was obvious someone was home? There must have been lights blazing. We need to find some evidence before we draw any conclusions.'

With utmost gentleness Ben slid the cover back over the deceased, treating the body with due respect. Taking care to not disturb things he made his way around the room, absorbing details, none of which were any help since the room seemed to be undisturbed. The layer of dust on every surface, except for the scuffs of recent footprints, attested to the absence of the owners for some time. Satisfied his team was scouring for the tiniest piece of evidence he left the room and took the stairs two at a time, his long, lean legs having no difficulty with the stride. He followed the sound of a loud drawn-out wail followed by silence but as he neared the room he could make out muffled sobs. Sounded as though the wife had no control over her grief. Who could blame her? Or was it an act? He hoped not.

Kathy Bates was lying curled in a foetal position on a queen-sized bed. First glance told him that she was about the same age as her husband; he guessed about fifty from the few grey hairs in her messy auburn waves. There were outward trappings of wealth but the room and her clothes were not gaudy, nor grandiose. The edges of a pale pink nightdress peeked from under a darker brushed nylon gown that had been placed over her, he guessed by the policewoman. Everything he'd noted so far was understated quality suggesting the Bates lived a quiet but financially comfortable life.

After a brief chat with the officer Ben knew the distraught wife was in need of sedation and unable to be interviewed at any length. Satisfied there was nothing to be gained by staying, he left the room then scouted around the upstairs area before returning to the lower floor. Nothing appeared to have been disturbed. There weren't even any footprints marring the sheen of dust, except for those leading to and from the main bedroom so what was the perpetrator looking for? Was it some particular item? Was there something more to this than his initial hunch indicated?

While trotting down the steps he glanced at his watch again then swore under his breath. Trish was going to be more than upset. In fact he'd be lucky if she was still waiting.

When Ben returned to the study John was chatting quietly with the coronial medical examiner. 'Do you need me, John? I'd really like to get away. You know the drill. I'll leave you in charge but call me if anything unusual crops up, although I can't see that we can do a lot tonight except collect evidence. Try to give me a couple of hours of peace if you can. I'll see you tomorrow.' He paused for a moment to give his men a chance to say whether or not he was needed. At a dismissive wave of his hand from John, Ben collected his sodden jacket from the hallway seat, shrugged back into it then dashed through the continuing downpour to his car.

Chapter Two

By the time he pulled into the car park of the swish city hotel, the rain had eased but he still wore the rain jacket to run through the puddles pooling on the bitumen. If he didn't take it, the perversity of fate would have it bucketing down when he left. Cold water splashed up his legs and made a mess of the gleam of polish on his favourite leather shoes. A frown at the mess then he nodded to the doorman who held open the glass doors then waited while Ben removed his jacket. After stamping his feet on the doormat he strode through the foyer, ran up the stairs then paused at the door of the restaurant.

It didn't take him long to spot the attractive, slim but curvaceous woman with honey gold hair pulled back into a neat chignon. Seated with her back to him, Ben noted the coffee cup Trish had just nestled on its saucer. His stomach muscles tightened at the thought of the reception he was about to receive but at least she was still here. The deep pile of the carpet muffled his footsteps as he drew up behind his date. Placing his long fingers on her shoulder he bent to kiss her cheek.

'I'm so sorry, Trish. Some poor bloke was shot dead and they put me on the case. I came as soon as I could. Did they pass on my message?' As he moved around to the other side of the table and settled in a padded chair, he watched her eyes to ascertain her demeanour. His apprehension intensified at her still features and the lengthy silence. It took too many seconds before Trish raised her eyes. They weren't sparkling and happy.

'Ben, I'm sorry but I can't do this any more. You are a really great guy and I more than just like you a lot but I can't live your type of life, never knowing if or when you are going to turn up. I truly admire what you do but your life is not for me. I've eaten and paid for my meal. I wish you luck and sincerely hope you can find the right woman but she's not me. I'm sorry, Ben, but it's over.'

Trish stood, her eyes downcast. He didn't know if it was because she felt embarrassed or if she was hurting, that she wasn't able to look at him. Removing her jacket from the back of her seat, she turned and left without bestowing a backward glance. Staring at her retreating back, gut instinct told him it would be useless to chase after her and a swank hotel restaurant was not the place to create a scene. He scoffed. If he was really honest with himself he had expected this, weeks ago, but it still rankled. He sat for a moment longer then glanced at the waiter he spotted hovering at a discreet distance.

'Sir, you will be eating?' the waiter asked in a subdued voice as he stepped towards Ben.

Ben thought for a moment. He hadn't eaten since breakfast at sun-up and the day had been long. He was hungry. Food was on offer. His body needed fuel and he needed time to absorb Trish's parting. 'Yes, but I think I'll move into the lounge bar if I may.' Scanning the menu, he selected the first item to take his fancy. 'Could I please have the seafood linguine served at the lounge bar?'

'Certainly sir, and a drink?' the man asked.

'I'll order wine at the bar.' Knowing the hapless waiter had probably seen and overheard Trish's public dumping and was being polite and discreet, Ben smiled at him. 'I apologise for the inconvenience and thank you.'

A sense of unease swept over him so he shot up and made his way into the piano bar across the passage. He'd been down this road before – too often – but never so publicly. That was a first for him. Well, he supposed that if you lived long enough then you'd experience most things life could offer. Now he could add another to his very long list. Dumped in public.

With habit making him observe his surroundings wherever he went, he gazed around. The gleaming white grand piano was silent, a spotlight highlighting it, but no pianist was sitting on the stool. Instead, background music played from a CD, the dulcet tones just loud enough to not impinge on muffled conversations amongst the few dozen patrons settled in comfy looking lounge seats around low glass-topped coffee tables. Not being in the mood to be the only solo person sitting amongst the groups of what appeared to be happy people, Ben perched his large frame on a padded stool near one end of the bar. Settling into the backrest he placed one leg on the foot-rail while the other remained resting on the floor. The barman, a suave looking man in his early forties, moved over to take his order.

'Red I think. How about a glass of Cabernet Merlot? I have a meal ordered.' He waited while a bottle was selected and the label shown to him then rested his elbows on the bar, a loud sigh escaping his lips as he dropped his head into his hands. Dumped. Again.

'You sound sad.'

Startled at the soft voice, Ben twisted sideways and took in the features of the woman he hadn't noticed. Shoulder length brown hair with a hint of red. In the dim light her eyes looked charcoal grey but he guessed they would be lighter in normal daylight. Medium height meant she had to perch on the bar stool with both feet on the rail. She was wearing a glittering top with streaks of shiny silver. Her plain black skirt moulded against shapely thighs then flared around her knees in soft folds. He admired the gentle swell of her breasts with the hint of cleavage above the top of the scooped neckline. No jewellery except for a fine, silver chain wrapped around one wrist. From the little he could see of her hands there was no watch or rings.

'What makes you think that?'

'Your sigh sounded sad. I'm a good listener if you want to talk about it. I'm Christine Mears. My friends call me Chris or Chrissie. I answer to them all.' The woman held out a slender hand.

Ben eyed the long but delicate fingers, taking in the neat trimmed short nails with a gloss that could have been natural or a colourless nail varnish. It was hard to tell. He grasped them in a warm handshake. 'Benjamin Somers, but I only answer to Ben.' He smiled at the dark eyes.

'And the reason for your sadness?' The woman asked without returning his smile, which disconcerted him. Why act friendly but not return a smile?

'Not so much sad, just resigned to the fact that I've just been told that it's over by the lady in my life, or should I say who was in my life. It was nothing more than I expected but it's still a shock. Trish couldn't handle my job or the irregular hours I keep. It's the same old story – you're a nice guy, Ben, but I can't handle your job. And I can't believe I'm telling you this.'

Feeling an unfamiliar tinge of embarrassment, he turned away from the penetrating gaze and contemplated his grasped hands, his thumbs pressed up against each other. He lifted his eyes to acknowledge the barman when a glass of wine was placed on a coaster and slid in front of him.

'What is the job all these hordes of admirers can't tolerate?' the soft husky voice asked.

'Hordes?' Ben snorted. 'I wish. Policeman. I'm a detective. When a serious crime happens I get called out to investigate. But serious crime never seems to occur between the hours of nine to five. The perpetrators always wait until I'm about to take a woman out on a romantic date, or take her to bed.' Pausing, he shot a quick glance at the woman to see if his crude comment had caused her any embarrassment. He smiled at her knowing grin. 'It's as though the criminals read my mind. Trish couldn't take any more broken dates.'

Ben sipped the wine, appreciating the pleasant taste then held the glass up to the light to admire the deep, rich red colour that showed its quality by clinging to the inside of the glass before slowly sliding downwards. For a moment the colour brought back the vision of Tony Bates lying in a pool of his own blood. He shook his head to rid his mind of the unwanted vision then turned back to Christine, a far more pleasant vision. 'And you? How come a beautiful young lady like you is sitting here all alone? Or are you waiting for someone?'

'No, I'm expecting no one. I'm working.'

His eyebrows shot up at the immediate thought of a more unsavoury occupation. Is she a hooker? She certainly didn't look like one. Too gentle, and dressed too discreet with just a hint of make-up, or maybe she wore none but there was a pleasant aroma of sweet perfume: floral musky scents that titillated his senses.

'And I need to get back to work right now. Maybe I'll see you later. It was nice talking to you. Try ringing your Trish if she means so much to you and flowers often work. She may change her mind.'

Intrigued as to what her work was, Ben watched in silence as Christine took her time to stand, turned left, ran her fingers along the edge of the bar as she took a couple of small steps to clear the end then moved with fluid elegance over to the vacant piano stool. He knew she'd heard his low chuckle when she turned to face him, smiled then licked the end of her index finger and made a score in the air before settling on the piano stool with her side to the bar. So the lady was intelligent and had a quick sense of humour.

She paused then sucked in a quiet breath, her raised shoulders indicating she was readying herself. Her fingers settled on the keyboard then began playing a soft, gentle melody, her long fingers gliding effortlessly over the keys. And talented, he added in his mind.

Remaining almost motionless on his stool, Ben noticed there were no music sheets in front of her before studying Christine's side profile. Watching the expressions on her face change with the emotion of the music, he again turned contemplative.

When his meal was served he angled his stool to watch the beautiful pianist while he ate. A few couples danced on the small, uncarpeted section of the floor while Christine created a romantic mood. Ben wished he had a lady he could hold close. Trish's departure hit home and he felt the too familiar loneliness welling up in his innards. This was a path he had walked down many times before and even though he figured he should be used to it by now, it still stabbed. Why couldn't he find the right lady to share his life with?

When he'd finished eating he strode across the floor towards the piano, approaching from the rear.

'Goodnight, Ben, I hope you catch your criminal and your woman.' Her quiet words startled him.

'How did you…?' he began.

'I have excellent hearing and I listen carefully to everything going on around me. Sleep well.'

'Goodnight, Christine, you sleep well too.' Lifting one hand he placed it on her shoulder and gave a gentle squeeze before leaving to spend another long night alone, pausing at the restaurant to settle his bill.

Chapter Three

Sergeant John Markham had spent the last half-hour briefing him on all the details of the previous night's murder. Ben read through the notes of evidence once again and sighed. It was so frustrating with so little evidence to work with. A second sigh escaped at the thought that he would have to question the wife. It was going to be gut-wrenching. Shutting the file, he then wound through the corridors to his car parked in his reserved spot to visit the hospital, hoping Kathy Bates was in better condition than she'd been the previous night. The fact that she'd been admitted to hospital in a distressed state didn't auger well. Some parts of his job he loved. Other parts he hated. This was one of the latter, interviewing newly bereaved family members with raw emotions.

As he strode through the hospital corridors he mulled over what little he knew. Gut instinct told him Mr Bates was killed through an unfortunate accident, especially since the couple weren't supposed to be home and according to the report, very little had been disturbed. What made him really uncomfortable was the fact that the killer fired five fatal shots to the heart. The perpetrator had to have been an experienced shooter to be so accurate. In an almost gunless society, who would have such skill? A sense of unease surrounded him as he neared the hospital room.

He paused before rapping on the closed door then waited for a response. Hearing nothing he pushed the door open a fraction then poked his head around the edge. Kathy Bates was sitting up, resting against a pile of plumped up pillows with her eyes motionless. Whether it was at him or at some far away place she was staring was difficult to fathom. He hesitated a moment, eased the door open and strode towards the shocked woman, his rubber soles squeaking on the linoleum floor the only sound penetrating what felt like a maudlin silence. Feeling as though he was an unwanted intruder, Ben paused before approaching the bed.

'Mrs Bates, I'm Detective Senior Sergeant, Ben Somers. I'm investigating your husband's murder. I need to ask you a few questions. Do you feel up to it?'

The bedside chair made a jarring noise as it scraped across the floor. He watched Kathy's hollow eyes as they slowly turned his way. She hugged her trembling body and squeezed her eyes shut as though his presence brought back unwanted memories of the previous night. Or maybe she was just trying to hold herself together. Her chest rose and fell several times as she took in deep slow breaths before her eyes finally focussed on him.

'I'm sorry, sir... '

'Call me, Ben. I know there's probably not a lot you can tell me, but if you could give me your side of the story we may garner some small clue. I'm really sorry about your husband.' Reaching out, he prised her arms from their death grip then gently grasped her fingers in an attempt to ease her tension as he asked pertinent questions.

After what he found to be a gruelling interview in which he gained nothing of value he called a halt when he realised the poor woman was on the verge of emotional collapse. Her reaction convinced him she was not responsible and had nothing to hide. Not leaving until the nurse he had summonsed was attending to the distraught patient he returned to the Bates' home feeling more than a tad wrung out and hating himself for having caused renewed distress.

Retracing his steps of the night before, he stepped under the crime scene tape and found the study, noting every detail while he scanned the room. He nodded to the two forensic officers still working then moved to the stairwell, searching for another bullet Kathy thought had been aimed at her. It didn't concern him that she had mentioned hearing only three shots. She had been asleep so probably didn't register the first few, especially if they were rapid fire – and they would have been rapid, given the panic of an intruder being disturbed.

He cast his mind back to her stilted version of events. After calling her husband's name she heard running, another shot then the front door slamming. He imagined himself as a burglar being disturbed, shooting out of fright, hearing someone calling, hurtling towards the door in panic, firing a wild shot at the voice calling from above. He acted out what he thought the movements would be then mounted the stairs while scanning the walls and ceiling for the elusive sixth bullet hole. It took a few minutes of intense scrutiny before he discovered what he was looking for hidden amongst the ornate moulding of the cornice.

He returned to the study and waited until an officer had finished taking notes. 'Constable, I found a sixth bullet hole.'

'Right, show me, Sir,' the other man said as he closed up his notepad and slid the pen into his shirt pocket. 'We thought it strange there were only five shots. Usually it's just one or two or they empty the chamber, depending on the gun. Five seemed like an odd number.'

Side-by-side they climbed the first set of stairs then stood on the landing. 'I thought the same. It's up there.' Ben pointed to the dark hole surrounded by small cracks in the cornice, the beautiful crafted plasterwork making it difficult to distinguish.

'Thanks. We hadn't got this far yet. We'll deal with it, Sir.'

'You always do.' Ben smiled at the man then the two descended and halted at the bottom. 'Deliver me all your findings as soon as you can. I'll let you get on with things.'

He was almost back at his office when Ben passed a florist shop, the sight causing his thoughts to focus on Trish and then to Christine Mears. Slowing, he pulled into the next vacant parking spot while recalling the final words of the lovely pianist. 'Flowers might work, if she means that much to you.' Ben contemplated for a moment. Was Trish really that important to him? Deep down he knew he wasn't in love with her but they'd had a close and warm relationship. She was fun to be with and had never made any demands, apart from her recent complaints about his work. In the end he figured she was certainly worth a try. At least having Trish in his life had eased his loneliness. Happy he was making the right decision, he strode back

to the florist shop where he made a selection of blooms, wrote out a message and asked that they be sent to Trish's place of work. Maybe she would give him another chance, he thought as he made a second purchase of half a dozen long stemmed scented roses, attached a note, *Thank you for listening,* and had them sent to the hotel.

A feeling of frustration accompanied Ben all afternoon. He scoured the reports from his forensic team, searching for a lead to follow, but instinct kept telling him the shooting was just an opportune burglary unless, and he kept harping back to the fact that there may have been a particular item the perpetrator had been looking for. Which meant that it was either an inside job or they needed to be searching for something a little more unsavoury as motive. Noticing John Markham walking past with a coffee in his hand, Ben called him into the office. 'John, what's your take on the Bates' case?'

'Burglary gone wrong was my first thought last night and I'm still leaning that way. No one expected the owners to be home. A back window was smashed to open the inside lock. A couple of pictures looked skewed as though they'd been moved. Could have been searching for a wall safe. Side tables downstairs had been rifled through but so far we've found no indication of any disturbance on the second level.'

'I feel the same but what about the accuracy of those shots? Five bullets reached their target with such precision any one of them could have been the fatal shot. Hell, if I was that accurate in target practice I'd be more than happy. Which means our shooter might be a pro, so I want you to make enquiries with gun clubs, shooting galleries and armed forces. Bullet type should be back soon. I found a sixth bullet hole. Mrs Bates thought a single shot was fired at her. It was in the far cornice of the stairwell. Anything turn up on fingerprints yet?'

'There were quite a few fresh prints from the same person but not belonging to either of the Bates. The prints are not on our local list. We're trying to get a match from other states. But we're not sure if other members of the family have been around to check on things while the parents were away. If it was a burglary it makes sense that the perp has done it before. Yet he must be an amateur to leave so many prints. We're running a match on any unsolved cases, especially recent ones. We can't be sure whether anything was taken until Mrs Bates returns home, which should be within a day or two according to the medical team.'

'What about the business?'

'The business appears,' he used his fingers to make quotation marks in the air, 'squeaky clean. They are genuine importers with regular buyers. We're delving further but I don't think we'll find anything. Customs go over their containers on a regular basis and they've always been clean. Import duties are up front and relevant authorities have never had any concerns. We're going through the computer now for any hidden or untoward files but so far nothing.'

Leaning back in his chair, Ben rested his heels on the edge of the uncluttered desk. 'Mrs Bates said something about a holiday home. Maybe we'd better check that out. Could be a second computer, who knows? Look into it will you? Here's the address.' He plucked one of several bright yellow sticky notes from the front cover of the Bates file and passed it across the desk. 'What has me puzzled is why the intruder broke in when there must have been lights burning.'

'May not have been any obvious lights. The wife had been asleep so that room would have been in darkness.

There was only a desk lamp burning in the study when we arrived and the curtains were drawn.'

'So it may have appeared that no one was in residence. The son is flying in tonight. Question him as well. Here are his details.' A second note was handed over. 'Keep me posted. I'm hoping for an early night so you can catch me at home if anything turns up.'

'No date with Trish?'

The rumble that escaped from Ben's chest sounded like a cross between a deep sigh and a groan. 'No, it's finished. She called things off last night. How did you find such an understanding wife?'

'I'm sorry to hear that. Trish is a nice lady and you leave my wife alone, she's one in a million. And you know damn well how I found her since you set me up on numerous dates with her and wouldn't give up.'

They grinned at each other. Ben had known straight away that Mary was the right person for John, but it had taken many dates for John to see what a wonderful woman she was. A vision of him standing as best man for John at the wedding day just over a year ago, flashed through his mind.

Ben's phone rang; the shrill noise an unwelcome intrusion on the only lightness he'd felt for two days. Leaning over, he lifted the receiver and listened to the message. Car keys were in his hand before the receiver was back in place.

'Come with me, John, we have an armed robbery. Two men critical from gunshot. So much for my early night,' he groaned as they raced down the passage.

Chapter Four

John had the portable emergency strobe lights flashing on the roof of Ben's unmarked car before they turned onto the open road. The shrieking siren paved the way for a speedy passage but still Ben had to weave through dense traffic, slowing at intersections in the busy rush hour congestion. After a short but harrowing drive they pulled up in front of a Building Society, parking next to an ambulance that stood with rear doors gaping. They rushed towards the paramedics then paused and waited in silence while they watched a sheet pulled over one victim's face.

'Damn it,' Ben muttered under his breath. His stomach muscles clenched as they strode inside, flashing badges to a young constable standing guard at the door. A second victim was being attended to by the medics. Ben winced then sighed as a different officer approached.

'Sir, we have an armed robbery. The teller pressed the alarm button. Most of the money was already in the night-safe. The robber wasn't happy with the amount he got so grabbed a customer as hostage demanding the safe be opened. Idiot wouldn't accept the fact that these days, safes operate on time-locks. That's the customer down there, three bullets to the chest.' The constable paused as he glanced to the floor where the man lay. 'He's in a bad way. The doctor works two doors down. Heard the shots and came running. Since they were closing, the teller didn't have any more cash to hand over. That's him outside - also three bullets to the chest. He died a few moments ago.'

'Any CCTV?' asked John.

'Three cameras.' The constable pointed them out. 'The manager is unloading the tapes now. We have a few witnesses outside who saw the getaway car. There were no other customers at the time, fortunately.'

'Gun?' asked Ben.

'Looks like a .38 handgun. Six shots, six hits.'

Ben caught John's eye. Instinct told him the same shooter from the previous night was responsible for this massacre. A desperate man was on the loose. They moved aside while the injured customer was wheeled to the waiting ambulance, the doctor working frantically to stem the freely flowing blood. With the amount of blood, Ben had serious doubts about the man's survival.

'Seal off the site and have guards posted. I presume the Forensics team is on the way?' A nod from the constable, who was jotting down notes, was his only response. 'Let me have those tapes as soon as possible. John, ring Mary, you're going to be late home again. Then find out about our two victims. Question the other workers here and get details of the witnesses outside. I'll be in the office for a few hours and after that I'll be home. I'm going to look at those tapes. I have a feeling this is the same man as last night.'

After collecting the tapes, Ben spent the next couple of hours studying the vision. He was pleased with the captured scenes from three different angles, although the perpetrator was well camouflaged right down to wearing swimming goggles over his eyes. It defied logic as to how the man managed to get within cooee of the teller, his get-up so obvious, even to the point of being ridiculous, which went a long way to confirming his suspicions of an amateur in desperate circumstances. After making copious notes, he attached a copy to the tape covers.

When he jogged down the stairs into the reception area he noticed a familiar flower arrangement on the front desk. He removed the large envelope on which his name was scrawled. After scanning the message, he screwed it up and slipped the ball of crumpled paper into the pocket of his standard navy trousers. Picking up the flowers Trish had returned, he turned to the female desk constable. 'How about taking this home? Someone might as well appreciate them.' Trish certainly hadn't, he thought as he forced a smile at the grinning woman.

Ben found himself running his fingers through his thick hair in frustration while driving home. When hunger pangs began gnawing he realised that apart from feeling bone-weary tired and infernally frustrated he was starving. Recalling the last time he had eaten was before sunrise that morning he figured he was in need of a break, not only in the case, but also in his life.

A sudden thought had him pulling over then executing a safe but illegal U-turn and heading back towards the city. Within fifteen minutes he was striding into the piano bar searching for food, a drink and some peace and harmony.

Settling on a stool at the bar he waited until the barman moved towards him before ordering the same food and wine he'd enjoyed the previous evening. He felt disappointed when there was no sign of the pianist.

'Christine not here tonight?' he asked the bartender.

'Yes, she'll be back in a minute. She's on her break. Are you the guy who sent her those?' There was an indicative nod towards the roses that had been placed in a large beer jug filled with water. They graced the end of the bar closest to the piano.

'Yes, Christine gave me a bit of advice last night and I wanted to thank her. She's a good listener.'

'She's certainly that,' the man murmured while he poured red wine with a twist at the end and handed it over. 'Your meal will be about ten minutes.'

While he sipped on the wine, Ben sat staring at the bare space at the piano, his concentration on the two cases he now had on his hands. He would bet a week's pay the two were connected. He was so deep in thought he didn't hear the arrival of Christine Mears until she brushed against him.

She moved to his side then wriggled her way up onto the same seat near the end of the bar. 'Ben, I didn't expect you would be back. Thank you for the roses. They have a gorgeous perfume and are much appreciated but it was your lady friend who I suggested needed the flowers.'

'Trish didn't have the same appreciation for her flowers. She sent them back with a very explicit note. They didn't work but thank you for the idea. It was worth a try but I don't think I'll be getting a second chance. It appears I am emotionally insensitive. I don't open up enough about my feelings.' His hand unconsciously moved to his pocket and fingered the crushed note.

'I'm sorry to hear that. And do you?'

'Do I what?'

'Open up about your feelings.'

'I thought I did. I don't really understand what she meant.'

'Did you ever tell her how you felt about her?'

'Did I declare undying love, do you mean?' His laugh sounded wry. 'I'm not into lying to a woman. I always thought I said the appropriate things, complimented her all the time. We usually had pretty special dates and I always let her know.' He paused as he thought. 'I honestly don't think I've yet met the woman I want to spend the rest of my life with. But I'm not afraid to tell people how I feel. So to answer your question, no, I never told Trish I was in love with her. How could I when I didn't feel that way?'

'So maybe she wanted more than you could give her and she knew you couldn't give it to her. Maybe her leaving was for the best.'

Ben sighed. 'You're probably right but she never said she wanted more from the relationship; never even hinted. I thought she was quite happy with the way things were.' A second sigh rumbled from deep down. 'It appears I was wrong.'

'You sound tired. Why don't you go home and get some rest?' Much as Ben had done with Kathy Bates earlier in the day, Christine laid her hand on his arm and gave a gentle squeeze as a sign of comfort and friendship.

'I've had a long, hard day, am in need of food and soothing music from a beautiful pianist to calm my frustration.' He felt bereft when she removed her hand and wished she'd forgotten it was there.

'So you haven't solved any dastardly crime today?'

'No.' He toyed with his drink. 'One dead victim last night and another today. There's a third critically injured and very few clues to work with. Not my favourite kind of day. It's the part of my job I don't enjoy.' He turned to her. 'How about you? How has your day been?'

'Pretty much the same as usual.' She turned and smiled at him. 'Except that some really nice man sent me some gorgeous yellow roses. Apart from that it was very normal. When I work late, I sleep late. But I enjoy this work. There's not much about this job I don't like.'

'The late hours, surely, must affect your social life. No dining and dancing with your partner?' There was an acute silence for a few seconds making him wonder if he had gone too far.

'Are you prying into my private life or was that just a general question? I'll take it as the latter because I don't believe you are the type of person who would deliberately pry. So to answer your question – no, the hours don't affect my social life.'

Turning at the hint of bleakness in her voice, Ben stared at Christine's profile while she sipped on a glass of water. Her answer created a whole heap more questions in his inquisitive mind and he didn't dare ask any of them. She had stirred up his curiosity so he glanced down at her left hand. No rings and no marks where any had sat. He wondered whether her 'no' was for everything he had mentioned – no social life, no dining, no dancing, no partner, or just no, it didn't affect her social life. Studying her features, he couldn't imagine her not having a partner. She was too attractive and far too gentle natured to be in the same partnerless situation as he. Lifting his hand, he wrapped his fingers around hers.

'The intent was not to pry and I apologise if my question came out that way.'

As Ben's meal was served Christine stood and stepped back from her seat. 'There is no need to apologise. Enjoy your meal. It's time for me to go back to work. I enjoyed our chat.'

After moving back to the piano Christine's fingers soared over the keys, creating an atmosphere of quiet romance. Most patrons stopped what they were doing to listen and appeared to be appreciating the gentle tones. A few stood and moved to the small square of polished wood then danced close to their partners. Ben listened while gazing at the long fingers as they ran without apparent effort up and down the keyboard. While absorbing the soothing tunes he thought about their all too brief conversation and about the brush of those deft fingers on his hand. Even after finishing his meal and savouring the final dregs of wine he sat for a while longer, taking in the serenity of the music and surroundings. He felt reluctant to leave but knew he needed a few hours sleep if he was going to function effectively tomorrow. He had a new spate of crimes to solve. Standing, he called softly, 'Goodnight, Christine.'

'Goodnight, Ben. Sleep peacefully,' she called back and sent him a gentle smile which moved something inside him.

Chapter Five

All reports for the case sat in a tray on one end of his desk when Ben stepped into his office early Saturday morning. He stared at the ragged pile and swore under his breath. Another Saturday spent working, which wasn't so unusual when they had a new case to investigate, especially when he had no woman in his life. But he used work to ease the gnawing loneliness that had permeated his life over the past few years. He always seemed to rationalise that he could take a couple of days leave when things quietened down, but he rarely did and couldn't remember when he had last been away on a holiday or taken annual leave. Maybe he should apply and go somewhere exciting to rejuvenate.

Huffing on a long sigh, he settled into his ancient but comfy office chair then studied every page of notes, storing away all the relevant information in the back of his mind while jotting down his own notes in point form, thus summarising every detail his officers had been able to glean. He paused for a brief moment when he reached the bright pink adhesive note informing him that the critically injured victim hadn't survived the night. Damn it. His thoughts centred for a moment's reflection for the innocent bystander mown down for nothing other than being in the wrong place at the wrong time. Shuffling through the papers, he sought the details of this latest fatality and wrote down the address of the wife then slipped the paper into his pocket, feeling the balled note from the previous night that he'd forgotten about. Sometime during the next twenty-four hours he would make a personal visit to the family for no other reason than to pass on his condolences. It was a relief that other officers had already had the grim task of knocking on the door to let the family know of the death. Or maybe the family had been at the bedside, anguished and praying when the man passed away. Such a waste and for what? He sat in quiet contemplation for a few seconds then shook his head to dispel the negativity before reaching for the final two sheets of notations that gave him all the information he needed.

The same gun had been used for both crimes. Fingerprints matched those of five other unsolved, recent burglaries. They had a rough description and partial number plate of the car. The car, he suspected, would have been stolen. They usually were, just to make an investigating officer's life even more frustrating. A few witnesses were able to give vague descriptions but the man, and they were sure it was a man, was well camouflaged. After viewing the tapes and knowing full well what the man looked like, he mused how each description given could vary so much. But that was normal, although not one person had mentioned the glaring and obvious goggles, leading him to assume they had been a last minute addition as the gunman entered the door.

Mulling over the facts, Ben's instinctive thoughts turned to drugs. This perpetrator was desperate for money so he either owed a lot to someone, possibly to repay a gambling debt, or needed it for drugs. And these days, crime from drugs far outweighed gambling debts. Reaching over the now neat pile of papers he lifted the receiver on his internal phone. After a short conversation he left his office in search of Detective Sergeant Robyn Mitchell from the drug squad.

He spotted his quarry heading towards him in the reception area of the Drug Squad. 'Robbie, where have you been hiding? I haven't seen you for months.' Instead of the usual handshake he would exchange with his fellow officers, Ben reached his arms around Robbie's shoulders and gave her a warm hug and a peck on her cheek.

'I could ask you the same thing. How's Trish?'

'Yeah, well… you know how things pan out in this job. She couldn't handle my hours. Are you still with Matt?'

Robyn grimaced, shrugged her shoulders then a wry grin crept from the corners of her mouth. 'We parted about two months ago. Same problem. Now how can we help you today, Ben?'

'I've got a couple of recent gun-shot fatalities associated with a burglary and an armed hold-up and my thoughts lead me to think the perpetrator is desperate for money. It could have something to do with drugs so I was wondering what your section was working on at the moment. They could be related. These are my details.' The two sheets of paper were perused as they walked side-by-side along a bare and dreary looking fluorescent-lit passage. 'Have you got anyone undercover at the moment?' Ben asked as they approached Robyn's office.

'Vince Gallati is sniffing around. We think a big haul came in a few weeks back but Vince hasn't been able to gain much information. He thinks there's a new big boss on the scene trying to muscle in. There have been some rumblings of discontent amongst some of our regular users and small time pushers and we have a feeling the bubble may burst some time soon. Come into my office and I'll show you what we have.'

Robbie turned into an open doorway and led Ben into the inner sanctum of her office where they sat hunched over files and computers for several hours, trying to match up details. Robbie wasn't as pernickety as Ben, resulting in there being little room amongst the untidy stacks of paperwork and files scattered on every surface including the floor: the clutter giving an aura of claustrophobia. No way could Ben work like that in his office. It would have him climbing the walls in frustration in no time at all. Every now and again one or the other wandered out to make cups of coffee in a cramped kitchenette, so small it didn't invite workers to linger so refreshments were carried into offices. Then they retreated for another round of intense discussion.

At one stage Robbie phoned her undercover agent to arrange for Ben to meet him later in the night. It was well after seven in the evening when Ben stood, stretched, and called a halt. 'Come on, Robbie, I'm bushed and I don't think my brain can take in any more at the moment. How about joining me for a bite to eat and then I'd like to show you something before I meet Vince? I've found a nice quiet place where one can relax and forget about work.'

'Lead me on. I'm starving.' Robbie paused as she glanced down at her outfit. 'Am I dressed all right?'

Ben eyed her up and down. Robyn Mitchell was about six inches shorter than he was, with a trim body clad in smart navy slacks, a white no-nonsense but lacy blouse tucked into her waistband and a matching jacket on the back of her chair. Her feet were embraced in black leather ankle boots with a low heel. She was not dressed for glamour but was neat and tidy.

'You look fine. It's a classy little joint, but we can flash our badges if they protest. I don't think they will.'

Ben waited while Robbie visited the ladies' room to freshen up. She returned with her shoulder length brown hair brushed back and tied in a neat ponytail at the nape of her neck and fresh make-up on her face. Giving her a smile of approval he grasped Robbie by her elbow and ushered her out to his car. They ate at a small eatery popular with members of their respective teams. The food was always good and they knew they would be well looked after and any overheard conversations were safe.

'Let's relegate work as a topic not to be discussed over a pleasant meal,' suggested Robbie as their meal was served.

'Sounds good. How's that brother of yours?'

'Married with their first child on the way.'

'I thought he was a student!' Ben set his fork on the side of the plate.

'That was five years ago!' Robbie laughed then lifted her glass of water to her mouth.

'Jeeze, time flies. How come we never dated?'

Robbie paused with a stunned look on her face then grinned 'Probably because you never asked me.'

Ben laughed. 'And would you have wined, dined and danced with me if I had?'

'Yes… maybe… no, probably not.' Her grin widened. 'You've always been more like a brother to me.' Robbie glanced at Ben's surprised face. 'Seems strange doesn't it but you never interested me in the romantic sense and I guess if you were in the slightest bit interested you would have asked.'

'I guess you're right but maybe I should've. I can't seem to get things right with any other woman.' He withdrew the crushed note still residing in the pocket of the trousers he'd worn the day before and opened it out. Using his fist, he flattened the creases. 'Trish said I was,' his finger found the words, 'rather scrimping with my emotions.'

'What the hell does that mean?' Robbie tugged the paper from his fingers and read the note in its entirety.

'I think she meant I never told her I loved her but I've never told any woman those words.'

'Never? Why?'

'Why tell someone those particular words when they're not true? It can only lead to heartache.' Ben snatched the paper back and tore it into shreds then toyed with the pile of tiny pieces to hide his embarrassment about his admissions.

'I can't believe you've never been in love. You're not gay are you?'

Ben burst out laughing, the noise attracting attention of other nearby diners. He felt his cheeks heat at the unwanted attention. 'Definitely not! I just haven't met the right woman yet. And I can't see any rings on your finger.'

'Yeah, well, I can't say it's because I've never met the right man.'

At the bleak tone of her voice, Ben eyed her lowered head then slid the tips of his fingers under her chin and nudged her head up. 'You've been hurt. What happened?'

'I lost my heart to a man a couple of years ago but he didn't feel the same and married someone else. So far nobody else has even come close. Unfortunately I still love him.'

Ben slung an arm around her shoulders and squeezed. 'I'm sorry.' He grinned. 'We make a pathetic twosome don't we. Let's get out of here.'

Ben drove Robbie to the same hotel he had visited the previous two nights. When they entered the bar, Christine was walking ahead of them arm-in-arm with another woman. A tinge of delight swept over him at the light tinkle of her voice as she laughed at something her friend was saying. The two women made their way to the end of the bar where Christine pulled herself up onto, what now appeared to be her regular bar stool as the same barman passed her a cup of frothy coffee, setting it with neat precision in front of her by spinning it around so the handle was to the right. The barman knew how to serve.

'I'll see you later, Chrissie,' said her companion as she turned and walked out of the room.

'See you, Maggie.' Christine paused for a moment. 'Ben, you're back again, and you have a lady with you.'

Surprised, Ben paused mid-stride. He hadn't thought Christine had seen them, since her back had been to them. He led Robbie closer then pulled out two stools to the right of Christine.

'Good evening, Christine, this is a work colleague of mine, Detective Sergeant Robyn Mitchell. She answers to Robbie.' Ben smiled as he recalled their introduction to each other two nights earlier. 'Robbie, meet Christine, also known as Chris or Chrissie Mears. She answers to all three names.'

'I'm pleased to meet you, Robbie but I sincerely hope you two aren't working right now. This is a place to relax.' Christine kept her hands around her cup of coffee as though warming them, but turned to face her two companions sending them a brilliant smile.

Robbie returned the smile. 'We've been working all day and I was worried I wouldn't be dressed appropriately for this place. It seems by the look of all these glamorous people that I was right but Ben assured me I would be fine. I feel very under-dressed.'

'Well only a man would know.' Christine turned to the barman. 'Mick, what do you think? Robbie wants to know if she looks beautiful enough to be in our company.'

'She looks pretty good to me.' After eying Robbie up and down, he gave her a cheeky wink. 'What would you two like to drink? The same red, Mr Somers?'

'I'll have a dry white if I may?' Robbie responded to Ben's questioning glance.

'Red for me and white for the pretty good-looking lady.' Ben laughed as he gave his order. 'How has your day been, Christine? You seem to have attracted quite a crowd in here tonight.' Turning his head, he glanced around the room. There were hardly any vacant seats available and he guessed the room could hold about fifty people in comfort, more if they squashed up a bit.

'My day was boringly normal and Saturday night is always a busy night. Did you solve your two murders?'

'No, not yet and we now have three murders. The other man didn't make it. Robbie and I have joined forces to catch the culprit. It's been a long day and I've promised Robbie that your music is a salve for overworked brains.'

'That sounds like my cue to get back to work. Have a pleasant evening, both of you. It was lovely meeting you, Robbie. You look after this man. I think he must work too hard because he always sounds tired.' Christine pushed the remains of her coffee to the centre of the bar, stood then made her way back to the piano. After flexing her fingers she settled them on the keys then began playing while the two of them watched and listened, taking occasional sips of their wine. It was a good half hour before Christine jerked to attention when Ben stood behind her. She ran her fingers down the keyboard to end the piece with a flourish before turning her head.

'Goodnight, Ben, maybe you'll be back in again.'

'Goodnight, Christine. I'll be back. I don't think I will ever tire of your music. You play extremely well and it is so calming after the tension of a day at work. Thank you.'

***

As she searched for the right note to begin her next piece, Chrissie felt the gentle squeeze on her shoulder, the warmth from Ben's large hand sending a tremor through her body. Then she heard him as he turned away and strode across the hard wood dance floor to the carpet which muffled his footsteps. Behind her she heard Robbie's laugh from the doorway and then silence telling her they had gone. Her shoulders and wrists slumped. Why, oh, why couldn't she enjoy the same sort of companionship? For a moment a deep feeling of sadness settled around her before she came to her senses and shoved it away. It was no good wishing, no good wanting what she could never have. A short pause while she sought out the correct notes, then she began the next bracket of tunes, determined to bring happiness she would never experience to her customers.

Chapter Six

After returning Robbie to her office, Ben continued on to his meeting with Vince Gallati. A walk along the cycle-path on the river's edge, sit on the bench under the large palm tree nearest the boatshed and wait, were his instructions. He ran his hand over the day old bristle on his face. Five o'clock shadow was supposed to look sexy, he'd been told but it sure felt darn itchy and it was way past five. Another few hours and his would be a day old. Glancing down at his rumpled clothes he knew he looked a little unkempt. He certainly felt that way. As he leant forward he dropped his face in his hands. Christine was right. He was tired, but not just in the physical sense. He was tired of being single, of the relentless pursuit of those who had little regard for the law and of his life in general. Heavens but he was in a rut. Maybe he should apply for leave and go overseas. Maybe he could do something out of character like climb a mountain or go skiing. Nah, that wasn't his thing. Trekking? Now that sounded better. Machu Pichu? Hmm, sounded good or maybe one of those walking tracks through Spain and Portugal. Sounded even better. But how much enjoyment would a holiday be without someone to share it with? Not all that much. Been there – experienced it and that was why he hadn't gone overseas since.

He was still thinking of the intriguing lady who created magic on the piano ivories when a hand gripping his shoulder startled him.

'Ben?'

'Yeah.' He jolted up straight and made to rise.

'Stay seated and act as though we have just met and are having a quiet chat. I don't think I'm under surveillance but I don't like taking chances.' Vince settled onto the other end of the bench with his arms outstretched along the top of the slatted wooden backrest, folding his ankles one over the other. Nodding his head he then reached over to shake Ben's hand as though they had just introduced each other even though they'd met several times before but neither had worked for the same section at the same time. The actions looked stupid up close but Ben supposed that any prying eyes would see it as a normal hello between two strangers.

Vince then settled back, staring out over the dark water of the river. 'Pretend you are just relaxing and we'll talk. Since Robbie's phone call I've been making a few enquiries to see if I can glean any more facts. But I couldn't find out much more than there's something big going on. I've heard mumblings of discontent about a few people owing big bickies to this new dealer. All supposition of course but I've heard rumours of death threats. Nobody seems to be able to give me any names. All I've heard are about are two men called Fatso and Stinky doing the leg work.'

'How long have you been undercover?'

'Not long enough to be trusted any higher up the ladder. I'm still the new kid on the block and not privy to secret dealings. I can't get it out of my mind that I'm going to need some undercover help. With your problem needing urgent investigation it's too big for one man. I've only just gained the trust of some small fry at the lower end of the hierarchy and don't have the time to work my way up through the organization.'

'Do you have anyone else who can go under with you?'

'Not really. Most people in our division are now too well known and would be recognised if we put them on the streets. We're in the process of recruiting new blood for undercover work but at the moment don't have any spare officers – especially single or unattached ones. So I asked a few questions about you. Have you ever gone undercover?'

He paused at the audible indrawn breath Ben had let slip. Then Ben grinned when he figured Vince already knew his comments would be startling.

'You're not known in the drug scene, either as an officer or any other way,' Vince added. 'I've been told about your excellent gut instinct and how good you are at solving crimes. We could use you on this one. How about it?'

Ben sat staggered. He'd been undercover on a couple of investigations a few years back but more in the corporate scene than the drug underworld. He wasn't surprised at the quick investigation into his capabilities but the request for him to work on this case was quite a shock. 'Hell, Vince, you sure know how to stun a man. What would I have to do?'

'Become a de facto dealer. We supply, you pretend to sell by making deals. I don't think I'll have any problem sourcing buyers. I can bring them to you. You gather info while we try to inveigle our way into the inner workings. We put you in an apartment in a not so salubrious part of the city than where you live now.'

The remark about his home hit its target but he'd inherited a substantial amount of money and had bought the house he'd taken to the minute he'd walked through it on the first inspection. He'd never considered selling it even though he would probably receive enough to retire on if he ever sold. 'Hell, I don't know. I've got my own investigations to make.'

'You'd have to hand it over. You can't be seen going to your office. The drug squad can second you for as long as it takes. We'll find you the buyers and bring them to you in public places.'

'But I can't just drop out from work.'

'You can go on long service leave for three months. Overseas. You need a holiday since you haven't taken one in years.'

Ben jerked his head around - flabbergasted at the amount of research the drug squad had done in such a few short hours. Not that any of the details were hidden away: the facts very simple to trace. 'How the hell did you find that out?'

Vince laughed. 'Your Super was very forthcoming when we dropped a few hints while discussing this with him a few hours ago.' He laughed again at the uncouth words Ben muttered under his breath.

'If you agree we can turn you into a well-to-do dealer so you can still visit good eating-houses, but preferably not where you are known. Find yourself a new woman and go out on dates. You still have to act like a normal red-blooded male.'

This comment drew a frown from Ben. How the hell did they know about Trish? Then he recalled his conversation with Robbie and how, during the afternoon she vanished a couple of times to make phone calls. 'Damn woman,' he muttered as he grinned. News certainly travelled fast and Robbie had outsmarted him. 'I'll get Robbie back for this,' he said then added, 'I suppose you know all my financial details as well!'

Vince couldn't hold back his laughter. 'No, we didn't need to go that far but you won't be able to return to your home at all. We'll change your appearance as much as we can; bleach your hair, change the style, coloured contacts, new I.D.'

'You know I would have to clear this with the Superintendent first.'

'Done. The powers that be have already cleared it. The decision is yours to make right now.'

'When would I start?'

'Tonight. Look, Ben, we have to catch this killer, and soon. He's a dangerous man and doesn't seem to care about taking pot shots at innocent people and unfortunately he is a damn good shot. To be authentic you will leave the country tomorrow as Ben Somers and come back a couple of days later as a new person. We'll leave a trail of Ben Somers travelling around the world. We have to get on top of this quick smart. I need your answer now. We'll have a man working with you while you change identity, who will give you all the details you need. Do you think you can do it? You're the ideal person to work on this. What do you say?'

'All right, I'm in.' Hell, why did he say that? The words had just slipped out before even thinking about it. Can't take them back now! Why not go with it? Trish had gone and there was no-one else to consider. It might give him something to think about, concentrate on, instead of spending so many hours in the office to alleviate constant feelings of loneliness. Lord, hadn't he just admitted he was in a rut? Well, what better way to leap out of it than by changing jobs for a while?

'Good. Welcome aboard. Go home and pack. Robbie will contact you with flight and other details. We could change your identity without leaving the state but having your passport stamped makes it more legitimate and if anybody makes detailed inquiries they'll find nothing but true facts. Besides we need to have your new persona arriving from overseas. Leave your mobile switched off, at home. We'll supply a new one. We can't afford someone finding yours loaded with police numbers. Get some sleep, because you won't be getting much over the next couple of days. We'll meet again when you return. I'll leave now. Give me ten minutes before you leave. Lock your car in your garage for a taxi driven by one of us will pick you up.'

There was a sudden silence apart from the splashing sounds of lapping water from the river that masked any footsteps. Without looking up Ben knew Vince had vanished with as much stealth as he had arrived. For the next ten minutes Ben sat staring over the dark water, enjoying the reflections of the myriad of lights from the buildings on the other side: the clear moonless sky seeming to make the brilliance even sharper than normal. The smell of diesoline from nearby charter boats and ferries almost overpowered the more subtle scents of damp earth from recently watered public gardens and the distinctive river water aroma. Wondering where his sanity had gone, Ben sat quietly excited, but also quite sure, now that he had time to think about things, he had taken leave of his senses. He was a damned idiot.

On his way home he rang John with final instructions. 'Can you visit the wife of our latest victim to pass on the Department's condolences?' He drew the notepaper with the details from his coat pocket and read them out. 'Something personal has come up so I'm handing the reins over to you.'

'Ben? What's happened? Can I help?'

'I have to leave the country tomorrow morning. I'm not sure when I'll be back. Probably in a few weeks.'

At the stunned silence on the other end of the line, Ben grinned. It was difficult holding back out and out laughter. Being best friends for many years, John wouldn't buy his explanation for a single second. John knew him far too well. Before any questions could be asked, Ben switched off his mobile phone.

Chapter Seven

Standing at the carousel waiting for his luggage, Ben was mentally exhausted. The past two days had been like a tornado whipping through his brain. Most of the time he had rued his decision to go undercover. His appearance had been altered so much he started at his own image each time he had stared in the small mirror over the bathroom vanity unit. The dark, brooding good looks had been altered to a windswept surfie type with soft grey eyes replacing dark brown. His longish but neat hair had been cut into a shaggy style then bleached to give a variety of colours ranging from dark brown to sun-bleached blond tips.

He reached up with one hand and ran the tips of his fingers over the Gel enhanced spikes standing on end. How he hated it. Glancing at his attire, he shuddered. His new wardrobe of clothes was scruffy but obviously expensive to indicate the wealthy drug lord but also the lifestyle of a world surfing freak. He sincerely hoped no one would ever ask him to demonstrate his prowess on a surfboard because they would be disappointed and he would be embarrassed. He had never attempted to even stand on a surfboard let alone ride the waves but he now knew the names of different types of waves, board types and movements and details about most of the better surfing spots around the world.

Leaning forward to scan the moving luggage belt, Ben wriggled at the uncomfortable expensive but garish jewellery that was now a part of his make-up. Heavy gold chains around his wrist and neck were not a part of his normal persona. He wondered if his skin would ever get used to the feel of the unfamiliar adornments. Gone was his sleek, elegant gold watch and replaced with a bulky stainless steel, waterproof abomination that he knew by the famous brand had cost the earth. Reaching over to grasp the handle of his brand new suitcase containing a whole wardrobe of clothes he despised, he figured he was going to have to get used to wearing the lot.

'Jaye Hammond?' Ben jerked around as a hand descended on his shoulder. It took a couple of seconds for his new name to register. The same taxi driver that drove him to the airport stood behind him. Ben knew the man was an officer but also knew better than to say anything whilst standing with a crowd of people milling around.

'Yes.'

'Your taxi is outside.' The dark, swarthy man slid the case from Ben's fingers then turned and began striding towards the revolving door. Ben followed, feeling uncomfortable at another man carrying his luggage but it was expected if he was going to carry off being Jaye Hammond. Jeeze why had he ever agreed to this madness?

He was driven to his new home, a penthouse suite of a recently completed complex. All he would need was in place – food, linen, toiletries, everything, and hidden where he was told it would be, a stash of confiscated cocaine that had his eyes ogling. He sent up a silent prayer that the state-of-the-art security system he'd been told was in place, worked and worked well. Hating anything to do with drugs, especially the way it wrecked so many innocent lives; he prayed there would never be the necessity to sell any. After unpacking his new clothes he roamed the rooms and moved items so that the unit took on the appearance of being lived in.

While waiting for the contact he scanned files on the laptop computer that had been set up. He figured by the time this job was over he would have intimate knowledge of every surfing spot in the world. His new mobile phone shuddered against the left side of his chest. He paused in his reading of the latest surf conditions in Hawaii to switch it on.

'Who's calling?'

'Vince. Meet tonight, site three, eleven o'clock and bring a sample. I have a contact.'

The phone went dead, which was expected since he'd been instructed to keep calls as concise as possible so there was no possibility it could be traced but he hadn't expected the messages to be quite so snappy. Closing up the phone with a shake of his head and wry grin, he reeled through his brain-bank for the details of the site three meeting point. A smile broke out. It would give him time to drop by the piano bar if only for a brief stop, to test out his new identity. Without saying a word he would know if Christine or Mick recognised him.

The latest trends in 'shabby chic' dressing didn't sit well. Ben felt beyond uncomfortable with his shirt hanging over his jeans. Hell, he felt plain uncomfortable wearing jeans of any description to an upmarket place but he was assured it was trendy. The only thing he liked about his appearance when he strode into the hotel later that night was the soft, black leather jacket he wore. It was better than his own. He hated the white loafers on his feet – especially without the comfort of normal socks. These half-mast excuses for socks felt as though they were forever slipping under his heels. He was still decrying his looks when he came to a sudden halt.

Christine's position at the piano had been taken over by someone else, and it wasn't Mick at the bar. Tuesday night, he thought, everyone has to have days or nights off. Settling at the bar he ordered a red wine, now certain no one present would recognise him but a deep feeling of utter disappointment settled around him like a shroud.

While waiting, he listened to the male pianist who wasn't nearly as talented as Christine and didn't have the same gentle touch.

'He's not as good as the beautiful lady I saw the other night,' Ben commented with a teasing smile when the barman moved towards him. 'But then again he'd probably have the women drooling.' The new pianist was slightly built but had ruggedly handsome features and was impeccably dressed in dark trousers, a dress shirt with a bright red bow tie and white dinner jacket.

'Chrissie? She's only in Thursdays, Fridays and Saturdays. She draws in far bigger numbers but won't give up her other job to join us full time.'

'What's her other job?' Ben was surprised there was a second job but was also curious to learn more about the delightful Christine.

'She teaches music three days a week at a private school. Says she loves the kids better than she loves us. She's a special lady.'

'Sounds like you have a hankering for her, mate?'

'Everyone has a hankering for Chrissie, she's that kind of woman but she would never mix business with pleasure. She's just a great friend and besides, my wife would kill me.' The man grinned. 'I only get to work with her if Mick calls in sick or goes on holidays. I relieve this bar on his nights off. Monday and Tuesday in here. You're new. I've not seen you before.'

'Yeah, just staying for a few months. I heard the music last Saturday and was impressed. Your Christine has a magic touch on those ivories. I might call in again when she's here and listen some more. Thanks mate.'

Feeling bitter disappointment, Ben downed the wine before leaving. He couldn't put his finger on what it was about Christine Mears that attracted him and her not being there put a dampener on the night. A glance at his watch told him he had time to kill so he called in at another seedier bar on his way to his meeting point, just to be seen, but at the same time to make his own observations. The place was well-known to the legal fraternity but not for good reasons.

Meeting place three was a private booth in a small but popular eatery in the section of the city well known for its nightlife and restaurants. Ben ordered a meal and coffee. One wine was enough if he wanted to keep his mind alert and he wasn't sure whether a social drink was going to be required when Vince arrived with the prospective customer. It didn't take him long to figure out why the place was regarded as a safe place to talk secret talk. The music was so loud it was difficult to even think let alone hear what someone else was saying. He hoped they wouldn't have to stay very long and had a sudden yearning for Christine, her piano and the ambient atmosphere she created.

The plates had just been removed from his table and Ben had ordered fresh coffee when two figures slid into the seats opposite him. Vince Gallati didn't appear to be in a very good frame of mind, his face indicating suppressed anger. Since he was late Ben wondered if the contact had kept Vince waiting.

'Gentlemen, can I interest you in a coffee or something stronger before the waitress leaves?' Ben asked as he nodded his head in greeting. When both men declined, Ben felt thankful. He said nothing else but waited for Vince to begin the conversation. After a good thirty seconds the tense silence was beginning to grate.

'Jaye, my friend here is interested in your goods.'

Suppressing a jolt at hearing the name he still wasn't used to, Ben cocked one eye while he studied the newcomer. Untidily dressed, the man was out of condition with quite a paunch around his middle and flab under the chin. He looked to be in his late forties with thinning brown hair, a very pasty complexion and didn't look at all well. Not seeming to have the appearance of the usual type of drug courier or dealer, suspicion niggled. Maybe he was just a user. He studied the man, seeking similarities to the goggle clad image on the CCTV film. Right height but wrong hair. Build was difficult to judge since the shooter had been dressed in an overlarge baggy tracksuit with a hood. The goggles had been tight, screwing the flesh grotesquely around the eyes. Nose and mouth? He'd have to study them side-by-side to judge.

'Does your friend have a name? He obviously knows who I am. I expect the same courtesy or my goods are not for sale.'

Both Vince and his friend looked startled at Ben's curtness, but he wasn't here to be pleasant. He needed to be the one in a position of authority or else nobody would believe he was the big boss with drugs to sell.

'Jaye, meet John.' Vince relaxed his stance.

The suspicious niggles heightened to sharp jabs. 'Ah, the universal name. How many John's are there in this country? Tell me your surname is either Doe or Smith and I'll really know you are telling me the truth. I think maybe I'm not interested in your money.'

'And I'm supposed to believe Jaye is your name? I don't think so.'

Ben was stunned at the sarcastic terseness from the stranger. Who the hell did he think he was? He spied Vince trying to mask the alarm from his face. This was supposed to be a very simple meeting but had all the makings of a nasty stoush. Ben noticed Vince's hand edge closer to the firearm hidden in a shoulder holster. Damn it all but things were going downhill at rapid rate. He needed to get things back on track and show he was the one with the upper hand.

'Well, my passport and birth certificate have Jaye on them, and so does my marriage and divorce certificates but that bitch who I was unfortunate enough to get shackled to, kept those two pieces of paper so I wouldn't be able to show them to you. Can you show me the same proof?' Pretending he was about to leave by making as much noise as he could while sliding his chair under the table, Ben stood.

'All right, all right, keep your shirt on. Des Casey is the name and to prove it, here.'

The man pulled out his wallet, opening it to reveal a driver's licence. Glancing down, Ben reached out and lifted the wallet for a closer inspection, memorising all the details shown before handing it back and settling back into his seat. The talking ceased for a moment while the waitress served Ben's coffee.

'Thank you, sweetheart.' Hoping he wouldn't be on the receiving end of a right hook to his jaw, Ben grabbed the waitress's hand and gave her backside a bit of a pat before he released her. Dear, God. He was acting like an idiot but he couldn't think what else to do.

'Now, where were we gentlemen? What can I do for you?' Even though he'd been told undercover officers would be serving him, he had no idea whether or not this woman was the real thing but she hadn't swung at him so things were looking up.

From the corner of his eye Ben spied the alertness in Vince's stiff stance then he seemed to relax, sinking back into his seat. Not understanding why the man was so defensive, Ben went on the alert. Something had upset Vince. Damn, but he was beginning to hate this whole scenario.

'I'm told by our friend here, you can supply me with certain goods.' Leaning forwards Des Casey spoke in a harsh but muffled voice.

Ben inwardly reeled at the stench emanating from the man. Strong garlic mixed with some other ghastly, stomach-churning odour. The man smelt as though he had never had a shower in his life but a memory of a man called Stinky teased its way to the forefront of Ben's mind. His smile might have appeared to be one of friendship but it was more of triumph. This was the first positive lead.

'I'm interested in quality and quantity,' Casey added.

'Quality is perfect. Test this.' Removing a tiny plastic packet from the inside pocket of his leather jacket Ben slid it over the table, keeping it hidden under the tips of his fingers while trying to keep his nose away from the man. He fought down the need to gag when he was forced to take a breath. Ah, Jeeze, this had better be the man they were after. 'As to quantity, I don't think you would have enough cash to pay for what I can supply and I only get paid in cash. Good night, gentlemen.'

Gulping down the final mouthful of coffee, Ben shoved his chair backwards as he stood. 'Our friend, Vinnie here, can contact me if you are interested. He knows the price and…' he paused for effect, 'get one thing very straight, I don't do special deals. The price is the price. Let me know within twenty-four hours or my goods go to my other customers first.'

Spinning on his heel, Ben left, striding down the pavement with the flow of traffic, searching for a taxi. A prickle of unease had the hair on the nape of his neck standing to attention. He was being followed. As he hastened his step, he glanced into the shop windows to see if he could make out a reflection of anyone watching. It was too hard, with burning lights inside most buildings and street lights and signs dominating the reflections. Turning to face the road, he glanced up and down as if intending to cross. There, to his left, a shadow ducked into a doorway.

The traffic was like a continuous gush of water making it impossible to find a gap to cross without getting splattered so he half-turned and sidled away from the doorway and held a hand up in a desperate bid to hail a taxi. As he trawled the kerb, he kept shooting glances at the doorway. The shadow remained – unmoving but it was a person.

Up ahead he noticed the intersection lights changing. He ran, hoping to catch the walk lights. As he reached the corner he caught sight of a couple exiting a taxi. 'Thank you,' he mumbled as he dived into the still open taxi door.

'Just drive,' he barked at the surprised image of the driver in the rear vision mirror. 'Someone tried to jump me,' he added when the driver did nothing but turn to stare at him. 'Please, sir, I don't really want to become a victim of a mugging.'

For way too long, Ben thought he might have to pull out his badge from an inside pocket but thankfully, the driver turned back, flicked his indicator and pulled away from the kerb. As they passed through the intersection, he scoured the footpath for his pursuer but the shadow had gone and could be any one of the dozens of people walking both ways along the pavement. He slipped his fingers into the inside pocket of his jacket and withdrew a small notebook and pencil and jotted down the details of Mr Des Casey he had memorised from the licence, not believing for one moment the licence was any less fake than his own passport and birth certificate. The man couldn't possibly be that stupid.

What concerned him the most was that he had been followed, which wasn't all that surprising as drug dealers and members of any criminal gang were prone to have back-up for safety measures. So how did they know who to follow? He'd left before Casey. Dumb question for any one could have followed Vince and Casey inside to get a peek-a-boo at the new dealer on the scene. They'd be itching to know what he looked like. Ben had just been stupid enough to not think of it beforehand.

He asked the driver to pull into a train station where he could see a small crowd of revellers waiting for a train. After paying with a note that had the driver's face break into a smile, he joined the crowd, hopped onto the next train with them then rode to the first station where he alighted as the doors were closing and picked up another taxi to take him home. He was about to peel off his garish garb when he felt the silent shudders of his mobile phone.

'Who's speaking?' He reeled off the two words as per instructions.

'Vince, licence details, site one, ten minutes.' The phone went dead. Short messages took on a new connotation.

Ben wasted no time in changing into a body hugging, bright tracksuit that he normally wouldn't be caught dead in, then shoved his feet into more comfortable runners that were even more garish in neon colours then jogged the short distance to site one; a bus shelter a few blocks from where he now lived. He sat next to the man already seated on the wooden slats but kept his eyes forwards as though he didn't know Vince.

'You can be an arrogant bastard at times can't you?' Vince chuckled.

'Only when I have to be. It worked, but I doubt the licence was genuine. Nobody could be that brainless.' His eyes gazed around in all directions to see if anyone else was around then he slid his hand along the seat until he met Vince's outstretched fingers. He tucked a slip of paper under fingertips then pulled his arm back. 'Where did you pick our friend up, the local piggery? I hope he showers before our next meeting.'

Vince laughed then rose as a bus approached. Without saying another word he climbed aboard and was gone.

Chapter Eight

Turning over as his eyes slid open, Ben jerked upright when sleep hazed eyes spied a man's shape sitting in a chair next to his bed. Vince was reading a book. Ben raised his eyebrows at his guest. 'At least you could have made breakfast,' he mocked with a grin.

'Why bother, it's almost lunchtime? The licence was bona-fide. The idiot showed you his real licence. We have someone tailing him now.'

'Which makes him a complete amateur and probably even more dangerous. Do you think he's working alone?'

'No, he said he was taking the sample to his partner for testing.'

Partner. So they were looking for two people: Stinky and Fatso. Thankful he'd left his underwear on, Ben swung his legs over the side of the bed then pulled on the jeans from the previous night before heading to the kitchen where he pressed the button on the coffee maker for his regular early morning caffeine fix despite it no longer being early. Vince joined him, accepting the hot mug by wrapping his fingers around it then sniffing at the rising aromatic steam.

With his own mug held motionless in mid-air, Ben stood deep in thought for a moment. 'How about humouring me and check out this Des Casey's past. If he is such an idiot he could be working for the gang to repay a debt. See if he is my shooter. The build is about right. It's too late to lift fingerprints from the booth we were in last night, it will have been cleaned by now but we could get him to handle something tonight. We'll order some drinks. You leave first and take him with you. I'll make out I've scored a date with our little waitress then collect his glass. Find out if he has any shooting history. My shooter must have had some sort of training.' As an afterthought he added with a cheeky grin, 'I'll need a set of wheels if I'm to be taking a girl on a date.'

'Your waitress is a cop and married to me, so make sure you behave yourself.' Vince raised one eyebrow at Ben's startled indrawn breath. Now he understood why Vince had become so testy.

'Sorry, you could have warned me.'

'Didn't have time last night. I'll chat to Jenny and organise a hire car for you to make it look authentic. There's a lockable garage at the back of these units. Same number as your door. A car will be left in there before tonight. Give Jenny the glass and Ben,' Vince paused until he had Ben's attention. 'Take care of her. She's three months pregnant with our first child. This is her last assignment.' Vince's voice softened so much Ben could tell by his tone and the look on his face that he loved her a great deal.

'You have my word she will come to no harm. But don't come out swinging when I chat her up. You'd better warn her because we need to make everything look real. By the way, I was followed when I left the eatery last night. You might want to have your boys follow anyone tailing me tonight. If they think I've got a huge stash of cocaine they might try to steal it when they find out where I'm staying. And now my friend, I'm going to find myself a decent lunch so I'll leave you to find your own way out since you had no trouble finding your way in, and I gather it won't be such a good idea if we were seen together. Ring me with a time when you hear from our delightful friend.' Scooping up door keys and wallet he left with Vince staring after him as he closed the door.

Later that night it took some time to find a suitable vacant parking spot. Two rounds of the local streets had frustration mounting so that when he spied a car leaving, Ben planted his foot to beat other searching drivers to the roadside bay in a side street near the eatery. Guilt stabbed at being so aggressive for it was something that usually went against his grain.

The minute he entered the restaurant, Jenny sidled up to him, took his elbow then ushered him into a different booth from the previous night. Having left plenty of time to set things up and wanting to still be eating when his guests arrived, Ben pondered over the menu before placing his order. He ordered a wine but drank little while he waited.

A mouthful of food was about to go into his mouth when his two guests arrived. Ben knew Vince had been waiting on the other side of the street for Casey for the past hour to ensure the gang didn't try to make contact with Ben any earlier than the time planned. Other backup officers were in the area in case anything went wrong or

Mr Casey brought along an accomplice. After the previous night it was more than likely. The moment he noticed the two men, Ben replaced his fork on the plate as he grunted a greeting to both. He then took a large swig of the wine and called out for the waitress. Jenny was there in an instant. Ben grabbed her hand and pulled her into his lap before wrapping his long arms around her then planting a quick kiss on her forehead.

'Sweetheart,' he slurred, 'how about another wine for me and also for my two guests? I'm looking forward to later.' He released his hold at her giggled response. Jenny ran her finger up his arm while sending him a seductive smile before she turned to the other two men and asked what they would like to drink. Vince ordered a beer accompanied by a frown, probably at the way his wife was interacting, thought Ben. It obviously didn't sit so well with Vince, even though he knew it was all for show.

When Des declined a drink, a frisson of unease settled into Ben's gut. Damn it, we need those fingerprints. 'My friend, its bad manners to refuse to join us in a drink if we are to do business and I don't like bad manners. I thought I pointed that out to you last night. If you don't want to do business, then leave now. I insist you have just one drink with us even if it something soft.'

He continued acting as though he'd had one too many, grunting his approval when Des asked for a beer, then he scooped up his last mouthful of food, placed it in his mouth then set his plate to one side as he chewed then swallowed.

'We'll wait for the drinks so we can talk uninterrupted.' He settled back into the bench seat, closing his eyes until Jenny returned with the three glasses. He waited while she served each glass then grabbed her again and planted a kiss on her hand. Giggling, she lifted his dinner plate and moved away with a seductive swagger to her hips. The look he got from Vince was searing.

'I managed to score a date and am looking forward to a long, hot night in bed. So gentlemen, talk. I'm eager to leave.' Picking up his glass he took a large drunken swig then felt like choking when the cloying sweet taste of something decidedly gross and artificial slid down his throat. A quick glance at Vince sitting back watching him with a rigid face set so hard in order not to laugh, told Ben that the other man knew what the glass contained. Vince's eyes slid skywards as he sipped on his cold beer. Ben made a silent bet that the beer was real.

Lifting his glass in an unsteady hand, Casey took in a large slurping gulp then leant forward. 'The quality is excellent and Vinnie here gave us the price. A bit hefty don't you think?'

The same disgusting stench from the night before swept into Ben's nostrils. It took strong force of will to keep his face impassive at the overwhelming putrid odour. The smell, along with the cloying bitter taste in his mouth had bile rising, which he forced down. 'I told you I'm not prepared to haggle,' he gasped then coughed to clear his throat. Jeeze was he going to die? 'If you want it, you pay the price.' God this stuff was awful. He coughed again. I need recompense for getting the stuff into the country.' His eyes began to water. 'It's not an easy task these days. I'm the one taking all the risks,' he managed to drawl in a clearer voice. 'Besides the quality is good enough that you can cut it down and still get top dollar on the streets. You'll more than double your money.'

'We want all you have,' Des blurted.

Ben straightened - staring at Des. 'Then you had better get your hands on a great deal of ready cash.' He paused while scrambling around in his mind for the right thing to say. For the life of him, with the taste still bitter and turning his brain into mashed spaghetti, he couldn't recall the amount he was supposed to ask for. With his mind completely blank he turned towards Vince. The man was sucking back a snigger of mirth. Bastard.

'My friend here,' he waved an open hand in his so called friend's direction and delighted in the panicked look as the attention shifted back to the swine, 'will tell you exactly how much you will need and how I like to receive it. You have forty-eight hours. After that, the deal is off. And now gentlemen, if you would be so kind as to leave me in peace, I have a date with a hot little number. Both of you have a good night, because I certainly intend to.' If he lived long enough. Shoving at the bench with such force it bounced on the wall behind him with an almighty loud grate and thwack, Ben stood then waited for the two to leave before settling back down in his seat to wait for his hot date. She would only appear when the coast was clear. He drained his water glass, swilling the water around his mouth to eradicate the foul taste then grimaced as he swallowed it down. Big mistake. He should have spat it back into the glass.

As he refilled the glass Jenny slid into the seat opposite, pulling on a pair of tight fitting latex gloves. While Ben repeated the process of cleansing a palette he thought had been desecrated for life, Jenny emptied the remainder of the beer from Des's glass into an empty one she had taken out of her largish shoulder bag. Out of the same bag also came a brush and powder. It took less than a minute for Jenny to lift several clear prints from the shiny surface. She placed the plastic film in an evidence bag. Ben sat back watching how efficiently Jenny worked. When she had finished, he stood as he picked up the grey powder smeared glass with a paper napkin.

'We'd better not leave this here in case someone is watching or comes back.' A sly smile hovered on his lips. 'I think we might want to get this other glass analysed as well to see what poison I just consumed.'

After handing Des's glass to a grinning Jenny, she dropped it into her bag along with everything else. 'Vince's idea, not mine. It's amazing what a few additives can do to raspberry cordial.'

'He'll pay,' said Ben as he slid an arm around Jenny's waist.

'That's what all the guys say but as soon as they come up with a prank to pay him back, he's ready with another. Jenny was wrapped up in Ben's arms, giggling like a young teenager on her first nervous date while Ben staggered as though rather tipsy.

'And you married him?' whispered Ben as they neared his car.

'He does have quite a few redeeming features,' Jenny murmured into Ben's ear as though she was whispering sweet nothings. He would have preferred the sweet nothings.

Ben's chuckle ceased the moment he neared the vehicle for a prickle of unease ran down his spine. They were being watched. He could feel the pressure of unseen eyes. Wondering if Casey had been miked up, he rained a couple of soft kisses onto Jenny's head. 'Can you feel eyes watching us? I hope Vince took me up on my suggestion to tail whoever was following.'

Not waiting for a reply he opened the car passenger door, handing Jenny inside as he patted her backside when she slid into the seat. Let Vince chew about Ben's actions. When he climbed in the other side, he placed one finger on his lips to silence Jenny. For some odd reason, he suspected the car had been bugged. But then he thought the idea ridiculous since he had arrived early and very few people knew his identity or the car he was driving. Hell, he hadn't even known what sort of car it was until a couple of hours ago. But damn it, they could have had scouts hanging around for hours and no doubt his description had done the rounds.

Jenny nodded in understanding then removed a pen and a scrap of paper from her capacious bag and scrawled the name of a hotel on the paper, holding it up for Ben to see. His heart began to thump when he recognised the hotel name and his thoughts turned to the lovely pianist who played there. Christine. The drug squad was putting the two of them up in a first class hotel. While he started the engine he realised that nothing less would be expected of some rich, big-time drug dealer. He would only want the best with high security for his night of debauchery with some wanton young waitress. The problem was it was Christine he was envisaging lying in his arms. He shook his head, wondering where the vision had come from and determined to get rid of it.

Jenny leant over across the console and placed her head on Ben's shoulder while murmuring sexy innuendos in his ear. Ben grinned then followed suit, making some quite lewd responses, eliciting giggles from Jenny. He prayed Vince was listening in and stewing. Payback time.

With his senses still prickling a warning, Ben kept glancing in the rear vision and side mirrors but with the heavy traffic it was difficult to figure out whether or not individual cars were following him in particular or just happened to be on the same road and going in the same direction. It wasn't until he was almost at the hotel that he picked up a darkish sedan that seemed to be scooting between lanes to keep on his tail. A shudder snaked across his shoulders when the car followed him into the underground car-park without waiting back. It was an amateurish manoeuvre. So maybe his car wasn't bugged. Maybe they'd just followed him from the meeting. It was easy enough to do. It amused him that the car pulled into a bay not far from them, close enough that he could send the number plate to his memory bank. At the same time he felt a sense of deep caution warning him to be careful. The driver was so damned obvious it was beyond ridiculous. Then a niggle of unease told him things just didn't appear to be right. They were way too obvious. The unease turned to gnawing. Were they going to take pot shots at him in the car park? He made a quick survey of the area. It was half full and like most underground car-parks, had a creepy aura. Bare grey concrete pillars threw dark shadows across car bonnets and presented umpteen dozen places to hide, or worse still to shoot from. What good would it do them to open fire? Surely they didn't believe he'd be carting around a cache of illegal drugs. Or maybe they did.

He used the side mirror to study the driver. The man was leant over the steering wheel with both hands gripping the top. No way could he be holding a weapon when all ten fingers were on display. The man was staring at Ben's car, probably waiting for Ben to make a move. He felt spooked but sitting there all night wasn't an option so he cautiously opened the door and alighted then sprinted around to Jenny's side, shielding her body in case bullets starting flying, not that he relished being the centre of target practise but he figured he'd be no use to them dead. But taking Jenny hostage would be of use. After slamming the door and pressing the remote locking device, he swept

Jenny into his arms then bent his head to make it look as though he was kissing her on the lips. 'We were followed and are being watched. Keep close in case they take a pot shot. Are you armed?'

Lifting his head he then eased his body between the grey sedan and Jenny while they walked the short distance to the lift. His survival instinct wanted him to run while logic told him to keep calm. Hearing Jenny's whispered 'yes,' he moved one hand close to his shoulder holster, ready to draw. At the same time he noted Jenny release her firing hand from his embrace, holding it on top of her opened bag where he assumed her weapon was residing. What else did she have in that bag?

After pressing the button to summon the lift, the wait seemed interminable. All the while he was expecting something to happen. He didn't know what it would be but the anticipation was nerve wracking. Both huffed out a sigh of relief when the elevator doors rumbled open, and they tumbled into the open doors still wrapped up together. They didn't ease off their embrace until the doors hissed shut.

Jenny pulled free. 'Vince has booked a room.' She smiled a small secretive smile. 'I'm to tell you it has single beds.' She grinned at Ben's shout of laughter. 'We go up to the registration desk to get the keys while looking as though you are asking for a room. It's all arranged. There's an adjoining room from which another operative will be joining us with more information. I'm leaving alone in the early hours of the morning after our night of unrestrained sex and you are booked in for two nights if you need them. Leave the car where it is; we have another for you in a side street because we were certain they'd post a watch on the car we were just in.' The doors opening into the main reception foyer prevented Jenny from saying more but Ben was impressed by the amount of forethought and planning.

Feeling much safer now they were amongst several other people, Ben ambled over to the reception desk holding Jenny's hand. 'You have a room for Jaye Hammond?' he asked.

Within minutes, they were ensconced in a large room near the top of the hotel - one with sweeping views over the river. Ignoring the magnificent scene, Ben reached for the remote control and switched on the television set before sinking down onto one of the single beds and slid his eyes shut. Jenny made use of the bathroom then found the tea and coffee making facilities and turned on the electric jug. 'Coffee, Jaye?' she asked.

'Do they have any hot chocolate there? I'm all coffee-d out. Any more and I'll never get to sleep.' He kept his eyes closed. Even though he was used to late nights he felt drained but knew it would be a while before he could relax enough to sleep. They had just settled down with their mugs of hot chocolate when the adjoining door opened and a stranger to Ben entered.

'Evening all,' the man acknowledged as he pulled out a chair from the desk, placed it backwards and straddled his legs across it, leaning over the backrest. 'Vince sends his regards. I'm Greg Williams and was in the car following your tail. Jenny has worked with me.' He sent a smile across the room to his co-worker. 'You have some evidence for us to process?'

After reaching for her bag, Jenny removed the glass and the film with the prints she had already lifted.

'Vince not game to show his face?' asked Ben.

Greg looked mystified.

'Ben had a taste of Vince's special brew,' Jenny said then turned to Ben. 'You're probably the last man on the force he's had a go at.'

'Want your stomach pumped?' asked Greg as he gave up any semblance of keeping a straight face.

'Do I need to have it pumped? What was in the concoction?'

'How much did you swallow?'

When Ben answered Greg laughed. 'You might want to stay close to the bathroom for the next few hours.'

'Fabulous, just what I need.' Sitting, he pulled both pillows from the bed and bunched them behind his shoulders. 'I had an uncanny feeling our car was bugged.'

'Yes, we watched him doing it but couldn't warn you. It's the same guy who followed you. I've never seen such an amateurish job in my life. It's under the driver's front wheel hub but we'll retrieve it since you won't be using that particular car again. It gave us a good laugh while we watched.'

'I was wondering how they could possibly know my car but I guess Casey gave my description and they would have had lookouts. Did you recognise the perp?'

'No, but we have a photo. Casey belongs to a gun club – clay pigeon shooting mostly. He has no record as such but his bank account was cleaned out a few weeks ago. His house was recently put on the market and his wife left him not long before that, so we figure you were right, he owes someone a lot of money. He owns a licensed .38 handgun as well as his club weapons. We assume it was the one used to kill your three victims.'

'He was carrying a weapon tonight. It wasn't very well hidden,' Ben said as he wriggled to find a more comfortable position.

'Vince spotted it as well. Vince was armed and kept as far back as he could in case the man got itchy fingers. We need to delay. We've kept a tail on this Des character but haven't been able to figure out for whom he's working. We are in the process of seeking permission to tap phone calls. It may not yield anything. I think they might be using pre-paid mobiles. We need the big man and not only Casey. We have photographs of your tail and are getting them printed. We'll spend the night looking through the files for a match. I didn't recognise the man. He's not a regular so we think he's part of a gang from the east trying to muscle their way in here. Are you able to come up with a valid reason to delay, Jaye?'

'Yes, not a problem, but I think we should use a different meeting place. They'll be expecting the same spot and will have lookouts planted again. Let's see how well they handle a complete change. What about site five? It's miles away from tonight's one and in a crowded place. It'll be easy for me to disappear into the crowd and surroundings. I'll be there a couple of hours beforehand to give me time to arrive without being tailed and to scout around for an escape route and hiding spot if I need it. I'm sure Casey and Vince will be followed but it won't give them time to set up any surprises. Say ten o'clock. I'll leave the car away from the premises, hidden well then hoof it back to the car when I'm positive I'm not being followed.'

'Talking about cars, give me your keys. We have a different car for you.' He reached over with a small plastic bag held in his fingers. 'Here are the keys and details of where it is. We'll leave the one you used where it is for as long as you're here and then for as long as it takes for them to realise you've flown the coop. You can stay here two nights: maybe wander around so they can see you're still here. Then go back to the unit after our next meeting. Good luck. Oh, and Vince says to behave yourself tonight.' As Greg Williams stood he replaced the chair then disappeared back through the door accompanied by Ben's loud laughter. As soon as he had gone, Ben turned off the television and settled on the bed, tossing the extra pillows onto the carpet.

'Goodnight, hot date,' he whispered as he turned his back on Jenny.

Jenny laughed then he heard the rustles and whumps as she settled.

Chapter Nine

Jenny had gone. Ben heard her leave but feigned sleep when she whispered good luck as she closed the door in the early hours of the morning. He knew she hadn't slept much because he'd heard her stifled giggles every time he'd had to rush to the bathroom. Vince was going to pay – somehow. Yearning for a clean change of clothes he didn't have, he instead showered using the free toiletries elegantly displayed on the vanity shelf. With no razor to be found amongst the paraphernalia, he rubbed his hand over the dark bristle on his chin as he peered in the mirror. So called sexy five o'clock bristle again but it didn't sit well and sure didn't feel in the slightest bit sexy. It felt damned itchy and aggravating. Purchasing a disposable razor and a new outfit was a priority and would give him something to do during the day for he hated doing nothing. He grinned. It would also give his tail something to do: follow and watch. Could be fun.

Ben smiled at the inept man waiting for him in the breakfast nook. The man reddened at being caught watching, an obvious sign. Ben chuckled, his laughter increasing as the man hid behind an open newspaper. The fact that the paper was upside down, which was highlighted when it was quickly turned the right way up caused Ben to bite the inside of his cheek to prevent losing complete control.

After a substantial breakfast of bacon, eggs, toast and fried tomato, washed down with fresh juice and hot coffee, he strolled through the city to a trendy men's boutique he favoured. He tried on a range of clothes before making his purchases including new underwear. He could handle wearing the same trousers three or four days in a row but not underwear or shirt. Each time he went into the change room he grinned at the number of times his tail walked past the window, peering in to see what he was up to. Opting to wear the new outfit that was not quite so outlandish but still a bit more *in your face* than he'd normally wear, Ben asked that the clothes he had been wearing to be placed in a carry bag.

Feeling devilish, he ambled out of the store as though he had all the time in the world. He stopped off in a pharmacy to purchase shaving cream and a razor then zigzagged down an arcade, peering into shop windows so that the tail could follow with ease. As he passed an antiques store he recalled knowing the owner and an idea struck. Using the windows as a mirror, he timed his approach to the shop. Waiting until a group of shoppers gave him cover, he slipped into the small antique shop and sped to the back counter. 'Mike, I need a favour. Can I slip out the back for a few minutes? I'll explain later.'

The man stared at him with a puzzled frown. 'It's me, Ben Somers,' Ben muttered when he remembered his changed appearance. He glanced out the window to ensure he hadn't been observed then dropped behind the counter when he spied his tail searching the windows on the opposite side of the arcade. 'I'm undercover and need to lose that dishevelled guy wearing the striped sweater,' he whispered.

'I didn't recognise you. He's looking this way. No... he's turning to go back up. No, he's peering in. Keep still, he's coming inside.' Mike sidled around Ben's crouched figure then stepped in front of the counter. 'Can I help you, sir?'

'Err, no, I was looking for someone. Tall guy, blond hair sticking up. I'm sure he came in here.'

Ben grimaced at the description of his hair.

'As you can see, there's no one else here apart from you and me,' said Mike.

'Damn it all to hell!' muttered the other man, then let fly with a string of profanities. There was a rustle then Ben heard the tingles and beeps of a mobile phone being turned on. 'Gerard? I lost him. What do you want me to do?' The voice faded moments before Ben heard the hiss and scrape of the closing door.

'Stay down,' said Mike. 'He's standing outside searching up and down while he's talking. You want to tell me what all this is about?'

'I can't but I sure appreciate your help. Do you mind if I sit in your back room until the coast is clear?'

'I have a better idea. There's a back door that leads to a narrow passageway for us owners. It goes the full length of the arcade. Your friend is headed uphill so if you go the other way there's a door opening onto the Terrace.' Mike shoved the door to his back room. 'He's out of sight.'

Not taking the chance to be seen, Ben duck walked into the back room then stood and shook Mike's hand. 'I owe you one, Mike.'

'Not a problem. We must catch up some time.'

'We must, it's been too long. Give me a call when you're free, or better still I'll call you when this gig is over.'

As Ben crossed the bare wood floor of the small storeroom, Mike returned to his shop and tugged the door shut. Keeping alert, Ben returned to his hotel. Before making a phone call to Vince to give details of the name he'd heard, he flew up to his room to deposit the bag of clothes. 'My tail made a phone call to someone called Gerard. It's not a common name but sounds French.' Hanging up after his brief message he then returned to the hotel foyer where he settled into a chair, right slap bang in front of the main doors, scanning the daily paper until he spied his tail walking through the doors.

Startled to see Ben sitting so close and staring at him, the man continued on around the revolving glass doors to go straight back out again. Trying to keep a straight face Ben refolded the paper and returned to his room, dissolving into peals of laughter in the elevator. He knew Greg Williams and his team would be having fun at the ridiculous naivety of the incompetent fool. At the same time he had a niggling feeling things were not right and he wondered if this man was a red herring. Otherwise, why would he be so darn obvious?

Chapter Ten

Confidence radiated as Ben entered the piano bar later that evening. He had lingered over a meal in the restaurant, all the while taking clandestine peeks at his tail, before picking up his half empty glass of red wine and ambling the short distance across to the lounge. Without seeming to be obvious he searched the room for a second set of eyes watching him. It unnerved him not knowing any more details about who, or what, he was dealing with. He couldn't remember ever being so unsure about an investigation and it didn't sit well. His pursuers wanted what he was supposed to be able to supply. Not paying for it would be preferable which meant once they figured out where the drugs were his life was meaningless to them, especially since he had seen at least two of them and one was a crack shot. But then again, knowing how the minds of serious criminals worked, these could just be two minions who'd shown their faces. If so, they didn't have a hope of surviving after they'd done all the dirty work. Ben wondered if these two knew they were scapegoats and would probably be done in.

Feeling confident he wouldn't be recognised by those in the piano bar, he perched on a stool right at the end of the bar closest to Christine. He felt his heart flip in his chest at the sight of her. She had her hair bundled up at the top of her head and held in place with a large, sparkling hairgrip. She wore a long, sleek, deep green gown that glimmered whenever she moved. During a quick glance around the room Ben noted a few dancing couples, while those seated on the plush padded chairs around the small tables were listening to the dulcet tones of the piano. Few spoke.

'Excuse me, sir, but that chair is reserved for the pianist. She'll be having a break soon and she likes to sit in the same seat.'

Twisting his upper body around, Ben stared at Mick but could see no recognition in the man's eyes. In one sense it surprised him for apart from the colour of his eyes, his face hadn't changed. But the hair – it was remarkable how it altered his entire look. Without saying a word he slid onto the next stool. At the end of her bracket of numbers, Christine moved to the stool he had just vacated.

'Coffee please, Mick. Is Maggie in tonight?' She wriggled her way up onto the stool. 'I have a companion tonight. I'm Chrissie.'

Ben released his held breath. She hadn't recognised him but before he had a chance to answer, they were interrupted.

'Hi, Chrissie, how are you tonight?'

'Maggie, lovely to see you again. Excuse me, Mr Mystery Man; I'll be back in a few minutes.' Sliding from her stool, Christine linked arms with Maggie and together they walked through the large opening on the other side of the room. A few minutes later they were back, laughing while they walked. Maggie left Christine at her stool.

'I'll catch up with you later, Chris. One of these nights you are going to have to take a longer break so we can really get a chance for a nice long natter.'

As Maggie returned to wherever she had come from, Mick set a cup of coffee in front of Christine while she wriggled her backside up onto her seat.

'Ah, my companion is still with me. You were going to give me your name,'

'Jaye Hammond, at your service.'

Christine paused for a moment, her head tilted to one side and her eyes quizzical. 'Ben?'

Stunned, Ben was at a loss as to what to do. 'How could you tell?' he whispered as he leant towards her. 'Can we talk in private for a minute?' He stood but a hand on his arm stalled him.

'Mick, can we have a few minutes privacy?'

'Sure thing, Chrissie, I need to clear a few tables in any case.' Mick left the bar with a damp cloth and empty tray.

'What's this all about?' Christine asked.

'I'm undercover for a while. How could you tell? Mick didn't recognise me. And please call me Jaye. If I'm being watched I don't want to blow my cover.'

'I always remember voices and scents but you've changed your aftershave. That threw me for a while. The aftershave doesn't suit you. The other one has a hint of spice and is sharp and clean cut. This one has a more cloying aroma and doesn't suit your personality.'

Amazed by her perception, Ben sat staring at her then shook his head in awe. 'You would make a good detective,

Miss Christine Mears. They could alter my appearance, but not my voice. You are very astute.'

'Thank you and it's Mrs, or was Mrs. My husband divorced me when life became too difficult for him. So, Mr Jaye Hammond, you are another new friend. I can play that game but let me know when we stop playing.' Two hands reached out to pick up her coffee. She held the cup mid-air for before taking a few sips.

As he watched, Ben sat thinking. He was told to find himself a new woman and act like a normal red-blooded man. A man in his supposed position would be seeking out the fairer sex. They had seen him on a one-night stand with Jenny so why not? He had no choice but to play the part. He slanted a sideways glance at Christine while possibilities see-sawed through his mind. Jenny was a cop and knew the dangers but he wondered if it was safe to ask Christine out. He wanted to take her out. There was an unusual tightening of his gut and his heart increased its beat at the very thought of a night out with the beautiful woman sitting beside him. No, not yet. He'd wait until the next meeting with Vince and Casey was over. Then he would have a better understanding of how things were going to develop.

After pushing the dregs of her coffee to the centre of the bar, Christine stood. 'I have to get back to work… Jaye. I hope we meet again soon.' She reached out, her fingers brushing against his hand before turning and walking back to the piano.

Even though her touch was no more than a flutter against his skin, it sent what felt like a shot from a stun gun through his body, and he'd felt one of those. All the officers had been on the receiving end so they understood how it felt. It wasn't pleasant. As he watched after her, he left his empty glass on the bar and moved back to a more comfortable seat in the rear of the lounge, hiding his amusement at the mad scramble of the man tailing him when Ben sat in the seat just a few spaces away.

Close up the man looked haggard with a whiskered face, which mystified Ben. Maybe this was just a small gang who didn't have the manpower to change watch on a regular basis. Were there just the two of them or was this man a ploy? The poor bugger had been watching him almost non-stop for over twenty-four hours. He smirked. Maybe he should go after him to let him know he would be going to bed soon.

Instead, he stayed, listening to Christine Mears while imagining what a dinner date with her would be like. Her slender arms moved in a rhythmical sway causing his body to react when he imagined those arms moving against his naked skin. Those long, strong but delicate fingers caressing the piano keys sent waves of shivers through his nerve endings as though they were caressing him. Pulling his reverie back to reality, Ben shoved his chair away from the table. It wasn't about to happen anytime soon – if at all and he needed to catch up on some much needed shut-eye - after a cold shower. The thought of sleeping alone suddenly depressed him.

On his way up in the elevator he made a decision. He would call down for a wake up call at four in the morning. If his intuition was right, he would be able to walk straight out the front door without being observed. His tail would be snatching a few hours of very welcome sleep and would probably be on duty again by six. It was what he'd do if the situation was reversed. He laughed at the thought of just how long the poor bugger would be waiting and began enjoying his new role a whole lot more. This undercover work had some advantages and was certainly a change from his normal duties. Maybe it wasn't such a pleasant change in one sense but the different situation sure wasn't boring or dull.

When he opened the door to his room, he wasn't all that surprised to see Vince sitting in the only comfortable chair, watching his television.

'You are a bit of a devil, Ben, but you are making our boys tedious tailing job well worthwhile. They asked me to tell you they have never had so much fun tailing someone.'

'I'm a bit of a devil? What about you? What on earth was in that drink you doctored?'

'State secret. Jenny told me the results.' He grinned.

'I will get you back.'

'Better men have tried. We believe Casey is your shooter but the gun doesn't belong to him.'

'Then how can you tell?'

'We have a match on the fingerprints found at the Bates' house and we know where he is staying and just about everything else there is to know about the man. He even used his own car.'

'You're kidding!'

'He's also responsible for three other recent burglaries. We suspect he owes a lot for drugs because our enquiries with the bookies and gambling joints doesn't have him anywhere near either and we can't find any financial loans in his name. We can pick him up any time.' Vince stood and paced across to the windows, which he glanced through before turning to Ben.

'Your shadow is from the east and is wanted there for a number of drug related crimes. We gather he also owes a huge sum of money, probably to the same guy. He goes by the name of Bobby, but my boys have already dubbed him, Booby.' Vince leant forwards.

'You wait until you see what I've got planned for him tonight,' said Ben as he perched on the end of the bed. 'Surely the idiots must know we're on to them. But then again I keep wondering if this man following me is just a decoy – he's so damned inept. I mean, if I was tailing someone I sure wouldn't be so overt. I'd want to remain unobtrusive. This guy isn't even attempting to be discreet, which has me concerned.'

'Okay, I'll mention it to my people. See if we can pick someone else up.'

'I'll be back in my unit by morning if you need to contact me, and my friend downstairs will be none the wiser. I'm guessing, and hoping, they are very short of men so we are only looking for three, maybe four people. We know Casey, we know this idiot and there is Gerard. There may be one more, possibly two. Let's hope that Gerard is the big man.'

Vince flicked off the TV. 'We have the boys over east searching for any Gerard who could be related to the drug scene. I'm off now to spend what is left of the night with my gorgeous wife. Thanks for taking care of her. Last night was her last official duty as a copper. I feel happier now she has resigned, but it was her choice. She figures it is better for our child to have only one parent putting their life on the line every day.'

'You're a lucky man, Vince. Take care of her. I'll see you later at location five. Let me know how long it takes for Bobby to figure out I've gone. With the car still parked below and me not making an appearance, it could take until our meeting.'

Vince was still laughing after he had closed the internal door between the two rooms.

Chapter Eleven

It was only a few minutes after the wake-up call when Ben emerged from the elevator in the foyer of the hotel. He carried his only belongings in the plastic bag sporting the logo of the shop from where he'd purchased his clothes. A quick glance around convinced him he wasn't being watched. Apart from the sole receptionist, the place was devoid of human habitation. After handing in his room key he strode outside, following the directions to his new set of wheels; a dark green version of the car he'd left behind.

The only interruption to his short walk was sidestepping a man who was leaning against a fence looking as though he was fighting back to need to retch. The man lurched back from the fence then started staggering and reeling down the footpath as Ben approached. Oh phew, the tall scruffy man reeked of sour whisky. A sudden stumble towards him and Ben reached out to catch the man but with only a brush against his side, the drunkard somehow seemed to find his balance and straightened again. Dragging his arms back down, Ben passed him by. A quick glance at the man gave him nothing more than an unclear view of his face as the head was turned downwards as though the man was searching for a safe place to land his next footstep or perhaps heave his guts.

Always on the lookout, Ben continued to check for any sign of a car tailing him but so early in the morning there were few vehicles around. A sole taxi trolled for a late night customer, a clanging rubbish truck emptied the previous day's refuse, two mechanical street sweepers had the nightly freedom to clean debris from against the kerbs and three cars were going in the opposite direction. The city was living up to its reputation of being dead at night. Even though he felt positive his journey back to his apartment went unobserved, he still maintained a rear mirror vigil. After locking the car in the garage allotted to his room he went upstairs, stripped off and fell into bed naked; his normal night-time attire.

Early the next evening Ben was drifting the streets of the port area, the large coastal town where site five was located. He was searching for a safe place to hide his car within a reasonable walking distance of the location and with enough cover so he could make his way back on foot. The ability to maintain cover amongst the streets and buildings was a necessity given the lack of knowledge of the adversity. Feeling certain there would be a tail on him the moment he left after the meeting he hoped it would be Bobby. Going on what he'd seen so far, it would be easy to lose the man plus Bobby would be tired and probably more than a little frustrated. Ben couldn't help grinning at the thought.

As he drove down a darkened street, Ben noticed a lean-to on the side of a business that had closed for the night. He brought the car to a stop then reversed back until he had good vision. The property backed onto an alleyway behind a row of old style houses. After reversing his car into the covered space, he locked it, jogged to the other side of the road then glanced over at the building. The car didn't look out of place and speckled shadows from overhanging branches melded the car into the background. Not too bad at all. Happy, he strode towards the main part of the town, all the time scouting around for hiding places and different accesses to the vehicle.

Although he felt confident about his anonymity, Ben glanced around. A trio of young ladies were laughing as the walked abreast of each other on the other side of the street, headed towards the night-life. He paused at the dark shadow of a powerfully built man who was moving from a car that had pulled into a drive at the far end of the street. He studied the shadowy figure until the man moved towards the front steps of the house while searching trouser pockets for keys. As Ben passed, the person stepped onto the veranda so Ben dismissed him.

Satisfied with his route, Ben continued on while giving the once over to revellers as he passed. Most were heading in the same direction and no-one snagged his attention as being suspicious. There was no sign of Bobby. It took less than ten minutes of brisk walking to reach the old but restored hotel where the meeting was to take place. Again the atmosphere was eardrum-splitting, with a loud rock band performing from a raised dais in one corner of the crowded main bar. Shuddering at the racket, Ben wandered around the premises, searching for the best place to settle down with a plate of good food: a place secluded enough for their meeting. He noted an arrow pointing upstairs so loped up the steps two at a time. Most of the old bedrooms had been converted into small dining areas with holes cut in the walls to make archways between each, creating semi-private alcoves. He selected the room on the end. It had the most privacy and was above the band so there would be enough noise to cover their conversation. Since Vince needed to know where he was, Ben rang him.

'Upstairs, on the end, above the band,' he said as soon as he heard Vince's voice.

Returning to the ground floor, Ben scanned the room for anyone watching him. They seemed an innocuous lot if not a tad rowdy. His eyes settled on a couple who had just entered the bar area. A flashy redhead was accompanied by a tall, well-dressed businessman with broader than normal shoulders. Ben surmised the woman was a hooker and dismissed her but a niggle of recognition had him casting his eyes over the man several times before he felt satisfied he didn't recognise the face. Maybe it was the shape that had taunted his memory bank. He ordered and paid for his meal plus a glass of wine, letting the waitress know where he was seated before mounting the stairs once again to investigate the place further.

Noting the door opened onto a balcony, Ben stepped onto the wooden veranda to scan around for an easy escape route if things went awry. He stood watching the action in the street below while waiting for his meal, only returning to the room when he heard the waitress setting down cutlery. His glass of wine was waiting, along with a separate glass, which was being filled with iced water from a large jug. Ice blocks chinked against the stainless steel then made plopping sounds as they landed in the tumbler. The waitress eyed him with a quizzical frown, and seemed satisfied she knew who he was for she pulled a badge from her pocket and flashed it in his direction. Ben nodded in acknowledgement, feeling happy the planned backup was in place.

After taking a sip of his Merlot, Ben set about re-arranging the room. He pulled two upholstered dining chairs nearer to the wall then shoved the table closer to them, leaving enough room for him to move with ease to either door but less room for his visitors. Then he removed his gun from the inside pocket of the leather jacket he'd grown rather fond of and wore every time he went out. Unclipping the safety catch, he placed the gun on the seat next to him and covered it with the jacket, ensuring he could reach the weapon in an instant. Another chair was set on the end closest to his jacket for Vince and a final chair opposite for Casey. The remaining two chairs he removed to the alcove next door. He didn't want Casey to sit anywhere else. The chair holding the gun was pushed in a fraction to make it look uninviting.

When his meal arrived he ate slowly to ensure he wasn't finished when his guests arrived. The steady, loud thumping of the drums from the rock band below began to grate on his nerves bringing to the fore a vision of a far more pleasant environment; the piano bar with the elegantly clad Christine Mears creating magic with her fingers.

A sudden scuffle from outside his booth sent the pleasurable vision shooting from his mind, bringing him back to full alert. What he didn't expect was the real live vision of Des Casey carrying a large suitcase into the room. He fought to suppress his utter amazement when the two entered.

'Good evening gentlemen,' he muttered as he indicated with one hand for Vince to sit on the end, thus forcing

Casey to sidle between wall and table to pull out the only other chair. Ben waited until the two men were seated before forking the remaining mouthful of food into his mouth then sat chewing. The entire situation felt bizarre and so far removed from what he'd normally be doing in the evening. To ease his sense of trepidation and try to appear as though this was an everyday occurrence for him, he leant back while his mouth worked. He slid his hand along the back of the chair next to him. Sending a quick glance in Casey's direction he noticed a band of sweat had broken out on the man's brow. Was he afraid or just plain over-heated? The man wasn't in the best physical condition and there was evidence he was under a lot of stress so maybe that was the reason for the perspiration.

Nobody said anything for way too long, which only increased the tension so Ben swallowed his over-masticated food to break the deadlock. 'Vinnie, my friend, I'm really disappointed in you for allowing an armed man to come in here. You know I deal on trust. Look, I'm unarmed.' To prove he had no gun hidden on his body he stood slowly, maintaining eye contact with Casey for even the slightest hint of the man reaching for the not so well hidden firearm, then spun around slowly while patting his trouser pockets, but all the time ready for the slightest twitch. After all, the man was a deadly shot. After regaining his seat he faced Des as he sucked in a breath of relief. Damn but he was twitchy but knowing how accurate the man's aim was had put the willies up him.

'My friend, if you want to discuss business any further, please allow Vinnie to remove that gun from your pocket?'

He noted the increase in sweat and a nervous twitch flicker near Des's left ear. Hell, the man was a nervous wreck – which made him all the more dangerous.

Vinnie moved towards him with care, every muscle in his body looking tense and alert for sudden movement. Then he gingerly slipped his fingers into the inside pocket of the man's coat, pulling the gun out and placing it on the table where it couldn't be reached without lunging. Smart man, thought Ben and thank goodness.

'I'm not sure I want to deal with people who don't trust me,' Ben continued in a quiet but firm tone. He had to keep the upper-hand; to show he was the one calling the shots. Any sign of reticence would show weakness. 'Now, please explain the case?'

As Casey shot a nervous glance at Vince his twitch became more pronounced. 'We haven't had enough time to gather together all the money, so I've brought half along and we'll take half the stuff now.' Des lifted the case onto the table and flicked the catches open.

Completely flabbergasted at the sight of the untidy pile of notes that looked to consist of elastic banded wads of $100 bills, Ben forced his features to remain calm but damn, it was difficult. He eyed the open case then turned to stare at Des. 'You don't honestly expect me to make a deal in the middle of a busy restaurant do you?' he hissed in an undertone then leant forwards to give the impression of aggression. 'You expect me to walk through the streets of a crowded town with several kilos of dope under my arm and then walk back down those stairs and through that crowded bar with a case full of cash?' He leant back and slid his arm closer to his draped jacket. Nothing about this situation felt safe. In fact, it was bizarre. 'You have got to be kidding me.' He paused for effect. 'You told me you wanted all I had. I've put off my other big buyers for you. The deal is off. You didn't keep your side of the bargain. Vinnie, get this idiot out of here and if you can't bring me serious buyers then our deal is off also.'

As he stood, Ben swept Des's gun off the table at the same time as he lifted his own, along with his coat, towering over the profusely sweating man. Casey was more than afraid; he was terrified, which sent a shiver of unease across Ben's shoulders.

'If you are serious, I'll be receiving another cache in three to four weeks. Keep in contact with Vinnie, but don't try any more stunts like this and for God's sake, have a shower. You stink like a sewer pit.'

Knowing he shouldn't have added the last sentence and regretting his spurt of anger, Ben strode out of the room, along the short passage then ran down the stairs three at a time, hiding both guns under his coat as he went. Once at the bottom, he turned along another passage leading to the public conveniences but bypassed them and shot out the back door he had noticed on his first search of the premises. A quick glance around to make sure no one was waiting for him, he shrugged his coat on, tucking a gun into each pocket.

A second cursory glance around and he decided to leave via the back fence. Jogging over to the back corner, he leapt onto a low stack of old bricks then vaulted over the picket fence, only to find he was amongst at least a dozen squawking chickens. As quick as he could, he let himself out of the chicken coop and hid by crouching behind an old incinerator when he noticed the back lights of the house flicking on. An elderly man dressed in an ancient dressing gown opened the door and peered out into the darkness. Ben figured the gentleman was too old and too afraid to take the chance of walking down his back-yard to investigate. He prayed he was. Waiting for the hens to settle, Ben remained motionless for several minutes after the man had retreated back inside and the lights had been switched off.

Ben crept down the driveway, out onto the next street then kept in the shadows of the many mature trees while he made his way back to his car. Even though he upset a few dogs protecting their back yards as he strode past closed gates, he was confident he had escaped unobserved and was even more re-assured when he could see no-one shadowing him during the drive back to his apartment.

Chapter Twelve

Ben had been determined to keep away but here he was walking into the piano bar late Saturday night, drawn by incessant thoughts of Christine that hounded his every waking moment and also invaded his dreams. He couldn't figure out why but he found it impossible to get her out of his mind. Finding his normal seat taken, he settled on her reserved stool to wait until she completed her session and went for a break. Mick moved over and was about to talk when Ben forestalled him.

'I know - the seat is for Christine. I'll move when she stops. A glass of red please?'

Mick studied him with a curious face. Ben cursed under his breath. His voice was what had twigged Christine to his identity. His nerves tense, he waited for Mick to associate the familiar voice with the man in front of him. Relief surged when Mick just shrugged his shoulders as he moved away to pour the glass of wine. Sweet mercy, Ben thought as he glanced around to see if those tailing him had figured out he might return to the same hotel. But no one else knew how intrigued he was by the lovely woman at the piano. Toying with the wine he didn't really want, he sat watching Christine, absorbed by the gentle music and her graceful movements. She really was incredibly beautiful. He figured he must have come in at the beginning of her session when forty minutes passed before she stood for a break. As soon as she moved, Ben vacated the stool and stood behind it.

Christine paused as she approached then smiled in recognition. 'Jaye, how are you? Just water please, Mick,' she added while climbing up onto her stool.

Shuffling around to the end of the bar, Ben stood beside Christine, placing his elbows on the highly polished wood of the bar then leaning forwards. 'All the better for seeing you, I can't seem to get enough of your music, or you.'

'You didn't come in last night,' Christine said with a shy smile that indicated she'd enjoyed his compliment.

'No, I was working last night. I don't know how to put this, because we hardly know each other, but there is something about you that keeps drawing me into this lounge. And it's not just your music. It's you. Christine, would you come out to dinner with me one night soon? I've been dying to ask you but haven't been able to pluck up the courage. I don't even know whether you're free to go out with me. You said your husband left you but for all I know there could be some other jealous man laying in wait. Please say so if that is the case.'

Apprehension hit when Christine paused for an inordinate amount of time. She appeared stunned by the invitation. A range of emotions flooded across her face.

'Are you sure about this?' Her voice wavered with hesitancy. 'I am unattached and I do like you a lot. You seem a very caring person and I guess if I'm not safe with a man in your position then I have a serious problem, but are you sure you want the bother of taking me out?'

He felt puzzled. Why would taking her out to dinner be a bother? 'Yes, I'm sure. I wouldn't have asked if I wasn't. Please say yes then tell me what night suits you.' Reaching out, he picked up Christine's hand and wrapped his long fingers around it, delighting in the sensations of her warm velvety skin against his rougher hands.

'If you're absolutely sure then I would love to go out with you.' Her radiant smile couldn't be suppressed and touched something deep inside. 'Wednesday night would suit me best. I don't have to get up early the next morning.'

'Wonderful, you've made me a very happy man.' After asking for an address and setting a suitable time to pick her up he lifted the hand he still had a firm hold of and settled a lingering kiss in her palm before releasing it. The warming sensation heated when Christine folded her fingers around the kiss. The simple action sent male hormones on a heated rush through veins and arteries, which stunned him. Never before had such a tiny action had such an effect on him but, damn, it sure felt amazing.

Just before she moved back to the piano for her next session, Ben wished her a good night and left, his innards doing strange things. His euphoria didn't blind his caution as he glanced around to ensure he wasn't being followed, wondering how the little gang of would be drug lords were handling the events of the previous night. It was obvious they hadn't been able to pick up his trail yet, although he was most surprised they weren't at this particular hotel. It would have been one of the first places he would have looked had the shoe been on the other foot. At the thought he slowed and made a more thorough sweep of his surrounds but he couldn't see anything out of the ordinary and not a single person twigged his memory bank. But that meant zilch.

When he opened the door of his apartment both Vince Gallati and Greg Williams confronted him. He wasn't really surprised for he'd been expecting one or the other but it did throw him a bit when he saw both were there. 'You two seem to continually keep late hours. What can I do for you?' he asked as he sauntered across the room and settled into a comfortable chair with one leg flung over the armrest.

'You wanted a report on your tail from the hotel you stayed at. He remained in the foyer until about nine last night. We don't think he had any idea you had gone until Casey met up with Vince. We figure both men are not over popular at the moment and might be getting desperate. Where did you get to after you left the hotel? You managed to even elude our boys. No one saw you leave.'

'Trade secrets.' Ben smiled as he reached over for the leather jacket to retrieve Casey's gun. As he drew it out the sound of a soft thud followed by tinkling had all three men train their eyes to follow the path of a tiny, circular, black and silver blob. Landing on its smooth, circular edge, it rolled across the polished wood floorboards, spun several times then flopped onto its flat face. All three recognised it for what it was.

'Christ!' slid from the side of Ben's mouth. 'Don't touch it without gloves,' he added as Vince bent to retrieve it.

Greg pulled a pair of latex evidence gloves, rolled up inside out, from his back pocket, dragged them over his fingers and tugged with a splat then squatted down next to the offending item. 'Well that answers one of our questions, you've been bugged, mate.'

Reeling through his brain bank, Ben swore again when he figured out when, who and how. 'Damn it, the drunk! He brushed against me. I knew things were too easy with Bobby. He was too blatantly obvious in his ineptitude. They've had a second man following me, using Bobby to put us off. Damn it but they're smarter than I've been giving them credit for.'

Squinting in concentration, he searched his grey matter for details about the drunk. 'Tall, well-built, untidy longish hair, but hell, knowing what I know now that could very well have been a wig. Taller than me by a couple of inches and I'd say quite a bit broader across the shoulders. Around one hundred and twenty kilos – could be another ten. It was hard to tell since he was hunched over. I can't give you any details of facial features. He kept his head down.'

'When was this?' asked Greg as his body tensioned.

'He was leant up against the wall of the hotel when I left in the early hours of the morning. Acted as though he was completely under the weather. He reeled down the footpath and brushed up against me. Stunk like a distillery but I guess he could have poured the stuff over his clothes. Damn, I should have realised.' He snorted in scoffing self-recrimination. 'They probably think it's a huge joke I didn't discover it sooner but I never put my hands in my coat pockets and hardly ever use trouser pockets. I keep everything in the inner pockets. The only reason I put this gun in my pocket was because I had two of them at the time. Lord, what a fool I am.'

'It could happen to any of us. None of us suspected a second tail.' By this time Greg had scooped the offending tiny piece of ultra smart technology into a small plastic evidence bag he slid from a different pocket. It appeared the man was always prepared.

'Yeah, but I'd already been suspicious of Bobby being a stooge. I just never acted on my suspicions.' Disgusted with himself, Ben flung his body crossways into a chair, leaving his legs dangling over the armrest. Feeling a lump under his backside, he felt around and tugged out the confiscated firearm. 'You might want to test fire this. I'm certain it was used to fire the bullets that killed my three victims. They'll find my prints all over it now. There was no way I could scoop it up carefully without relaying suspicion.' He paused for a moment. 'Your prints will be on the end as well, Vince. I trust you guys have kept my department up to speed with developments so they can stop wasting time searching. Any leads on Gerard?'

Grabbing the gun with his still latex clad fingers, Greg slid it into a second plastic bag. 'None. The name has no meaning in the east. We're trying immigration. It's a French name so we're looking for anyone with that name who has come into the country over the past six months but odds are it's a false name. And we have informed your mate, John Markham that we know who the killer is but at the same time he can't have him just yet. We also let him know what you were up to because he was asking too many questions about your whereabouts. It seems the man knows you too well. There is no way on this earth Ben Somers would have taken any leave at such short notice. In fact, there is no way you would have taken any leave, period. I could use a man like you on a permanent basis.'

Ben let out a shout of laughter. 'Not interested. I like my own job too much, although I've enjoyed toying with Bobby. I can't believe they were stupid enough to walk into the hotel with a case full of money. How much did they have?'

'Just short of a million.'

'You're kidding. How much are we asking?'

'Two million.'

'Are you telling me I'm sitting on two million dollars worth of drugs?'

'No, not any more,' said Vince as he prowled around the room. 'We've sent it away for safekeeping and what was here was no-where near worth the asking price. That's why we're both here. Your alarms went off. Someone was attempting to break in but the force owns this entire floor and we had someone living next door for this very reason. I guess this bug,' he waved the plastic bag around in the air, 'showed them where you're camped out. I've left a couple of small sample bags in the safe just in case we need them. If they do manage to break into this place, it will be relatively clean and what drug lord would be keeping his stash in the same place he was living? Now, until the next contact try to be seen around, but be careful. You have two desperate amateurs that you have taken the Mickey out of, looking for you. We have a permanent tail on both, hoping they will lead us to Gerard. Keep your mobile phone on. Greg's number is the third one on your list. Try not to call us unless you have information or need some help. Your phone has GPS. I assume you know how to use it.' As Ben nodded the two men headed towards the door. Why in hell's name would he need a G.P.S.? He lived in this city. Knew most of it inside out – especially the seedier haunts.

Chapter Thirteen

Nervous apprehension had Ben on tenterhooks. He had never looked forward to a date as much as he was this time but he felt edgy, which was unusual. Hell, he'd been on hundreds of dates so why should this one be any different? To ensure an interruption free occasion he had chosen a quiet restaurant out of the city - one with an excellent reputation. Feeling confident his enemies could no longer keep tabs on him now that the tracer was gone and minders were keeping both Casey and Bobby under tight watch, he felt certain Christine would be safe. He'd been out driving a couple of times and had seen no indication of being followed. It still unnerved him that he had no idea exactly what any of the other gang members looked like, especially since it was now obvious they had been tailing him around the clock. And here he was calling them amateurs.

A few minutes before the agreed time, Ben pulled up in front of the neat little unit that was Christine's home. He felt on top of the world as he strode down the short coloured concrete pathway to knock on the door. Christine must have been waiting for him because the door opened before he'd had a chance to pull his hand back. He sucked in his breath at the sight of her.

'You are a very beautiful woman, Christine Mears.'

A shy smile crept from the corners of her mouth. 'Thank you, come on in a moment, I just need to let Angel go free.' Turning on her heel, Christine walked back into her sitting room, bent down to a black Labrador then paused at the sudden gasp that slipped from Ben's throat. An eerie silence followed while she released Angel from a harness.

Ben was completely stunned. 'That's a guide dog?' he asked, when he had caught his breath.

There was a visible tremble all the way down her body as Christine rose. 'I thought you knew,' she whispered in a desolate, anguished voice. She paused as though waiting for Ben to speak. When he didn't, she turned her back on him. 'I think it would be better if you left. I understand completely that this is all too hard for you. My husband left because of my disability and the problems it created.' Her voice broke on a sob. He figured she was fighting back tears.

Ben headed for the door to shut it but as he turned back he noticed Christine sink down to the floor with her arms wrapped around her knees. He spied a few tears gliding down her cheeks. When Angel nuzzled her owner, Christine laid one hand on the dog's soft head. His heart hitched as his innards tightened.

'Taking out a beautiful woman for a meal is not hard, whether she can see or not.' Ben spoke from the doorway, startling Christine. His footsteps echoed on the tiled floor as he neared. He bent over and grasped her hands then drew her up from the floor. He refused to release her even though she tugged at her hands.

'No, I had no idea, and yes, I was shocked to see Angel. In fact you knocked me for six, leaving me speechless. I'm supposed to be the detective noticing all these details but I'd not seen the signs. You cope extremely well. I'll leave, if you really want me to but I believe you promised to come out for a meal with me. I'll be very disappointed if you change your mind. A lot of things have just fallen into place. Why Maggie walks with you, I assume to the rest rooms. Why your senses of smell and hearing are so acute; why you always sit on the same seat; why you don't use any music – a host of things. But you not being able to see doesn't alter the way I feel about you.' Releasing one hand, he crooked his index finger and brushed the few tears from under her eyes.

'It altered the way my husband felt about me,' she murmured as she fisted away the remaining moisture. 'I have retinitis pigmentosa. Without going into any detail it means that as the disease progresses, contraction of the peripheral fields eventually leads to blindness. I can still see a tiny bit as in tunnel vision but am legally blind. I will lose all sight in the not too distant future. My husband walked out soon after I was diagnosed.'

'Then he didn't love you.' He had no idea where his bald statement came from but Ben knew without a doubt, it was true. A man in love would support his partner without hesitation and not leave her to fight her way through life. 'Christine, we are going out for a meal. How hard can that be? If I need to make some adjustments, so be it. Let's just go out and enjoy each other's company. Tell me what I need to do to make the night enjoyable for you. Please don't make me leave?'

Her face lifted with a look of such hope that it twisted his innards. 'Ben, are you absolutely sure about this? I would love to go out with you.' Her damp eyes were so direct in her stare that Ben wondered how much she could actually see. Then a thought flashed through his mind. How long had it been since some-one had taken this beautiful woman anywhere?

'I'm positive, as long as you remember to call me Jaye in public, but only for the next couple of months. I must warn you though, I've upset a couple of crooks over the past week and they are searching for me. At the moment they have no idea where I am and where we are going tonight is, I feel sure, safe. I am also armed. It has to do with the three men who died when I spoke to you last week. It's a lot bigger than I ever imagined and I have been seconded to another department to work undercover. On the very remote chance they find me, your safety will be my number one concern. If I need to tell you to do something, don't ask any questions, just do it. I promise I will protect you with my life. And now my beautiful Christine, you can opt out of dining with me.' He winced. He'd gone too far but she had a right to know the facts.

Christine cocked her head to one side with a soft smile on her face. It was so good to see that wisp of a smile instead of the despair she'd shown when she thought he'd left.

'I'm willing to take a chance with you if you are willing to do the same with me.' Her smile broadened when he drew her against his chest. Damn but she felt good.

'Wonderful, let's go and enjoy the evening.' After a brief hug he released his hold, immediately grasped her hand then turned towards the door.

She pulled back. 'Ben, the best way to lead a blind person is this.' Tugging her hand free she placed the fingers of one of her hands inside his elbow. 'Remember to warn me when we approach any steps or uneven ground, otherwise you'll find me grabbing hold of you while I trip and sink to the ground. Since I can't see so well, it could be embarrassing where I grab.' There was a hint of innuendo in her voice.

Ben laughed. 'Not that I want you to trip, but I wouldn't mind in the least if you grab hold of me. In fact I would enjoy it a great deal.' A bright tinge of pink bloomed across Christine's face.

He waited while she locked her door then guided her to his car, handing her into the passenger seat. Even concentrating on taking care of Christine, he managed to search around for any signs of a tail. There was a young couple jogging towards the park on the opposite corner with their leashed dog looking much happier than them at the exercise. A couple of teenagers were skate-boarding on the opposite footpath. As they drove past an SUV pulled against the kerb under the shadows of a spreading tree at the end of the street, Ben noted the dark shape of what appeared to be a woman, sitting in the driver's seat. She was studying an open book that looked to be a road map, with a small torch. Under normal circumstances Ben would stop to offer assistance but he wasn't overly familiar with this part of town and a legally blind woman wouldn't be much better. Although the way she negotiated the piano bar he figured she would be a greater help than he imagined. He still couldn't believe he hadn't noticed the signs. Said a lot for his detecting skills.

He kept up a patter of general conversation until they arrived at their destination then silence ensued while they walked through the car park, then under the cover of the entryway. Coming to a couple of steps, Ben stopped. 'Much as I'm looking forward to your arms grappling around me, I guess I'd better tell you we have three steps going down, then we have about two metres of paving and a rather heavy glass door.'

Chrissie smiled while she descended without falling and waited for Ben to push the door open. Pulling her chair out for her, he waited until she was settled before moving to his own seat. When the waitress offered them both a menu, Ben murmured, 'I will be ordering for my lady.' He smiled at Christine's gasp and guessed her husband had never been so considerate of her disability. 'That's if it's okay with you, Christine. What takes your fancy? Is there anything you don't eat or any favourites?'

'Nobody's ever done that for me before. Thank you. To answer your question, I don't eat any kind of shellfish. Apart from the fact that they don't agree with me, can you imagine trying to de-vein a prawn when you can't see it? Describe the rest for me.'

'You have a point there but one would hope the prawn is already de-veined before it's served. You've just completely put me off the shellfish.' In a quiet but clear voice, Ben read out the other items on the menu, making humorous comments about some of the ingredients and eliciting a few laughs from his guest. When the waitress came to take their order, Christine made her choice but insisted on no gravy, sauce or dressing on her salad.

'Try eating a piece of meat smothered in gravy with your eyes closed. And you can't see the mess the gravy makes when it falls.' Chrissie commented after she'd heard the waitress walk away.

'I can see I have a lot to learn but don't be afraid to let me know, Christine.' He reached over to seek out Chrissie's hand, lifting it up then wrapping his fingers around hers.

'Why do you call me Christine?'

The question startled him. 'Because it suits you, and it is your name.'

'So I can call you…'

'Jaye,' Ben interrupted. 'Only Jaye.'

Christine cocked her head to one side and grinned. 'Very well, only Jaye, tell me what you look like. I already know you are tall, broad shouldered, quite lean, have a deep, sexy voice, are wearing the aftershave I like and have a great sense of humour. Fill me in with the rest of the details.'

'Before or after the makeover, Miss Know-it-all?' For a brief moment he felt relieved she couldn't see his face because he had felt it suffuse with colour at some of her description. How she had sussed out so much, he had no idea. She had to be able to see a lot more than he had imagined.

'Now.'

'At the moment I am a world travelled surfie with the most awful streaked, bleached hair that is forever messy. Grey eyes, lighter than yours, thanks to coloured contact lenses. Still six feet tall. I couldn't alter my height without them chopping off half my legs and no job is worth that. My clothes have been described to me as shabby chic. To me, shabby is the operative word. I can't abide walking around with my shirt hanging out over my pants, but it is. It's supposed to be the trendy layered look. Feels downright messy. None of what I am wearing is the real me. Listen to this?' Lifting his forearm from the table he rattled the chains on his wrist. 'Ghastly. And I'm told it all costs a small fortune. I'm supposed to be very wealthy. I can assure you, if I had that sort of money I certainly wouldn't waste it on clothing of this type.'

Christine laughed, a sweet tinkling sound that fascinated Ben. 'And before?' she asked.

'My grandmother was Spanish. Like my mother, I have her ebony black hair and dark brown eyes. I like to be neat and well dressed. No jewellery apart from a watch.'

'Ah, tall, dark and handsome. When we leave here will you let me feel your face so I can see in my mind what you look like?'

'I don't mind at all. You can feel as much of my body as you want.' He paused then whispered, 'our food is arriving.'

Reddening at Ben's cheeky words, Christine sat still while the plates were served. Then she looked embarrassed.

'What's the problem?'

'Jaye, will you describe my plate as in a clock. For instance, mashed potato at three o'clock. It helps me eat without making a total mess.' The way she said it, humble and hesitant, did another good job of twisting his innards into a tight knot. She needed a confidence boost so he was patient as he described her dinner plate then watched while she moved the plate in line with the edge of the table, felt for her napkin and tucked it into the top of her dress. Made sense. She then felt for the large knife and fork, discarding the entrée cutlery she didn't need. A glass of red wine was set at a particular distance from her plate and she unerringly found it each time she took a sip. Amazed at how accurate she was, he tried to imagine doing the same with his eyes shut. He'd have the tabled littered with dribbles and splatters in no time at all. While they ate he kept up an amusing banter, enjoying it every time he heard her sexy, tinkling laugh.

After the dinner plates had been removed, he asked Christine if she danced. 'There's a small dance floor of which other people are taking advantage.'

She grinned. 'I've not danced since losing my sight but I'm willing to give it a try if you'll forgive my stumbles. But don't spin me too much because I could lose my sense of balance.'

He hadn't thought of that. There was so much to consider. 'I think it will be me begging forgiveness every time I step on your toes.' Ben stood then guided Christine to the floor. She soon relaxed into his arms while he shuffled her around the floor. His taut body muscles pressed against and welcomed her softness while he held her close. He smiled at her closed eyes as he relished the feeling and watched a range of expressions flitter across her face. He couldn't help but wonder what she was thinking. Should he ask, or would he be intruding? Her features softened then he felt delighted when she dropped her head onto his shoulder, causing him to tighten his hold around her waist and draw her even closer. Unable to resist the temptation, he planted a soft kiss on her hair just as the music ended. It was a few moments before he found the strength to release her.

Before they moved back to the table to order sweets and coffee, Christine drew in a deep breath and stood hesitant.

'What's the problem?' Ben asked.

'This is the hard part. This was one of the things my husband couldn't handle. It embarrassed him too much. I need you to guide me to the ladies' room, or to ask a waitress to take me if you find it too embarrassing. I only need to be shown to the door, I'm fine after that. If they have separate facilities for the disabled it would be even better as all the buttons and handles have Braille markings.'

With her quiet voice sounding almost apologetic he figured she was feeling embarrassed about having to ask. 'That's not hard. I certainly don't have a problem with that. I chased a woman into the ladies once and created quite a stir amongst those inside. I had to break the door down of the cubicle where my quite nasty little trollop had locked herself. I handcuffed her while she was standing on the seat, screaming blue murder at me. Trouble was it was she who had committed the murder. She was one little spitfire. I ended up with scratches all down my face and hands. She is now doing a twenty year stint.'

Reaching out for Christine's hand, he placed it on his elbow then led her down the passage, moving a discreet distance from the door while waiting for her and trying to figure out what there was to be embarrassed about. Any man with an ounce of manners and respect would keep his partner safe and do all he could for her. He then led her back to their table where he read out the dessert menu.

'I'm not one for sweet things,' she murmured, 'but if there is cheese, I wouldn't mind some to go with a really hot, white coffee. I have quite a passion for good cheese.'

'Sounds good to me, I'll join you,' and he placed the order. Things were getting better and better. Who would have guessed that this woman shared his weakness for good cheese? So far he hadn't found one tiny thing that he didn't like about Christine. Even her inability to see didn't put him off.

When the platter arrived, Ben sliced up the three different cheese varieties, placing a small wedge onto each cracker on the plate before sliding the plate in front of her.

'You have a blue vein at noon, soft Brie at three and a sharp cheddar at six. Three pieces of each on crackers, with a mixture of dried fruits and nuts at nine o'clock.'

'Thank you, would you care to share it with me?'

'I'll only help you out if you promise me another dance before we leave.' Ben reached over and grasped Christine's hand.

Several dances later interspersed by imbibing the cheese and coffee, Ben suggested it was time to leave since the room was emptying at a fast rate. He felt saddened the magical night was about to end.

At Christine's unit, Ben glanced around for any sign of someone following or laying in wait, before assisting her to her door. 'Allow me,' he said when she removed a key from a small evening-bag. Slipping the key from her hand he unlocked the door then pushed it open.

They stepped inside. 'You promised me you would let me feel your face.' Christine murmured hesitantly as though afraid of asking.

'Go ahead.' He kept still while she lifted her hands and gently ran the tips of her fingers over every feature of his face, starting from his hair then moving down. When she reached his cheeks, she smiled as the tips of her fingers searched around the slight depression and then made just as thorough search on his other side.

'You have a dimple, but only on your right side.' Smiling in bemusement, she ran the fingers of one hand along his lips. Ben couldn't resist lifting his own hand to press her fingers closer while he planted a soft kiss on them before releasing her hand to let her continue her exploration. He smiled at the sound of her indrawn breath and the pink blush rising up her face.

'I knew you were tall, you said you were dark, and now I know for sure about the handsome. You are a very good-looking man. Thank you for a glorious evening. It has been a very long time since I've had such a wonderful time.'

Her words had him wonder again if any man had taken her out on a date or if her disability deterred them from issuing an invitation, which to him would be reprehensible. 'It was my very great pleasure, Christine. But before I go, how about me returning the compliment? I want to know if one particular part of your face is as soft and warm as it looks.' Without waiting for an answer, he sought out Christine's mouth with his, brushing her lips while he wrapped his arms around her, feeling her tremble under his touch. Her response had him deepening the kiss until his own body's reaction told him he had better let her go, very soon.

'Far softer and warmer than I ever imagined,' Ben whispered as he eased his hips away from her middle lest she realise just how his body had reacted. 'And the sweetness is very intoxicating. Goodnight, beautiful lady. I sincerely hope you will agree to come out with me again, very soon. I'll be in the bar sometime over the next few nights. Sleep well, Christine. I look forward to our next meeting.' He released her and stood back, waiting until she locked her door from the inside before returning to his car.

***

Once alone, Chrissie expelled a long loud sigh. Angel padded over to her, snuffling her wet nose against the hand Chrissie had dropped down in greeting. Together, they walked side-by-side into the lounge room, Angel's excellent training not allowing her to lollop in front of her mistress, or jump up in exuberance. Instead, Angel waited with practised patience until Chrissie was seated, then she plonked her head in Chrissie's lap. She ran her fingers behind Angel's ears and ruffled her fur.

'I had such a wonderful night, Angel. We danced – and it felt so good. Ben was ever so kind and gentle and he didn't seem to mind having to help me. I know it was just one dinner, but Angel, one dinner out with a really nice man is a thousand times, no a billion times better than no dates at all. I know he was probably just feeling sorry for me, but Angel – he kissed me. That felt so amazing. His arms were so warm and so strong… and his lips… wow, Angel! He did say he wanted to go out again but I don't really expect it to happen… but it's nice to dream. You go to bed girl; we'll go for a walk in the morning. Goodnight, Angel.'

Chapter Fourteen

The euphoria of her fantastic night out was still zinging when Chrissie woke early then breakfasted in the tiny courtyard behind her unit. Angel stood next to her, crunching on the cupful of biscuits she was allowed each morning while Chrissie munched on toast and sipped black tea. With still a brisk chill kissing her cheeks, she felt that the sun's rays hadn't yet reached her back door, so she knew it was still quite early without having to resort to feeling the hands on her special watch with a glass that opened out and which had raised numbers so she could feel the hands against each numeral.

The earliness of the hour didn't bother her. She preferred to walk Angel when fewer people were milling around. It made it easier to negotiate the walking track through the nearby park and not get harassed by the cyclists who gave her status no consideration at all. When they beeped their bells, most expected her to move out of the way, even when they saw Angel in harness. When she didn't move from the path, some would issue a mouthful of abuse as they veered off the edge to avoid a collision. It shouldn't be like that. She had been shocked when told it was normal treatment of people with sight impairment by some callous people.

Her hunger sated, Chrissie rinsed her few dishes and put the breakfast items away in their regimented places. 'Angel,' she called then held out her hand, shivering when the cold dampness of a wet nose brushed against her skin. She knelt then slipped the working harness over Angel's hairy but smooth back and strapped it into place.

'I don't know what I'd do without you,' she murmured as she ruffled the hair around Angel's head. She tugged on a pair of socks and sneakers then tied a sweatshirt around her waist in case the light breeze strengthened. A sleeveless T-shirt clung to her body. She felt both sides of her head to ensure the two bunches she had tied her hair into were still in place just behind her ears and were relatively even. Happy, she ran her hands down her legs to rid close fitting sweat pants over a pair of shorts, of any wrinkles and to make sure the bottom of the legs were even against the tops of her shoes.

She grasped the stiff harness. 'Walk in the park, Angel.' The command was all the dog needed to lead Chrissie safely along the regular track. It was a route Angel knew well and rarely needed any commands to complete.

As she made her way down the side of her street then across the road to the large park, her usual route for their daily walk, she couldn't erase the smile of sheer euphoria from her face. She hadn't felt this happy in way too long. At the sound of someone falling into step behind her as they emerged from a connecting road, she swung her head from side-to-side to gain an impression of the type of person that was there. Was it some-one regular she could chat to? The heaviness of the footfalls indicated two men, but they were strangers, the rhythm being unfamiliar and most regulars acknowledged her as they passed.

The sounds of the native birds foraging for their early morning delights heartened Chrissie as she commanded Angel to find a seat, so she could linger and enjoy the songs of the wild birds waking up to a new day. Having walked in the same park so many times, she knew exactly where she was when she felt for the back of the park bench where Angel had stopped. She felt the ridges and fine gullies of the wood beneath her fingertips. Plonking herself down, she edged her way along to the middle of the wooden seat before releasing the harness, allowing Angel to lie by the side of her feet.

By holding her head still she was able to focus and see a tiny pinprick of what was in front of her. The sounds of the water tumbling over smooth rocks in the stream a few metres in front had her listening intently for the different quacks and honks of the water birds. Then she sought out each one, overjoyed when she managed to focus. It delighted her each time she managed to catch early morning rays glinting off feathers. Soon she would have to rely on memory or imagination to visualise such beauty. When she heard the two men who had followed her go past, she called out, 'Good morning.' They both mumbled an indistinct reply as they continued on down the pathway. The footsteps faded into the distance as she sniffed the air, absorbing the dank moisture of rotting reeds on the edge of the stream, which was a haven for mating pairs of birds. It was the wrong season for young chicks; the last lot were on the verge of reaching maturity. An occasional splash told her that either a fish had jumped out of the water or a duck had dunked its head underneath scrounging for tasty morsels.

Two cyclists passed, heading in the direction she'd come and three joggers pounded past in the opposite direction. A fresh gust chased a few leaves down the path and there was an answering rustle higher in the branches.

A low growl from Angel interrupted the delightful sounds of nature. Alarmed, Chrissie dropped her hand down, fumbled around then grasped the handle of the harness. 'What is it girl?' she whispered as her blood swarmed.

She felt Angel stand and tense, her next growl louder and more insistent. Chrissie felt a wave of fear sweep up her body; a surge of adrenaline had her muscles tighten. She stood, turning back the way she had come. 'Walk, Angel.'

Angel began leading Chrissie along the path accompanied by deep-throated growls. Chrissie felt the agitation in her dog and knew something was wrong by the unusual behaviour. 'Faster, girl,' she urged, her free hand reaching for the personal alarm around her neck.

They reached the area of the park where there were dense bushes along the sides of the pathway: the more muffled sounds of the water and the scents from the close grown shrubs her indication. With less background noise, she was able to make out the scrapes of footsteps behind her. They were keeping pace but nearing. Panic surged. She urged Angel to go faster still while she listened with intense concentration. Slow jogging she could handle but an out and out rapid run holding the harness without losing her balance and tripping was beyond her. Focussing was impossible with so much jolting up and down.

She jogged as fast as she dared. The footsteps increased their pace to match hers. Two people were following. The heaviness of footfalls indicated men - the two strangers?

Panic turned to terror at the sudden onrush of the two sets of feet.

Angel's barks intensified.

Chrissie's fingers tightened around the personal alarm. She often felt stupid wearing it but the people at the Association for the Blind had drummed it into her that it was a necessary evil. She never believed anybody would take advantage of a person's disability to accost him or her but now she was more than glad she continued to sling the alarm around her neck whenever she stepped out of her door. Feeling for the button she pressed hard, emitting a shrill, ear splitting sound.

Two strong arms grabbed her from behind. She screamed.

Angel's barks grew louder and more frantic.

A rough hand clamped over Chrissie's mouth to silence her as she was dragged to the ground, her gasp of pain muffled by the fingers pressing into her mouth. The alarm was ripped from her neck, tearing skin in a searing burn as it was yanked without a care. Beads of warm sticky blood trickled down her neck melding with the damp dirt she was pressed into. Feet stomped on the alarm until the strident noise was silenced.

She heard the frenzied barking of Angel, and then a loud thud, followed by a yelp then a whimper. She bit down hard on the fingers pressing into her mouth, hurting her. At the loud yowl of pain from the owner of the fingers as he loosened his hand, Chrissie yelled, 'Angel!' There were a few more loud thuds and then silence: an ominous silence, then the sickly metallic smell of blood.

Tears sprang to Chrissie's eyes but they disappeared the moment her legs were grasped by one pair of hands and her arms by the other. There was no escaping. Then an overwhelming odious stench almost overpowered her as the person holding her arms panted with effort, putrid breath fanning her face. Both men grunted and puffed while they carried her just above the ground, her backside scraping along the rocks and bushes. She screamed again and again.

She was dropped with a heavy thud onto the rough ground then a fist whacked her across the side of her mouth to shut her up. Whimpering in pain, she squeezed her eyelids tight together as she tried to exorcise her terrified mind from her hurting body. Jagged stones and bushes jabbed into her from underneath as a rough, foul tasting hand clamped over her mouth again, pressing down hard while another hand grabbed hold of her T-shirt, tearing it upwards, the blast of cold air causing goose bumps to rise on her bare skin. The other pair of hands grasped the waistband of her track-pants.

Kicking every which way as hard as she could, one foot contacted with bone and muscle. There was a strong accented curse then a sudden painful punch to her abdomen in retaliation. Agony tore through her body. She had trouble trying to catch her breath after all the air had whooshed from her lungs from the heavy punch. A rough hand grasped one breast through her lacy bra, squeezed hard, the searing pain blindsiding her, while two more hands jerked her track pants down to her thighs. Her shorts rode down with the pants but her briefs stayed put. With her writhing from side-to-side, the hand on her mouth released a fraction, giving her an opportunity to screech out for help. There was a tug at her scalp as her hair tangled with the leaves and twigs from the trampled, crushed bushes. An all out effort to wriggle free caused the man to release his hold on her mouth giving her the opportunity to screech out an almighty scream. She was rewarded by another hard blow to the side of her mouth that knocked her head sideways so hard, it felt as though her head was parting company from her neck. Whimpering in pain, she could feel and taste the blood flow from inside her mouth where her teeth had penetrated the soft skin inside her cheek.

Large, thick fingers pressed against her knickers, rubbing at her most private parts. Not gentle caresses that a lover would make, but harsh grating movements that really hurt, while another hand held down one leg. This wasn't just about rape: this was going to be torture. 'Why?' she whimpered as tears flowed from the corner of each eye. She sniffed to fight them back but the moisture kept on leaking.

'This is a message for your boyfriend,' was growled into her ear from the accented voice.

'But I don't…'

'He will understand.'

Feeling confused since she didn't have a boyfriend but frantic with fear, she wanted to just give in and let them kill her. Then she wouldn't feel anything. But that wasn't her. She was determined to fight so lifted her free leg and kicked with all her might, arching her back to gain more momentum. The accented voice cursed again, 'Keep still you bitch if you don't want to get hurt.'

If she had been able to she would have laughed in scorn for she knew for certain she was going to be hurt regardless. She'd already been hurt. So she kept fighting by squirming from side-to-side, bucking her hips and shoulders and trying to free her limbs.

In the distance a cyclist dinged the bell on his bike so Chrissie made a final effort to writhe her mouth free and managed to let out another yell for help. A male voice called out in response from not that far away. Her two attackers paused then released their hold. The very instant she felt freedom she screamed again and continued screeching even while she received several hard kicks to one side of her body and her head. She let out a final scream as she heard the running footsteps moving away from her, crashing through the bushes then she sank into dark oblivion.

When she became aware of her surroundings, there were hands on her body. Her attackers had returned. She screamed out at the top of her voice in a determined desperation to writhe free but the hands pressed down on her again to still her.

'It's all right. You are safe now. I'm a paramedic and you are in an ambulance on your way to hospital.' A calming masculine voice, so different from the others, came from near her head while a gentle, warm hand grasped hers.

Her eyes burned with unshed tears as she recalled the frenzied attack. One tear escaped and was immediately brushed away with a soft cloth.

'Angel? Where's Angel?' Chrissie whispered. Her mouth felt really sore and swollen and she barely recognised her own voice.

'Who is Angel?' the voice asked.

'My guide dog, where is she?'

Chrissie felt the tense silence. Memory surged. Tears welled up in her eyes then flowed unchecked down her face. She knew what was coming but didn't want to hear or believe it.

'I'm sorry. Angel was already dead when we arrived on the scene. We could do nothing for her. The police collected her body. Do you have a name? I'm Pete.'

'Chrissie, Christine Mears. How... how bad are my injuries?' They must be bad for everything hurt, even breathing. 'I feel ghastly.'

The tears continued. She had no control. A hand wiped the salty moisture from her cheeks with a soft cloth but regardless of the gentle touch she winced in pain.

'You have quite a few rather nasty bruises, cuts and abrasions, but we'll need the doctors to check you more thoroughly for any internal damage. The blows to your head need further examination to check for fractures and concussion. Try to relax. We'll be there in a couple of minutes.'

The hand that continued holding hers was warm, large and gentle giving her a sense of comfort. But Angel - her heart hitched and she slid her eyelids closed. Her brain began to recall more accurate details and an overwhelming sense of shame and anger enveloped her. She tried to turn over, but couldn't, so instead turned her face away from Pete, and switched off. Her tears dried up, her mind slipped into an empty blackness.

An awareness of a lot happening about her tickled at the edge of her consciousness but her numb, shocked brain absorbed little. There was a sensation of movement and the voice of Pete reported her condition.

'Christine Mears, a blind lady, spoke coherently for a short while then went into a state of shock.'

Shock, she was in shock? What did shock feel like? All she could feel was pain. During a thorough examination and treatment, the female doctor talked to her the entire time, telling her what was happening and why. She heard but didn't take much in. Her tattered, torn clothes were removed from her body and replaced by a hospital gown.

Police visited and were given details that were known about her by the nurse by her bed but she answered no questions. Words were beyond her, which felt ridiculous that they wouldn't form. It felt weird, as though she were in some vast vacuum and was disconnected from reality.

A different voice murmured something about a change in her condition and that she appeared to be aware of her surroundings. She didn't feel any different – her brain was still mush. A buzzing sound came from next to her head then a few minutes later, clacking footsteps approached. They stopped at her bedside and her hand was grasped. The fuzziness in her head didn't feel so fuzzy but was still there.

'Christine, I'm Dr Rachael Woods.' When nothing more was said Chrissie turned towards the voice. She could make out a large shape standing next to the bed. Pink. She was wearing pale pink. 'You are in hospital. Do you remember why you were brought here?'

Chrissie nodded a couple of times while fighting to hold back a renewed rush of tears. She knew. It had all flooded back. She'd been assaulted and Angel… 'Oh, God, Angel!'

There was a grating noise sounding like a chair being dragged across the floor followed by a hush of fabric then a creak. The doctor was sitting beside her.

'Christine, is there anyone I can call? Any family? Friends?' The voice was gentle.

'I have no family here. What is the time? I have to go to work.' She made to sit up but a sharp pain tore through her abdomen and she fell back on the pillows, gasping.

'You won't be going to work for at least a week. The police have notified your school and the hotel where you work. They made enquiries with the Association for the Blind to garner details about you. The Guide Dog Association have been given details of Angel's demise. The police want to ask you a few questions. Do you feel up to it? I'm to let them know when you come around but I can put it off until later if you like. I've ordered you a meal.'

Chrissie shook her head then regretted the movement when a sharp pain galloped through. She said nothing. Despite the agonising pain, she turned over and put her back to the doctor who lingered for only a few moments then left the room. The last thing Chrissie heard was the doctor speaking to someone outside in the corridor. She assumed it was the police. 'I'm sorry but Mrs Mears is not well enough to be interviewed yet. Try again in the morning.' A brief sense of relief overshadowed her shame.

Chapter Fifteen

Ben wriggled over for the umpteenth time, thumped his pillow into submission and groaned. Sleep had been sketchy. Thoughts of his evening with Christine kept swamping his brain, re-living every moment, every detail. A vivid image was the bleakness of her face when she thought he'd left: something that had never been an option when she had asked him to go. All he'd done was turn around to shut the door and when he turned back… sweet mercy, the look of utter devastation on her face! It had shocked him to the core. How often had she been hurt because of her disability? How often had people turned away just because one tiny part of her body didn't work so well?

He recalled how his body had quivered then hardened when her fingers ran over his face, her gentle touch further inflaming every nerve ending in his body. And the kiss!

Even thinking about how she had kissed him back, gave him an instant reaction he found impossible to ease. No woman, and there had been quite a few, had ever affected him so profoundly in such a short time.

After finally falling into an exhausted sleep, Ben slept later than normal. One glance at his clock and he shot from bed. His trousers were at half mast when weary brain cells began functioning. He wasn't required to go to the office. He was undercover and had nothing to do. Just the thought of having a day without investigating crime and filling out endless reports sent his innards on edge. Not being one to sit idle he had to do something. Without stopping for breakfast, he drove out of town to his favourite park then went for a hard, physically draining run, pushing his fit body to the limits to try to ease the emotional tension from the previous night. Exhausted but still needing to occupy his time, he found a quiet café where he lingered over lunch. Still antsy, he returned to the apartment, showered then surfed the internet to fill in time. There was no doubt he would be spending most of the late evening sitting at a certain bar waiting for the brief moments he would have to talk to Christine, be with her, touch her. He cursed for forgetting to obtain her phone number.

Full of confidence, Ben strode into the piano bar that evening. That same confidence whooshed out of him when he came to a grinding halt only three steps inside the doorway. It was the sound of the piano that alerted him. Something was very wrong. Instead of the soft, gentle arpeggios that dominated Christine's playing, more strident staccato notes of her colleague grated against his eardrums. He glared fiercely at the piano as though it was an aberration on his senses. Gathering his wits about him, he strode over to Mick. 'Where's Christine?' he demanded.

Mick stepped back looking shocked at the ferocity of the demand. 'I don't know a lot about what happened, but apparently she was attacked early this morning while she was walking her dog. She's in hospital and won't be back for at least a week.'

Mick's last few words were spoken to mid-air. At the word hospital Ben spun around and ran out of the bar. He was on the phone to the nearest emergency hospital before he reached the stairs. Asking about the condition of Christine Mears confirmed where she was but standard procedure was that unless you were a relative, no details could be given except to inform him she was as well as could be expected: a comment that told him absolutely nothing except that she was a patient. As well as could be expected for what? Had she just fallen, been punched, assaulted or even raped?

Less than ten minutes later Ben was asking for her room number. A blank look of ignorance when he mentioned Christine's name told him a lot. The hospital was not giving any details. If she couldn't talk, then she was seriously hurt. Not caring about his undercover role, he drew out his badge from an inside pocket and flashed it.

'I'm in charge of investigating Mrs Mears' attack and I need to make sure she is all right. I'll only be a minute. I need to confirm one minor detail with her because we think we have her attacker in custody.'

His blatant lie gave him the results he wanted and within seconds he was riding the elevator to Christine's floor. The ride up three floors felt interminable, giving Ben time to wonder why the hospital elevator was so plain and boring. Cheerful pictures and messages were a definite requirement to make terrified, anxious visitors feel more at ease. It felt like forever before the doors hissed open and he scanned the signs for room numbers, turning the way indicated by arrows.

What took less than a minute felt like an hour as Ben sped down the corridors at a rate that was only just below an out-and-out run, searching for the correct number. Spying the number twenty-four on the closed door, he paused, sucked in a deep breath in an attempt to calm rampant nerves then pushed open the door far enough to ensure Christine was inside. His heart melted at the sight of the huddled figure lying on her side, her legs drawn up into the foetal position. Even from the distance he could make out her badly bruised and swollen face in the soft bedside light. What felt like a ten tonne slab of concrete settled in his chest at the sight. He flicked the switch at the door knowing full well the sudden brightness wouldn't affect Christine very much, if at all, but he wanted to see how bad her injuries were.

'Christine?' he managed to squeak out.

Instinct told him she was awake and had heard. For a brief moment, her eyes fluttered open then she turned over to face away from him. Noting the difficulty she had in moving he knew she was in a great deal of pain, further wrenching his innards in a way he couldn't recall ever happening before. He moved towards her, slowing as he approached then stood beside her bed. She had turned her back on him and covered her face with her hands as though ashamed. Hurrying around to the other side of the bed, he reached out with one hand then with utmost gentleness grasped the fingers of both her hands. With his other hand he ran one finger down the side of her bruised face, barely touching her. His heart clamped tight.

'Dear, God, Christine,' he whispered as he knelt on the floor. He drew her hands away from her face, bringing them up to his lips where he settled a soft fleeting kiss on her fingers before just holding them against his mouth as he studied her. The pain in his heart, when he saw the injuries to her face, was agonizing.

'Christine, please talk to me? What happened?' His eyes followed one solitary tear as it escaped from the corner of one shuttered eye. After tracing it with the tip of one finger, he leant over and gently kissed the eye it had come from. A second tear followed the first, and then another and another until there was a steady stream. It wrenched his insides at how she was unable to hold back her distress. How long had she been holding back her emotional pain? And what the hell happened?

Drawing back the covers, Ben took utmost care in gathering her up into his arms then carried her around the other side of her bed to the only chair in the room. He settled with her in his lap, cradling her head against his shoulder with one large outspread hand. Gripping the edge of the open-weave, cotton blanket, he yanked it out of its restrictive tucks then wrapped it around her to keep her warm. It didn't take long for the tears to become an uncontrolled torrential flood, soaking his jacket and shirt. He said nothing but allowed her to cry out all her hurt and misery.

The nurse, who came by to take observations, saw what was happening, smiled and then closed the door behind her. So if Christine could miss a round of obs then her condition wasn't critical. The knowledge in no way eased his angst.

When Ben felt the sobbing ease, he reached over to her bedside table, whooped a pile of tissues from the box then mopped the worst of the moisture from her face, taking care to not put any pressure on her cuts and bruises.

'Ben?' she whispered with a hiccough.

'What is it, Christine?'

'They killed Angel.' Sucking in his breath he tried not to tense his muscles. Anger filled every fibre of his being. Who did this abominable thing? Why?

'I'm really sorry to hear that. Have you spoken to the police yet?'

She shook her head against his chest.

'How many people attacked you?'

Two fingers edged their way out from the hem of the blanket.

'Men?' asked Ben as he tried to dampen down his ire and keep his voice calm. Inside he felt like exploding from anger.

'Yes.' A tremulous answer gushed out. A deep sob followed.

Ben ran his fingers down the side of her face to ease her tension then kissed the top of her head. 'Tell me what you can about either, or both of them. I know you didn't see them, but your other senses would pick up more than most people. Let me know if you want to stop but the more you can tell me, the easier and quicker it will be to catch them.' He hated asking the questions, hated her having to relive her terror but to catch the perpetrators he needed as much information as he could glean, very quickly.

'One had an accent, probably Dutch, maybe German. He was tallish and had very large hands with thick fingers. His hands were abnormally large.' She shuddered. Feeling her trembles against his torso, Ben tightened his hold.

'He carried my feet and pulled my tracksuit pants down. He tried to... Oh, God... Ben... he touched me... hurt me.'

Clamping his mouth shut, Ben held her close while finding it hard to breathe. Inside, he was seething and his heart physically ached.

'Would you recognise the voice if you heard it again?'

'I'll never forget it!' Chrissie gasped out. She wriggled then sniffed. 'He said it was a warning.'

'A warning for what?'

'I don't know,' she whimpered. 'He said my boyfriend would understand but I don't have a boyfriend.'

'And the other one, what can you tell me about him?'

'Rough hands. He held my hands and punched me here.' A shaking hand brushed against the worst of the bruises on her cheek. 'He was the one who pulled my top up. His fingers were rough on my… Oh, Ben… it was so awful. He squeezed my breasts, really hard. It hurt so much. I remember biting his hand to make him let go. The other one I kicked. The worst thing I remember about him was his ghastly breath. He stunk so bad.'

Jerking upright, fear ripped through his gut. This was his fault? He'd been followed again. But how did they know where he was going? His eyes slid shut as he drew in a long breath. Sweet mercy, how on earth was he going to handle this? How to tell her? Rising with her still in his arms, he placed Christine back on the bed and tucked the blanket around her.

'I have to make an urgent phone call. I'm sure I know who it was and why. Oh, dear God, I'm so sorry Christine.' He swept one hand through his hair then down his face trying to wipe away the guilt and shame. 'I'm going to leave you for only a few minutes but I promise I will come straight back. I'll send a nurse in to keep you company. I don't want you to be alone.'

As his mind scrambled for the best course of action he stared at Christine. Her face was a mess. One cheek was swollen and black, the other not much better. The lower lip had a bloody split in one corner and there was an egg shaped lump on her brow. Nausea swirled. Bending down, he brushed his lips against her swollen mouth then left as fast he could without making his rapid departure obvious. He grabbed the first nurse he could find, flashed his badge then insisted Christine be watched until he returned to the room, explaining why he felt her life was in danger. He sped to the Chief of Nursing in her office, once again showing his badge, requesting to use her phone. First he called John Markham and gave him a run down, demanding a twenty-four hour guard be placed outside her door. His second call, on the mobile he had been given, was to Vince.

'What happened to the tail on our targets? Christine Mears was sexually assaulted and beaten to within an inch of her life by Casey and Gerard – who is, by the way, probably Dutch and not French. He is tall with abnormally large hands. I think he's the same man who planted the bug on me. I want Casey picked up now and charged with aggravated assault. I've rung John on a separate line and have ordered a twenty-four hour guard for Christine.'

'We can't do that. He hasn't led us to the big man yet.'

'Well if your frigging men had been doing their job this morning they would have caught both of them together, raping and belting the life out of a defenceless blind woman and her guide dog. If you don't pull that bastard in now then I'm off the case. Throw the flaming book at him. You've got him for three murders we know of, a pile of burglaries, attempted rape, attempted murder, aggravated assault. What more do you flaming well want? He's too dangerous to be left loose any longer. How many more deaths do you want on your hands? I'll give you one hour to have him in custody or I'm going back to my job and I'll arrest him myself. If you need me, I'm at the Royal hospital and I intend staying here all night if I have to. Ring me in one hour.' Slamming the phone shut in utter frustration he then leant on the cluttered desk trying to calm his racing heart and cool his temper enough to face Christine. Dear God, how could he face her? Would he ever be able to rid himself of the terrible guilt tearing at his innards?

'Damn it all to hell!' he yelled before demanding to see the report on Christine's injuries. His stomach muscles tensed tighter and tighter while he read through the extensive list of severe bruising and swelling. Damn, and he'd held her. She must have been in agony with that many bruises to her torso. His greatest fear was that she had been raped, as it was obvious from what Christine had said that rape had been the intent. A sigh of relief whooshed out when he read the last sentence. There was no sign of sexual penetration. But she had been sexually and physically assaulted despite there being no penetration. The knowledge didn't in any way alleviate his massive guilty conscience.

Some very deep breaths as he walked, lots of self-talk, a brief pause outside Christine's door, then Ben ambled into her room as though he didn't have a care in the world, to relieve the nurse of her watch. He sank back into the chair he had occupied a few minutes earlier, lifted Christine's hand and beamed her a broad smile, even though he knew she wouldn't see his face. But he had a vain hope his voice didn't give away the deep anger and remorse that was stabbing at his conscience.

'I've got my best men on the case and I'm posting a guard outside your door until they release you from here.'

Christine sighed then winced as she turned her head his way. 'Then what am I going to do? I can't teach without a guide dog which means I'll have to give up my job. I'll be trapped in my home almost twenty-four hours a day. I won't be able to go shopping, walking, anything, unless I drag someone out with me.'

'What are the chances of getting another dog?'

'It takes months and months to train them to specific needs, if there is one available. It costs a lot of money to train each one and there is such a demand.' Her eyes stuttered then slid shut. 'Poor Angel, she tried so hard to protect me. She didn't deserve this.' She swept one hand down her face and sniffed. There was a gulp and then tightening of her facial muscles as though she was fighting back a new bout of tears. 'I'm going to miss her so much. She was my best friend.' Her voice broke on a sob.

Ben waited as she fought for control, his thumb running gentle soft circles around the inside of her palm. 'Do you have any family, any other friend who could come in for a while?' He leant forwards, his fingers on his other hand brushing a few stray tendrils of hair from her face. His heart lurched when he watched her shake her head.

'Well, try not to worry. I'll sort something out. Now, why don't you try to get some sleep? I'm staying until they send one of my men to stand guard. If I'm not here when you wake, it's because there is a guard outside your door and I'm on your case. But I will be back. I promise. Don't talk to anyone other than John Markham or myself and especially don't mention my name. John is my second in command. He's a good man; one you can trust implicitly.'

Sitting in silence with Christine's hand in his until he was certain she was asleep he waited for the phone call from Vince. When he left the room to meet Vince at the bus stop around the corner from his apartment, he noted the plainclothes guard stationed at the door. He knew the man well, as one of his, and was pleased when Jack Grimshaw didn't recognise him as he sidled past, keeping his face shadowed.

Deep thoughts settled then swirled while he waited for Vince. Things had to change big time now Christine's life was in danger. Somewhere along the line he had missed a tail, which meant either Gerard or a fourth and possibly a fifth person had taken over shadowing him and apart from the vague description of the drunk, he had no idea what either person looked like. They were certainly better at their job than the other two. What he couldn't figure out was how they knew where Christine lived since he'd found the bug before he'd been to her place. Something still wasn't adding up.

He sensed Vince sitting on the other end of the bench. 'Tell me Des Casey is in custody.'

'He is. I gave the information to your boys and John Markham pulled him in. That way, it isn't related to the drugs, only to the assaults and burglaries.'

'Well things are going to change as from tonight. Christine is almost totally blind and has no one to care for her. Because of me, and you when it all comes down to the facts, she was badly hurt and needs protection. Therefore, from first thing in the morning, Jaye Hammond has gone back overseas to catch some big waves and organise his next purchase while Ben Somers is back at work. We have no more meetings for a few weeks in any case. By then, I pray we have been able to get enough information out of this scum so you can catch Gerard. I didn't mind when it was only my life on the line, but now they have Christine as their target, we either do it my way or I'm out. You figure out the details of the travel, but I want all my gear back in my own house by morning and my house and car keys in the unit. I'll leave everything in the apartment and ensure I leave the area unobserved. Right now, Christine needs me more than you need Gerard.'

'You're quite taken with her aren't you?'

He sighed. 'Yeah, there's something about Christine that draws my heartstrings pretty taut. She is a very special lady and she sure as hell doesn't deserve the treatment she received. Christine is an innocent bystander who has become entangled in a frightful mess – because of me. I'm finding it pretty hard to live with myself right now and if anything else happens to her, well, tell me how you would feel if it was Jenny lying in that hospital bed.'

There was a lengthy silence after Vince's indrawn breath. 'Okay, I'll do the paperwork on travel documentation. I'll keep in touch through Robbie to keep you up to speed if anything develops. I know it doesn't make things any better, but I'm real sorry about Christine. I know I would feel the same if it was Jenny. My boys lost their target and have had the riot act read to them. I've told them that if they stuff up again, I'm transferring them to your division to work under you and that right now you are pretty livid with them. But I didn't quite use those words. The words I used were quite a bit more colourful but I'm pretty sure they got the message.'

'Could I suggest we also pick up our other suspect and get him sent back to where he is wanted by the authorities? That way Gerard either has to deal with us alone, or find some other poor scapegoat. It will give us more time and it may even bring the big boys out in the open.'

Vince mulled the suggestion for a few moments. 'Yeah, I'll give the details to your boys and you can have him. Good luck.' Without another sound, Vince stood then ambled silently into the darkness. Ben remained where he was for a few minutes before jogging back to his apartment where he broke protocol to ring John Markham for a special request. John's mouthful of jesting abuse showed he wasn't pleased to be dragged from a deep sleep in the middle of the night for such an idiotic item.

Chapter Sixteen

The first rays of sun hadn't yet reached the horizon but the night had lightened. Ben left the apartment with nothing but the clothes he'd purchased and his own firearm. He'd made a thorough search of every item of clothing in case he had inadvertently picked up another electronic tracking device but with nothing there he still had no idea how they'd found Christine.

Keeping to the shadows he moved on foot. By the time the sun had fully emerged over the ranges in the distance to wake up this part of the world to another day, he was back in his own house waiting for the arrival of John Markham. Feeling edgy he unpacked the two suitcases sitting inside his front door, just for something to do. Relief surged when he heard John's voice on the intercom not long after the first stores had opened. Glancing around before unlatching the door, there was no evidence he had ever been away, not that it would matter with John.

John eyed Ben's hair as he handed over his purchase, a packet containing black hair rinse.

'Don't even dare think about making a comment,' Ben growled. 'Give me all the details on Casey while I use this.'

Ignoring John's grin, Ben read the instructions on the package on the way to the bathroom, leaving the door wide open. He pulled out a pair of latex gloves that were pretty well standard equipment for his job and he had hundreds of them. Then he slathered on the sticky substance and rubbed it into every strand of hair to ensure he covered every hated speck of blond. The making and sipping of coffee filled the required time for the dye to work before he rinsed the acrid smelling gunk out. A towel took out most of the water before he inspected the result in the mirror. Thank goodness the horrid streaks had gone. It wasn't as dark as his natural colour but it was a one hundred percent improvement. It startled him to realise just how much the different hairstyle and coloured lenses had altered his appearance. While he worked he chatted to John about all that had happened and laughed when John complained about having to be the one to interrogate their new prisoner.

'It was his sickly odour that got him arrested,' he called from the bathroom as he yanked on clothes. 'When Christine described his breath I knew who it was. My guess is that if he were medically examined, we would find he has cancer and is rotten on the inside. He looked real pasty when I saw him so maybe doesn't have long to live. Sorry, but you are going to be the one who does all the questioning. Even back to my normal appearance my voice will be recognised by him and we can't afford to let him know who I am in case he tips off the others. We'll be arresting one of his offsiders but I want them kept well apart. They're not to know that each other is in custody. You'll have to deal with him as well. We're after the big guy, Gerard. When she's feeling up to it, I'll have to bring Christine in to positively identify Casey. She bit him on the hand. Get a match from her teeth to the bite. She will need to feel his hands and smell his breath for a positive I.D.'

When Ben emerged from the bathroom, his hair still damp but neatly groomed without the ghastly stiff gel, he was beginning to feel more like his old self, especially dressed in his own clothes. 'My next stop is the hospital to see Christine. I'm going to need today to organise things for her. Did you track down what happened to her dog?'

'Yes, it has all been taken care of. The dog had to be autopsied first, for evidence. You can pick up the ashes tomorrow. Why did you want it cremated?'

'For Christine. Angel was her best friend. It might help ease her grief. Somehow the Police Department is going to have to find another guide dog. Ring me if anything crops up. I'll try to call into the office later this afternoon. Give Casey a real grilling and see if he will let anything slip about for whom he was working. God, he was stupid enough to show me his real driver's licence, use his own car in the hold up, carry a million dollars cash into a crowded restaurant, amongst other things – he should be easy enough to break.'

The two men left the house at the same time; John heading for the office while Ben went towards the hospital.

A nurse was carrying Christine's untouched lunch out of her room when Ben arrived. He frowned then grabbed the tray from the nurse's arms and held it in one hand when he entered the room using his hip to nudge the door open. He set the tray on the bench hanging over the bed. 'Not eating is going to get you nowhere but to stay in here a lot longer than either of us wants. I presume your breakfast went back untouched as well.'

A dark blush of guilt rose up Christine's face.

'So either you eat it yourself or I feed you. You choose.' He placed the knife and fork in her hand, described her plate then sat in the chair next to the bed, watching intently while she toyed with the food, placing small amounts in her mouth every now and again. He could see the action of chewing hurt but didn't relent until he was satisfied she had eaten enough to sustain her.

'Good girl,' he murmured as he removed the plate, strode across the room and placed it on the floor outside the door.

'Now we can talk. By the way,' he whispered into her ear, 'Ben Somers is back. Feel this.' Reaching for her hands he placed them on his head allowing her to feel the new sleek hairstyle minus the disgusting sticky gel. 'And it's back to being black, thank heavens.'

'You can be bossy, can't you?' She sounded miffed.

'Only when I have to be. Now, how would you like to get out of here?' He smiled at her obvious delight. 'There are conditions attached. I rang your doctor who informed me she would release you in the morning, only if there is someone to look after you full time until you have recovered, which means you can't go back to your place.' He eyed her raised eyebrow, which must have hurt to even move it. 'We have one of your attackers in custody but the other one remains free and since he knows where you live you wouldn't be safe there by yourself. Plus I wouldn't even consider you being stuck inside hour after hour with no way of getting about. Please don't take this the wrong way, but how about moving in with me until we can get you back on your feet. I have stacks of room and we can organise the furniture and cupboards to suit your needs. You'll have your own private bedroom and bathroom. I've spoken with the Association for the Blind and they'll send someone to help us sort things and train you as to where everything is. You will be a lot safer. And I have another surprise for you. Her name is Honey. She is still in basic training, but will be yours.'

'How did you manage that? I know how hard it is to get a guide dog.' She reached around feeling for Ben's hands, stunned amazement lighting up her battered face.

He obliged by lifting his hands to a place where she could grasp them. 'Sometimes being in a position of authority helps. It's our fault Angel was killed; it's up to us to replace her so I pulled a few strings as well as rank.' His mind flashed to the hefty amount he donated from his personal account to ensure Christine moved to the top of the list, but that was to be kept from her. 'You've not commented on my proposal.' His fingers around hers felt good and damn but it felt right.

'You don't know how hard it would be. I can't clean to start with. I can do it, but can't see whether or not anything is actually clean.'

'That's not a problem. Because of the long hours I work, I have a lady come in every week, so therefore it makes no difference. What's your next argument?'

'Your furniture will have to be re-arranged so I have a clear path to walk. I can't impose on you like that.'

'Christine, I don't even use half of my furniture. It's a very rare occasion when I watch television. I relax in the same lounge chair every night, eat at the kitchen bar and sleep in my bed, and you wouldn't be imposing. Believe me, I would enjoy the company. I live by myself in a huge house and work long hours because I no longer enjoy the loneliness of being by myself. At least at work, I have someone to talk to. You would be doing me a great favour. If you say yes, I can have you out of here first thing in the morning. We can go via your place to pack whatever you need. I guess I should outline the alternative. They are thinking of putting you in residential care until you get Honey.'

The speed with which her look changed from concern to absolute horror didn't surprise him. He'd reacted the same way when he'd been told. Residential care meant she would be a young, fit and lively woman stuck with elderly people needing almost full time assistance.

'That doesn't leave me with a lot of choice does it?' Ben winced at the bleakness in her voice.

'I'm not that hard to live with,' he said, making out his feelings had been hurt, but at the same time teasing her. 'We could at least give it a try for the short term. It has to be a lot better than the alternative.'

'Only on one condition.'

'And what would that be?'

'You have to promise me faithfully you will let me know if my being there gets too hard for you.'

Ben couldn't help drawing her into a warm embrace but was careful to not compromise her injuries. 'I promise. Now, I'm going to leave you for a few hours. I'll be back to tuck you in before you go to sleep and… I'm going to check that you eat your dinner. I know it's painful to chew, but you have to eat.' He laughed. 'You're going to need all your strength to put up with me.' Leaning over he gave her another gentle hug. He'd already pushed the boundaries on what is appropriate but heck, his body wanted a closer connection and his body was winning the war against his brain. He needed to take a step backwards so pulled away.

'I thought you said you weren't hard to live with,' she laughed as she settled back into the mound of pillows, wincing as she moved, which sent his feelings of shame and remorse sky high again.

'You'll just have to wait and find out, won't you?'

***

Chrissie could tell Ben was leaving by the fading of his voice. After the snick of the door she heard him chatting to the guard outside then silence. Because it hurt so much, she took care to move, hesitating every few seconds as she pulled herself up in bed, wincing at the sharp twinges in her side and head with each movement. Finally making it to a more comfy position she settled back into the pillows. Thoughts about all Ben had just said centred in her brain. Were they the only two alternatives or had he just used those two to get her to agree? She would have been able to manage to live in her own flat by herself, she did it every day. But she would never be able to leave unless it was by taxi, and even then she wouldn't be able to walk around anywhere without a guide dog. Six months ago she would have coped. The tunnel in her vision hadn't been quite so narrow. But now? No way, with not much more than a wide pinprick of vision left. Much as she yearned to be independent she knew that without a guide dog she would be totally dependant on other people to do everything for her. The thought of having someone else to keep her company gave her a sense of elation but she knew Ben would be at work a lot of the time, and she still had her job at the piano bar. Teaching would be out of the question and the thought saddened her.

She snuggled down into the pillows to ease the ache in her sore ribs where she had been kicked. Remembering how Ben had held her as if she were precious sent a warm glow of utter contentment deep inside: feelings she thought she would never experience again. Releasing a satisfied sigh she reached over to find the television control. After several failed attempts at pressing various buttons, she managed to find the correct one and what sounded like a news broadcast, came on. She tried to follow the programme but thoughts of Ben kept taking over. She kept convincing herself to not make too much out of their friendship because in the end, nothing more than companionship would become of it. And she certainly needed friends.

Most of her old friends had treated her as though she had the plague and not just a gradual loss of sight. Some had maintained contact for up to a year but now not a single one ever rang her any more. It saddened her to think about it. Just because one part of your body didn't work properly anymore, people thought you to be unapproachable or not worthy of their time, yet nothing else about you changed. You were still the same, had the same needs, desires, skills, thoughts. Ben was the only person she had met, apart from those at the Association for the Blind, who treated her as a normal human being. Well, so did Mick and Maggie and a couple of the teachers at school. But that was only at work. They never invited her to any functions or rang her or asked her to join them for a chat over coffee.

A short laugh escaped. She still couldn't believe Ben hadn't realised she was blind until he saw Angel. Oh, dear, Lord, Angel. Dear, sweet, Angel. She switched off the TV and let thoughts of her best and only friend wander through her mind.

Chapter Seventeen

It had been a hectic afternoon. Ben felt exhausted. After making umpteen dozen phone calls he spent the afternoon rearranging furniture in his house to accommodate his new house-guest. He hadn't looked forward to anything so much for a very long time. Before John went off duty, Ben called in to ask a favour. 'Would Mary be prepared to spend a few hours a week keeping Christine company while I work?'

'I'll ring and ask.' John moved to his own office to call on his personal mobile and returned a few minutes later. 'Mary would be delighted and said she would round up a few of her friends to make up a roster.'

'That's more than I hoped. Tell her how much I appreciate her help. Now what's happening around here?'

'Bobby is in custody, awaiting extradition to the East.'

'Before he goes I want him to have a thorough grilling. You do the interview while I watch from the observation room. Has he committed any crimes in this State?'

'None that we know of but that's not to say he hasn't. There are outstanding warrants from two other states. That's what we used to arrest him.'

By the time Ben returned to the hospital, heavy rain had begun tumbling again and he'd been caught out without a suitable jacket to shield him from the torrential downpour. Of course, all the parking bays near the entrance to the hospital had been taken which meant he was forced to park a block away. He sat for a while, waiting for a break in the never-ending deluge, but finally decided he would be there forever unless he made a dash through the downpour.

Grasping a white paper bag in one hand, he slammed the door, pressed the remote on his keys and ran, dodging under the scant shelter from trees as he made his way to the entrance. Before advancing inside he shook under cover of the entryway to rid himself of most of the water. Once inside he didn't hesitate, eager to see Christine again, and loped up the stairs instead of waiting for the elevator. As he passed the nurses station he enquired as to whether Christine had eaten her dinner and smiled at the response – half of it. He then asked what time he could pick her up in the morning to take her home.

The latest guard at the doorway cracked a joke with Ben, which delayed him a few moments. Knocking but not waiting for an answer, he shoved the door open with his shoulder. 'People who eat their dinner deserve to be rewarded,' he said as he made his way towards the bed. He tugged the trolley over her bed then opened out the paper bag he had protected from the worst of the rain. While he worked he dipped his head and pecked Christine on her better cheek and grinned at her gasp but she didn't pull away. Good. A smile spread across his face when he watched her nose quiver slightly as she tried to work out what he had. 'Stop cheating. This is supposed to be a surprise. Your reward for eating most of your dinner.'

'You're wet, and you've got cheese.'

Ben ignored her while he removed the plastic film from the plate. 'Open wide. Since you're so smart you have to tell me what variety it is before you get another piece. Every time you miss I get the next piece and I should warn you, I bought my favourites.' He delighted in hearing the giggle from Chrissie before he popped the first piece into her barely open mouth, avoiding the still fierce looking cut.

She allowed the cheese to sit on her tongue before she chewed then thought about it. 'Brie or Camembert, and you have left it out long enough for it to begin to melt. You know about cheese.'

'I can see I'm in for a challenge here. I love cheese. Try this one.' He took care in tweaking the end of her nose closed so she couldn't smell the sharpness of the aroma first then watched her face while she tasted.

'Ooh, that one is strong. It has to be a blue vein, but which one? It would go well with a slice of apple.'

'Open.' He slid in a piece of already sliced sweet apple. 'You have to get it right or I get the next piece.'

'I give in, but it is very creamy under the blue.'

'That's good because this is one of my favourites and I get the other piece. It's Stilton. Remind me to cook you my chicken and Stilton casserole one night.'

Christine smiled while Ben savoured his piece of cheese and apple, making exaggerated murmurs of appreciation after he swallowed the titbit down.

'I'll give you a clue on the next one. Think Europe, but not the two countries we've just tasted.' This time he placed a piece of cheese on a thin sliver of apple, reached for her hand then placed it in her outstretched fingers.

She felt the cheese for its texture and then sniffed before placing it in her mouth. 'Holland. It's smooth but sharper than Edam or Gruyere and has much smaller holes. I'll go Vollendam.'

'Damn, you are too good. Are you sure you don't want to join me in my job? I'm positive you won't get the next one.' Hoping he had dulled her tastebuds by giving her a couple of strong cheeses he moved back to a milder one. He watched while she tasted, his hopes dashed when she smiled so wickedly.

'You shouldn't give me my favourite. This one is definitely camembert.'

'I can see we are going to be fighting over a cheese board. It's my favourite soft cheese as well. But it needs a good port to wash it down. Do you drink port?'

Christine nodded, a grin splitting her face, which was good to see but he didn't like the wince of pain that followed.

'Looks like I'll have to put a lock and key on my little cache of vintage ports. Have you had enough, Miss Piggy? I can leave the rest for later if you like. I've put each piece on some apple so don't leave it too long. It's covered with plastic film.'

'Thank you for everything. Now tell me why you are so wet.' Her fingers explored his shirt to more thoroughly feel the dampness. Her touch raised disturbing tingles of pleasure, eliciting a sharp, drawn in breath of delight.

'Because it's pouring rain outside and the whole world is visiting patients in here which means I'm parked a block away. A question. Would you prefer your bed or mine?'

Eyeing her shocked face, his own cheeks heated as he perceived the innuendo. 'Sorry, that didn't come out quite right. Do you want me to have your own bed brought over to my place or are you happy with the one already in the room you will be using. I can guarantee it is comfy.' To ease the disturbing feelings her touch was eliciting, he grasped her hand and drew it away from his chest but then kept the hand firmly ensconced in his.

'I'm happy with what is already there. The only thing I'd really like to be carted over is my keyboard. I need to practise every day to work on new pieces. I'll play when you aren't there so I don't disturb you.'

'Then I would be extremely disappointed. I love listening to you play, it helps me relax. Now, I've spoken to your doctor and you can be discharged after her rounds in the morning. She wants to check you over before you leave. I'll be here at eight. Make sure you eat your breakfast because I have another little surprise if you behave yourself.'

Drawing the hand he was somehow still holding up to his lips he settled a gentle kiss in her palm. 'Sleep well,' he whispered. Without waiting for a response, he placed her hand on her bed and left.

'I need some clothes to go home in,' she called.

Spinning on his heel he returned to the side of her bed. 'I can pick some of yours up on my way home. Have you got your house keys or did they take them away with your clothes?'

'I was told my keys were in the bedside table.' As she reached over she collided with Ben's arm when he reached out at the same time.

'Allow me,' Ben murmured, swallowing down his gasp of pleasurable shock from her touch. He found the single key. 'What would you like to wear?'

'Jeans and T-shirt will be fine and I need a pair of shoes.'

Reaching over, Ben kissed Christine on the top of her head. 'Goodnight. Sleep well. I'll see you at eight.'

She murmured a quiet goodnight, which he only just heard over the soft squeaks of his shoes on the polished linoleum floor as he left.

Chapter Eighteen

Unable to restrain building excitement, Ben was jogging up the steps to the third floor of the hospital much earlier than he'd said. He whistled under his breath while striding along the passageway but stopped at what sounded like a muffled voice call out his name. Sneaking over to a nearby door, he leant with his ear close to the panelling but all was quiet. Convinced his thoughts of Christine were overtaking his senses, he shook his head to clear it of confusion then continued the few steps to the door, nodding at Mac, the guard on duty.

'She's not in there, boss,' Mac said as Ben pushed the door with the flat of his hand.

Ben paused. 'What do you mean, not in there, where is she? You're supposed to keep her in your sight at all times.'

'The nurse took her to the treatment room. Over there.' Mac pointed to the door Ben had paused at. 'No-one has come out yet.'

'How long ago did she go in?' His stomach muscles contracted into something tight and mighty uncomfortable. A stab of concern surged because he couldn't figure out what Christine would need treatment for. There were no bandages or plasters to be changed. She had quite a few minor cuts and plenty of heavy bruises but nothing requiring treatment. His instinctive gut feeling began churning around with the force of a tsunami.

'Just a few minutes.'

'Did you recognise the nurse? Was it one of the regulars?' Turning he studied the door, his stomach tightening even more to create a very uncomfortable pain that felt like rats gnawing.

A nurse shot out the door then sped down the corridor away from them.

'Get her!' yelled Ben. He dropped the parcel of clothes and drew his gun from a shoulder holster as he raced towards the door.

As Mac chased full pelt after the nurse, Ben flung the door open with an almighty shove with one hand while the other hand had his gun aimed. The door gave a resounding bang as it was flung back on its hinges then whacked against the bench behind it. The noise echoed. Ben scanned the room which was larger than expected, running three times deeper than wide.

Empty. No Christine.

Dread settled into the pit of his stomach. His eyes dropped to a wheel-chair facing away from him. A skewed sheet draped over something lumpy. Tentative, he reached over and hurled the cover back then recoiled. Hell, no.

Christine's body was slumped in the chair.

Oh, hell, please don't be dead? He spun around to make sure no-one else was in the room, his eye straight down the barrel. Satisfied they were alone he reached out one hand to feel Christine's neck for a pulse. His held breath whooshed out at the slow but faint lub-dub under the pads of his fingers. It wasn't a normal healthy heartbeat, it was too slow, but at least she was alive. His own racing heart made up for the sluggishness in Christine.

Shooting out to the passage he yelled for a doctor and some assistance then returned to the chair. Turning it around with one hand, he kept his gun aimed at the door. Christine's comatose body began sliding forwards. He grabbed her around the shoulders to prevent her from tumbling to the floor. Keeping his arm in place he shuffled the chair to the door with his legs.

A nurse arrived, horror distorting her face at the gun aimed towards her head. Recognising her, Ben lowered the firearm. 'Someone tried to kidnap Christine. She's unconscious. Get the doctor, now! I suspect she may have been given some sort of sedative.' And please, let it be a simple sedative and not something more sinister.

The nurse scuttled down to the nurse's station then tore back with the doctor on duty. Ben had Christine in his arms and was on his way to her room. He laid her on the bed then stood watching with a heart that felt as though it wanted to hammer a way out of his chest while the doctor examined her.

The doctor fingered a small blood spot on Christine's upper arm. 'She's been injected with some sort of sedative. I'll get an immediate blood screen done. She's breathing fine but is heavily sedated.'

'Stay with her for a minute, I'll be back soon.' Striding to the door and continuing on into the treatment room, Ben scanned the entire area searching for a syringe. He was about to leave when he noticed a bin tucked under a shelf, pushed to the back but on a skewed angle as though shoved in a hurry. His fingers shook as he nudged the lid open. Damn it. He picked up a towel before reaching in to retrieve a used hypodermic.

Back in Christine's room he held it up. 'Can you test this here without compromising fingerprints?'

The doctor shook her head.

He swallowed then sucked in a long breath in an attempt to bring his feelings of angst under control then reached into his coat pocket and drew out his mobile phone. As he was finishing his call to John Markham for a forensics team and some backup, Mac returned.

'I lost her,' he panted. 'There was a white van waiting outside a side entrance with the motor running and the rear doors standing open. There were too many people around to fire a shot. I managed to get the licence number and have rung through a description for a trace. The blue and whites are on the lookout. Sorry boss. How is Christine? Is she all right?'

'She's alive, thank God!'

Unable to figure out how they knew details about Christine, Ben wracked his brain for any hint. What had he missed? After finding the planted bug, he had been extra vigilant checking both his car and all his clothes with a thoroughness that bordered on manic. A sudden thought had him holding up one finger to his mouth to silence everyone then he made several hand gestures to Mac, indicating that the room might have been bugged. Cocking one finger towards the nurse, he beckoned for her to follow him outside. The doctor trailed after them until they were well away from the room.

'I want you two to go back in there and have a regular conversation about other patients, without naming real names. Whoever did this knew what time I was coming in but I was an hour early and scuttled their plans. Mac and I will search for a small surveillance gadget. Say farewell to Mac and me as though we are leaving the room but don't mention Christine's condition at all.'

The faces of both women were creased with anxiety but they returned to the room and followed instructions, their voices quavering at first while Ben and Mac searched every possible place a microphone could be hidden, which could be anywhere since they could be so tiny. With silent nods of encouragement from Ben the conversation eased from hesitant to amiable, even including a couple of laughs when the nurse added a corny joke she had heard in the staff room. Ben had to stifle his laughter to the better than usual joke and he could tell Mack had appreciated it as much.

After a comprehensive search revealing nothing, Ben was stumped but felt certain the room had to be bugged. They were missing the obvious. Christine's whereabouts and condition after her attack would have been quite easy to ascertain, but to come in so early to kidnap her was above being co-incidental. Logic told him the night hours would have been easier for a successful human heist with fewer people around but wheeling out a patient would have been too obvious during the night – especially with an unfamiliar nurse doing the wheeling. Early morning with its breakfast rush, handover of staff and busy rounds was a far more logical time.

To double check, Ben swapped places with Mac to re-scour each other's search places. He had almost given up after coming to the conclusion his hunch had been wrong. He stood with one hand on his hip, the other brushing in frustration through his hair when he spotted the card on an arrangement of flowers. Moving closer, he leant over to read the handwritten words. *All my love, Jaye.* Knowing damn well he hadn't sent any flowers he instantly figured where the arrangement had come from and something Christine had said about her attack jabbed into his mind: a warning to your boyfriend. He fisted his brow for stupidity. They were seen together and his alias, Jaye, was assumed to be the boyfriend. Being new on the scene nobody would have known whether or not Jaye and Christine were old friends. Damn, damn, damn. They had followed him to Christine's place either when he picked her up or later when he took her home. How had he missed that? His mind scrambled back to that night: the dog walking couple, the skateboarders and the lost woman. It must have been on the way home. But how? Nobody but he, had known where he'd made the reservation and he hadn't used his real name. To top it all off he could recall scouring the area when he'd taken Christine home and had seen nothing out of place. But it was now obvious he had missed something vital.

Holding up a hand to indicate he had found the bug, he read the details on the card. The flowers had been purchased in the hospital gift shop on the ground floor. Made sense and could give a lead. The sender didn't need to know what room she was in. Reception or the florist would have delivered it and the tracking device would have told whoever, exactly where Christine was. They could even have gone into her room to check. She wouldn't have seen them. He took meticulous care in lifting the arrangement then carried it out of the room. Once in the corridor, he stood thinking. Where to put it? Spotting a sign a few metres down the corridor, he grinned. Perfect. It didn't take long to stride the distance then shove open a door with his shoulder. One sweep of the room and Ben was more than happy. It was ideal. He lifted the flower arrangement and perched it against the back wall on the partition between two cubicles in the visitor's male toilet, praying that until the forensics team removed the microphone and arrangement for examination, all the men using the room had severe wind, diarrhoea or constipation.

By the time Ben had returned to Christine's room the corridor was awash with his team of men. He greeted John, who had come in off duty. 'The treatment room is to be thoroughly examined, as well as Christine's room. I want Christine transferred to a different floor, a blood sample taken and two armed guards posted outside her door.' He snorted. How many different fingerprints and DNA would be found in a treatment room of a busy hospital? What was even more frustrating was that no doubt the room would have been disinfected on a regular basis. Maybe the handles of the wheel chair would be the best option.

As an aside to John, he mentioned the hospital florist and one man was sent to make enquiries. After the syringe was sent to the forensics lab, Ben handed over the investigation to John then mounted the stairs to the next level. He snuck across the floor of the private room he'd insisted on, and drew up a chair next to Christine's bed. As he sat he fought back the itchiness of unfamiliar threatening moisture swimming across his eyes. This beautiful woman had been an unwitting victim twice now in less than twenty-four hours – because of him. While the fingers of one hand wrapped around her curled fist, his other hand gently caressed the uninjured parts of her face. He stayed there - even after he was handed the initial results from the test that confirmed and detailed the sedative used. There were no fingerprints on either syringe or the wheelchair handles. He sent a silent message of thanks skywards that the drug wasn't something deadly. A groan rumbled from his chest. It could so easily have been fatal.

After several hours, Christine began to stir. At last. He felt bewildered by the intensity of his feelings for her: sensations and emotions he had never had to confront before. At the sound of the tremulous, 'Ben,' when Chrissie began stirring, he realised that he'd never felt this way about a woman before, sending all his past dalliances fading into an obscure background of insignificance.

'Ben?' Her eyes fluttered open.

As he watched her attempt to focus drug hazed eyes he pressed the call button to summon the doctor. 'You have given me one hell of a fright, Christine. What do you remember?'

She shook her head from side-to-side as though to clear away the fog. 'Oh, my head hurts.' She eased back against the pillow. 'Where am I?' She rubbed her eyes then her temple.

'In hospital.'

'Oh, yes.' She blinked then rubbed her eyes again.

'Can you recall what happened?'

'Umm… let me think. I heard you walking down the passage. You were whistling. I called for you.' She paused as though searching for memories. 'The nurse… she stuck something in my arm and… I was afraid… that's when I called out to you. I don't remember any more. What happened?'

'Do you remember receiving a flower arrangement from me, or should I say from Jaye?'

'Yes, but I thought it was strange you didn't write from Ben, since you'd already told me Ben was back.'

'That's because I didn't send the flowers.'

'You didn't then…'

'They came from the gang we have been chasing for the past couple of weeks. It appears they had no idea Jaye and Ben is the one and same, and I hope they still don't. The arrangement contained a hidden microphone. I presume they heard our conversation last night and knew what time I was supposed to be coming in for you. You have no idea how glad I am that I was early.'

'Why, I don't understand?'

'No nor did I until I remembered something you said. The message for your boyfriend.'

'Excuse me?'

'Remember, one of your attackers said that the attack was a message for your boyfriend.'

'But I don't have a boyfriend.'

'They don't know that but I'm almost certain we were seen together the other night when we went out to dinner. I could have been followed. No, change that, I must have been followed, and led these thugs to your place. I'm so sorry, Christine, but for some reason you have been caught up in a rather nasty crime. These people are the ones responsible for the attack on you. They tried to kidnap you this morning. I think they were going to use you as a bargaining tool with Jaye, to get their hands on a rather large cache of fictional drugs. To them, you are worth around two million collars.'

'Two million what?' Christine shot upright at the same time as she spun her head around. 'Oh, it hurts,' she gasped as her hands slid up the sides of her face. Taking a steadying breath, she settled back into the nest of pillows.

The doctor entered, bringing the conversation to a halt. 'Mrs Mears, you've finally rejoined us. How do you feel?' Her hand was lifted and pulse taken.

'I feel very groggy and my head hurts like crazy, like a dull but insistent headache. In fact everything hurts,' Christine said as she turned her head, more carefully this time, to face the new voice.

'You were injected with a powerful sedative and will probably feel groggy at least until morning. We can give you something to alleviate the pain if you like. The other aches are from your attack and you'll probably feel pretty bad for another twenty-four to forty-eight hours and then things should start to ease as your body heals. Would you like a painkiller?'

Christine winced. 'No thanks. I think I've got more than enough foreign substances floating around my insides. I'd rather sleep it off as long as I know I'm going to be all right.'

'Doctor, can I take Christine home?' Ben asked as she settled back again. 'She will be a lot safer and I promise someone will be with her every minute of the day... and night.'

'Under normal circumstances I would rather keep her in for observation, but after what happened this morning, I guess I can hand her over to you for safekeeping. I would only be concerned if there was any concussion but thankfully there isn't. Ring if you have the slightest concern about her condition. Mrs Mears will probably sleep a lot until the sedative is out of her system but that will be a good thing. She has painkillers for the injuries she received; the dosage is on the packet. I'll have a nurse come in.'

Half an hour later Christine was discharged. She was wheeled to a back entrance in a wheel chair since her legs were so shaky. Ben lifted her out of the chair then settled her into his car. They didn't go straight home. He made a detour.

'I promised you a small surprise today. I hope you will like it.' She swayed as she stood after alighting from the car. Ben wrapped an arm around her shoulder to guide her through a doorway of a double storey building. He settled her into a vinyl armchair in the reception area while he sought out the person he'd phoned earlier in the day to explain why he would be in later than expected. When he returned a few minutes later he knelt in front of Christine and handed a small container into her fingers.

She looked puzzled until Ben guided her fingers to the tiny metal nametag that had been printed in Braille.

'Angel,' she gasped, tears brimming across her eyes.

'I had her cremated for you. These are her ashes for you to do with as you want. I know how much you loved Angel and felt it important you could have some closure.'

'Oh, Ben, thank you so much.' She leant forwards and rested her forehead on his chest. Somehow, as though it was a natural reflex, his arms wound around her shoulders to hold her close for a few minutes before he eased her out of her seat and guided her back to his car. The box was clasped tight against her chest as though it was worth millions. It delighted him that his judgement had been correct. At last he'd managed to get something right with this woman. Yet it was because of him that the box even existed. It didn't sit well, churning his stomach contents at the thought.

From the street, Ben realised his house didn't look much. Despite this he described it as they approached. 'There's a high, red brick fence surrounding a modern built Federation style house. Remote controlled doors give entry to a double garage. They open onto the road at one end of the property.' As he pressed the remote, one door whirred as it rose. 'The garage is the most used way of entry into the house. There's a small electronically operated gate leading from the pathway to the front door. To gain access, visitors are required to press a button and then speak into the slatted panel by the gate. If I'm not here, no access can be made unless the person has the key to the gate.' He nosed the car into the garage.

'Why so safety conscious?' asked Christine as the car slid to a halt.

Ben cut the engine. 'Despite the fact that it was already installed when I purchased the house, a lot of police officers have heightened security just because of their position. Unfortunately, sometimes crooks caught for illegal activities don't take their arrest lightly and seek retaliation.'

'Doesn't sound fair.' Christine unbuckled her seat belt and eased it back.

'I agree and most petty criminals accept their punishment but it's more the hardened and serious offenders that have this skewed idea about being caught for their crimes. The security system inside is state of the art. Anyone trying to breach the system sets off an alarm at the security firm with a direct link to my office. Once inside the gate, there is a small front garden that usually looks rather unkempt.' He winced at the thought of exactly how often it was nothing more than a patch of dead weeds. He really should take more leisure time. There was silence apart from the sound of him opening the door, alighting then his footsteps as he rounded the boot and approached the passenger door.

'You don't like gardening?' asked Christine as her door opened and she made to get out, pausing as she bumped into Bens' outstretched hand. She grasped his fingers.

'I work long hours so a lack of leisure time prevents me from doing much. Every now and again I dedicate an entire weekend to putting the garden to rights. It looks trim and neat for a few weeks before falling into a state of neglect again.'

As they walked through an interconnecting door into the house, Christine paused. 'Tell me about the actual house so I can picture it.'

'The house is large; larger than I need. Four huge bedrooms and a central open living area, with the modern kitchen at the back overlooking a shaded patio, then lawn. A long granite bench separates the kitchen from the massive front room I've divided into two.' He stopped walking and stood behind her. 'We are standing in the middle. Grasping one of her hands from behind, he guided it to indicate the directions. 'To your left is a formal lounge area with a more casual entertainment section on the other side. This is where I prefer to relax.' He turned Christine around. 'Straight ahead, across the bench is the kitchen. On one end, to your right, is a dining area. I can count the fingers on one hand the number of times I have used the dining room for eating as I much prefer to eat perched on one of the stools at the kitchen bar.' He glanced into the so-called dining area. At the moment it looked more like an office with a laptop computer and piles of files stacked next to it. With Christine here, he would have to knuckle down to cleaning it up. Not being one who liked a lot of clutter, he kept his home tidy – well maybe apart from the dining table.

'As I mentioned before, a cleaning lady comes in once a week to undertake the major cleaning jobs.'

Taking her arm he led Christine down the short passage dividing two of the bedrooms, explaining the layout as they went and allowing her time to feel her way with inquisitive fingers. One room was set up as an office cum storeroom cum ironing room with the ironing board in a permanent standing position to press a fresh shirt each time he required one. The other room was normally a guest bedroom but now had the honour of housing Ben but he wasn't about to tell her he had moved rooms to accommodate her. His old room had an en-suite bathroom, whereas he would be using a separate bathroom adjoining the guest room. He described each room as they passed while continuing on through the house until he reached the main bedroom.

'This is to be your room while you are here. It has an en-suite so you will have privacy.' While Christine felt around the room with outstretched hands, Ben stood close by, nervous at first in case she tripped but he soon realised she was more than capable of finding her way around. 'I'll leave you to explore while I collect your gear from the car,' he said as he retreated.

Chapter Nineteen

Chrissie felt her way into the bathroom then edged her way around by using the tips of sensitive fingers to find all the features. It always amazed her how more aware she was of her sensation to touch and how it had developed so acutely since her sight began diminishing. Even more amazing was her sense of hearing. The slightest of sounds had her ears honing in to figure out what had caused it and from which direction it came. Background sounds she would have previously ignored were now pinpointed and assessed to figure out whether or not danger was imminent. Two thuds indicated the dropping of the two large suitcases they had packed earlier. She eased her way to the end of the bed and sank into the mattress.

'Ben, we need to talk. Please come here?' She beckoned then patted the bed next to her. When she felt his weight settle into the mattress she turned to him. 'This was your room. I don't want to put you out. I'm happy with any of the other rooms. I don't need so much room.'

'It makes little difference where I sleep and all the bedrooms are the same size. I'm at the other end of the house and have my own bathroom. This room gives you privacy. All I did was swap the beds around and my cleaning lady made sure everything in here was spotless for you. Don't disappoint her. She put her heart and soul into this. And how did you know it was my room?'

'I knew it was your room the moment we walked in. Your soap, your aftershave, the aromas linger.'

'Detective Mears on duty again, eh? Now, how do you feel? I'm going to cook us some dinner. What would you like to do?'

'I'm still feeling rather head-achy but I'd like to sit where we can talk.' Placing her fingers on the inside of his elbow, he led her out into the lounge and settled her on the sofa to rest, plumping up a couple of soft cushions under her shoulders and head. Then he turned on some very quiet background music that wouldn't intrude while they chatted.

***

When Chrissie woke from her drug-induced sleep the next morning, the fog had lifted from her brain but it still took her a few moments to remember where she was. In a normal situation she could have walked to any point in her own home without bumping into any objects. Now she had to feel her way around the edge of the room until she found the doorway to the bathroom. It wasn't just her inability to see that made her move with so much caution: her body felt as though it had been wrung through a wringer then pounded by a pile driver so she tried to use as few muscles as possible.

The house sounded silent when she returned to the bedroom, which was a problem since she needed to find a clean set of clothes. Assuming Ben was still asleep, she stumbled around the room until she found the two suitcases at the end of her bed. Not being the one who had packed the clothes, she had no idea what items were in which case so after unzipping the first she ran her fingers along the top of the pile of clothes while trying to fathom out the contents. Footwear wrapped in plastic bags and her classier evening wear. Delving deeper, she searched for underclothes. Not finding any she shoved the case to one side then drew down the other case, her body protesting at every movement.

Running her hands over the outside, she searched for the zipper only to discover the case was upside down. To turn it over she had to stand, causing sore muscles to protest. Because Ben hadn't zipped the case closed after removing her nightclothes the night before, the case opened out, spilling garments all around her. Frustration and pain had her close to tears but she gritted her teeth in determination, refusing to allow even one to fall. She grabbed any item she could find, fingered it to feel what it was then shoved it back into the open case while cursing under her breath.

'Has something happened to your voice Miss Independence?'

Chrissie jumped at the voice from the doorway.

'I told you I would help you unpack.' The voice neared. 'You didn't have to do it all in one foul swoop and I was planning on placing everything in the cupboard, not on the floor.'

She could feel him standing over her then felt his warm breath fan against her cheeks at the same time as his hands slid into her armpits and she was hoisted from the floor then set in a chair. 'Why didn't you call me?' He was squatting in front of her.

'I didn't want to disturb you.' Chrissie felt chastened so her response came out as no more than a mumble, which made her feel even more of a dill.

'Let's get one thing straight right from the very beginning.' His fingers lifted her chin. 'I was fully aware of the assistance you would need and fully prepared to give it, when I asked you to move in here. It will be easier after next week when your aide comes in to sort things. Until then, please don't be afraid to ask.' His hand dropped. 'Now I presume we are looking for clothes to wear today. Any preference? I guess I should tell you we are going for a drive up the coast with maybe a bit of beach walking.'

She heard the soft swish of clothes moving around. 'Here, matching knickers and bras.' Her hand was lifted and the two items pushed into the curled ends of her fingers. Her cheeks heated.

'There's no point in being embarrassed. I was brought up with three older sisters. I was beyond being embarrassed by the sight of women's lacy underwear at a very early age. Mind you, in my latter years I've received a lot more pleasure in personally removing them. What would you like? Skirt, shorts or slacks?'

Her face felt as though it was being incinerated before she managed to get out, 'A skirt please. I'm sorry, Ben.'

To further inflame her heat she felt Ben lean towards her then a kiss was planted on her brow, about the only place she could feel on her face where there wasn't a cut or bruise. But the kiss was nice and Ben didn't seem to have the same inhibitions she had about showing affection. Or maybe it was just him being friendly. Regardless, she would take as much affection as she could even if it meant nothing to him for she'd sure had a dearth of it since being diagnosed.

'Here's a skirt with matching T-shirt and don't keep telling me you are sorry. You have nothing to be sorry about. I'm the one who should be apologising.'

'Why?'

'It's because of me that you're in this pickle. And believe me, I'm finding it hard to live with the guilt right now.'

The next two items were placed over her arm. 'Now, what about footwear?'

'Sandals will be fine.'

'I'll leave them on the end of your bed. How about getting showered and dressed while I clean this up so you don't trip when you come out? Call me when you're ready, or no more cheese.'

She heard and felt the air change as he stood then he lifted her into his arms. She squealed at the suddenness of his actions. He just laughed as he stepped over the upturned pile of clothes before depositing her in the bathroom, the echo of his footfall and the change in grey light telling her where she was.

***

Ben refolded rumpled clothes as he dropped them back into the case. Standing them out of the way he returned to the kitchen to finish preparing the late breakfast.

At a muffled curse, he glanced up and shook his head at her cussedness as he spied Christine extracting her toe from around the castor of a chair. Her sandals were hooked over one finger. Then he watched her tentative foray across the lounge area, arms outstretched. Damn woman. Too proud to ask for assistance. He remained silent to see how long it would take her to ask for help. Not being able to handle it any longer after she bumped into the glass-topped coffee table, he made his way around the kitchen bench, moving up behind her.

'Now, you are being stubborn,' he whispered in her ear. She squealed and jerked in fright.

'Don't sneak up on me.'

'Then don't be so obstinate. You have more than your fair share of bruises already. Why add to them? You seem to find it hard to say four simple little words, so let's try practising them. Please help me, Ben? Now let me hear you say them.'

'Ben?'

'That's only one word. I want to hear all four.'

'Don't do this to me, Ben,' she whispered.

'Wrong. You only got two words right that time – me and Ben. Try adding the other two.' Standing a few steps away from her, he planted his hands on his hips while he waited.

'Ben?' Chrissie put out her hands to touch him but he slid sideways, just out of her reach.

'You've gone backwards, that was only one word. Have another go.' This time he stood on her other side and watched as her head swung his way. She turned to face him with unerring accuracy, her arms reaching out again. How did she do that? He hadn't made a sound. He stepped behind her.

'Ben, please?' Giving in, Chrissie hung her hands by her side. She looked so cute imitating a chastened puppy.

'You're improving, sweet Christine.' Leaning over he placed a hand on her arm.

'Why did you call me that?' she asked.

Ben paused for a moment. There was no way in the world he could tell her how deep his feelings for her were. Not when she had just moved into his house. She would think he had ulterior motives and wouldn't learn to trust him. Vowing to be more careful he ignored her question.

'Come on, four little words. The only one you haven't been able to get out is help. I wonder why that is? You had no trouble calling it out the other morning. Your cyclist saviour told us in his statement that he heard you yelling for help. You had no problem in asking me to help you when we went out for dinner, so why the big deal now? I understand your need and desire to be as independent as you can, but you are in a strange environment. There is no shame and no weakness of character in asking for some help when you need it. And until you know your way around here and your aide has been in, you need assistance.' He softened his voice. 'Please, I don't want you to get hurt any more.'

Relenting at her sad face he grasped her hands in his. Thinking it wasn't the wisest of moves since her very touch sent his libido zinging he released his hold and returned to the kitchen. 'Breakfast is ready.' He watched from the other side of the bar while Christine appeared to mull over his words.

'Please help me, Ben?' He couldn't help but smile when he heard her almost imperceptible plea.

'That wasn't so hard, was it?' he murmured after he returned to her side and placed her hand inside his elbow, leading the way into the kitchen. While settling her onto the bar stool he described the layout.

Chapter Twenty

Soft popular classics wafted from the car's CD player while Ben drove north along the coast. Every now and again he would describe the surroundings in detail. Chrissie had wound the window down a fraction so she could smell the crisp salty air and feel it blowing through her hair. She could see more than usual – a pinprick circle of blue indicating a bright sun but with no peripheral vision she had to turn her head both sideways and up and down to make out any of the scenery but by the time she managed to focus, it had passed in a blur. It wouldn't be long before even this miniscule amount of vision was gone. It still dug deep that fate had dealt her this blow and even though she tried not to dwell on it, the knowledge rankled and every now and again her positivity seemed to take a long hike and get lost.

She knew when they pulled into a car park for Ben detailed the scenery, something she was more than grateful for. It was still hard to believe that this man hadn't shied away from her once learning of her disability. Most people did, which hurt a lot more than she would ever disclose to anyone. She also knew it was because the general public didn't know how to approach or treat a person with disabilities. She'd been told it was because they felt uncomfortable in case they said or did the wrong thing but hey, all she wanted was to be treated as a normal human being and a few friends would be a bonus so she wouldn't be so darn lonely - especially at night.

Within minutes she was walking alongside Ben with her hand in his elbow. He described the features of the sandy path through coastal bushland until they reached the beach at the mouth of a river. Wanting to feel the sand, Chrissie paused to remove her sandals then wriggled her toes through the warm soft granules. They felt a bit rough like fine sandpaper and yet at the same time tickled. Ben followed suit then wrapped one arm around her waist, his sandals in his other hand while they walked along the water-hardened sand on the edge of the waves. Every now and again, a wave raced up the beach swirling around their ankles. She was taken by surprise by the first one. Ben hadn't warned her but laughed when she squealed at the cold foam kissing her ankles. It didn't take her long to work out the bubbling squish as the waves ran up the sand just before they hit. Better still, she liked the sibilant popping as the water receded.

To maintain her balance Chrissie slid her arm around Ben's waist then hesitated, scared he might think her to be a bit forward. When he said nothing she left it there. He raised his arm to her shoulders, tugging her closer. The tingle of pleasure that enveloped her was beyond description. How long had it been since a man had held her like this? Way longer than when her husband walked out. All of a sudden she realised that Richard hadn't shown much affection for almost two years before her diagnosis. Maybe Ben was right and Richard had never really loved her. The thought rankled but then deep down she had always suspected he'd only used her to get better known and gain a better position. She'd been used. It hurt. And now, because of her disability, she'd never enjoy the closeness of a loving relationship. Men didn't want a woman with flaws.

When she felt her head drop to Ben's shoulder she jerked it back upright. A hand came up and gently pushed it back. 'Leave it there. It feels right,' was murmured in her ear. Mortification hit but she left it there for it did feel right and so good even though she felt really self-conscious about the intimacy of her action. But how long before he found life with her too darn hard? It had taken Richard two months. What rankled the most was that her sight was relatively good when he'd walked out. She'd give Ben two weeks.

***

When they returned to their starting spot Ben suggested they sit on the sand for a while. He waited until Christine sank down before settling behind her, his knees bent, legs apart, drawing her between his legs where he held her against his chest. She tensed.

'Relax,' murmured Ben in her ear. 'There are dozens of people around. I'm just holding you close to protect you.' Liar. 'I have this constant fear that our friends will attempt to kidnap you again. I feel guilty enough already that my knowing you has caused you so much trauma and put your life in danger. Although our gang of crooks are not after you because of knowing me, they are after you because of Jaye. I have to keep you safe. Feel this.' Taking a hold of her hand he pressed it against the side of his chest. She yanked it away at the feel of his holstered gun.

'I'm armed twenty-four hours a day, except at home. But even there, my gun is within close reach. Until we catch the rest of this gang your life is under threat. I need to tell you a few other things. I'm returning to my regular work tomorrow but you will have your aide in every day to sort out my house to suit your needs. You are safe inside and it is imperative you stay inside until I return home. Don't even go out either the back or front door and don't answer the door to anyone. I'll leave you my contact number if you have the slightest suspicion of anyone hanging around. If you need to go shopping I'll organise one of my team to accompany you. My men will drive you to the hotel, remaining on guard while you work then bring you home again. I hate having to do this, but your safety is my number one concern.'

Christine squirmed then removed her hands from being wrapped around her own legs. One hand landed on Ben's thigh. He slid his fingers over her hand to hold it in place. Big mistake for her touch sent his hormones zinging. The only way to ease the effect was to stand. Reaching down he pulled her to her feet. As she straightened, she glanced up then gasped. Thinking she was hurt, Ben scowled. "What's wrong?' he asked when he noticed a single tear in the corner of her eye.

'Nothing is wrong, everything is right. Stand still. Please?' With her fingers shaking she reached up with one hand. Soft fingertips touched his cheek then ran down the side of his face.

Completely mystified, Ben stared at her face, which was moving up and down then sideways with unblinking eyes following the trail her fingers were making along his skin, creating havoc with already oversensitive nerve endings. Her finger paused at his hated dimple then a wondrous smile spread across her face.

'I can see you.'

It took a moment for her words to sink in. 'You can?' he asked as he jerked away in surprise.

'Please, don't move?' she begged as she re-focussed by moving her head closer. Velvety fingers continued on their path of exploration, searching every single curve, plain and hollow of his face then up through his hair. 'You are a beautiful man,' she whispered in awe. 'The bright sun shining on your features gives me enough light to make out every detail, but only as a narrow tunnel of sight. I have no peripheral vision at all. Turn around.'

It took enormous restraint to not hug her tight as he turned slowly, allowing her to explore with her gentle touch creating sweet torture. He felt the silken brush of her fingers run down his arms, causing his dark hairs to stand on end. She ran the palms of her hands across his shoulders then down his back. Then he sensed her squatting behind him. He shivered as her hands ran over his butt then down one leg all the way to his foot.

'Cute backside, turn around again,' she called from somewhere close to the back of his knee.

As he turned he spied a group of onlookers gawping at them. Very little fazed him in life as he'd always been self-confident and experienced a lot of things most people wouldn't have but a heated blush rose up his neck then spread to his cheeks as he realised they must look almost obscenely intimate, especially with Christine running her hands up his bare legs as she rose. He sent up a silent prayer of thanks when her hands parted as they approached his crotch, then he placed an addendum on his plea that her eyesight wasn't clear enough to notice the reaction her intimate ministrations had caused as her hands run up the outside of his hips to his waist. Thank goodness his shorts were not tight fitting, although they were feeling too damned tight. Her hands met again at his abdomen then spread across his chest with enough pressure she was able to make out the muscle structure underneath his clothes.

Glancing down at her face, he blushed again at her cheeky smile, realising she was more than aware of what she was doing to him. 'Are you quite finished? We have an inquisitive audience that I'm sure can see what you have done to me.' The wench grinned even more.

'It's not often I can see this clearly, I'm making the most of the opportunity. I want to imprint every detail about you on my brain. I'm just sorry you're wearing so many clothes.'

Heaven help me, he begged as he blushed again and grabbed a firm hold of her tormenting hands and held them against his chest. 'You know damn well what you're doing to me don't you?' Her laugh told him he was right. 'I'm expecting to be arrested any second for indecent public display.'

'Then you can flash your badge.' Her voice had a hint of humorous innuendo as she reached up and planted a brief kiss on his chin.

'Which will cause a public scandal. I am sworn to uphold the law, not use my position to escape the law.' Stepping away from her tormenting body, he maintained his tight hold on her hands to prevent any further exploration. 'I think we should get away from here before I completely lose control. You have a bit of devil in you.'

'No, I'm sweet and innocent,' she said then giggled.

'Innocent, my foot,' he grumbled as he stepped to one side and linked elbows to guide her across the sand. Not game to walk too close for longer than he had to since his libido was in overdrive, he drove the short distance to the casual restaurant where he had booked a table for lunch.

Chapter Twenty-One

Felicity Smythe called through the intercom at the front gate before eight the next morning. As he let the lady in Ben introduced himself, even though he had spoken to the aide from the Association for the Blind several times over the phone. Tall and slender, she looked to be in her mid-thirties. What pleased him the most was her charming smile that appeared to be a permanent fixture. Christine needed someone with a positive, friendly attitude. With Christine still asleep Ben showed Felicity around while imparting detailed explanations about what had happened and stressed the importance of the pair of them staying inside.

Once in his office, he examined every detail of the investigation into the attack and attempted abduction, as well as Tony Bates' death and the armed hold-up. Long discussions with John Markham outlined how he wanted the interviews undertaken. For the rest of the day he was an unseen observer and occasional consultant while Des Casey was grilled in the interview room.

It took five gruelling hours, but Casey finally broke under intense pressure. 'My business was going down the gurgler. Almost bankrupt. I tried to borrow money from all the regular financial institutions. None were willing to give me added finance. Then I met a private financier. After signing up I discovered the interest rates were astronomical. When I couldn't meet the repayments I got deeper and deeper into debt. When my wife discovered I had emptied our bank account and mortgaged the house, she walked out. I was coerced, no forced, into repaying the loan by working as a drug courier. I was so petrified. Then I messed up the first job by losing a small package of drugs. I think they were nicked on purpose to tie me in deeper. This further increased my debt. They threatened to kill my wife and kids if I didn't come up with the money. I had no choice but to turn to burglary. None of the deaths were planned; they were unfortunate accidents.'

Ben's ears pricked up when he learnt that Gerard was not the top person.

'I took my orders from Gerard, but he received orders from someone else.'

'Give us details. Where does Gerard hang out?' asked John.

'I swear I don't know. We always meet in a different public place.'

Despite constant hounding, Casey didn't give any more details about Gerard except for a description – which was not a lot more than they already had but verified what both Christine and Ben had described. Watching from his hidden room, Ben was inclined to believe Casey in that he couldn't give them a surname or whether Gerard was a real name. At the same time he felt certain Casey knew more – a lot more. Who was the financier? He must have met the guy to sign papers, must have a description but he wouldn't disclose a single clue. Maybe the threat to his family was enough of a warning to keep his mouth shut.

After a brief discussion with Ben while Casey was allowed a bathroom break, John continued the interview with a change of topic. 'There was an attempt to kidnap a woman from the hospital. What was your involvement?'

Casey's eyes flew open in surprise. 'I don't know anything about any kidnap. I swear.'

By the startled look on Casey's face, Ben believed him.

'But you were involved in the attack on Christine Mears.'

'That bitch!' he hissed. 'She's quite a beauty. Pity we were disturbed. I would love to have had my way with her. Nothing less than the whore deserved.

'Whore?' John asked as he shot a glance in Ben's direction.

'That's her trade – a paid whore.'

Ben's teeth gnashed before he gritted them together and flexed muscles that wanted to punch the man for it was what he deserved. Instead he paced back and forth in an attempt to ease building tension. John's back was turned away and from what Ben could see, John's jaw was clenched. After a lengthy silence, John blew out his breath and spun around.

'What do you mean, a paid whore?' asked John.

'How else would a blind bitch like that, earn a living? What else are they good for?' answered Casey. John stilled, as did the other officer standing guard in the room. Ben felt bile rise as his stomach twisted and tensed into a vicelike grip. Give me two minutes alone with the man, he thought. There was a burning desperation to barge into the interview room to thump the living daylights out of the scumbag, even though he'd never used physical force against anyone. But now he was sorely tempted. Instead he pounded his fist on a desk, flinching at the pain. Fighting back his inward fury, he moved closer to the glass to listen.

'Gerard followed her home to see where she lived. She stole Gerard's wallet after a night of sex. We laid in wait for her to pay her back. A bit of nooky in the bushes, a bit of a touch up to show her we meant business then she would have returned his money.'

Huh! Ben was stunned. None of Casey's explanations made any sense. Either Casey was spun a whopping yarn by Gerard or he was keeping things back and making up his own story. But it did explain how they knew where she lived. So one of their little gang had seen him with Christine in the piano bar, or maybe they were watching her place the night they went out to dinner. Jeeze this was getting more and more frustrating.

'I don't believe you,' John said. 'You planned to abduct the woman, hold her to ransom.'

'No way! Why would we do that? Ransom for what? She's a hooker!' There was a prolonged silence. John glanced towards the mirror, his face telling Ben that he believed Casey. So did Ben, which made no sense. What in hell's name was going on? Did these guys all belong to the same gang? Or were they so disorganised that one didn't know what the other was doing?

'After all, she can't see, so she would never be able identify us.'

Ben jerked his head up at Casey's smug comment. Anger surged then he smiled at this misconception; he had news for Casey. Then he wondered how he was going to convince Christine to face this odious man to identify him.

After another couple of hours of intense questioning, Casey was sent back to his cell. John and Ben had a short discussion before Ben left for home, in an uneasy frame of mind. Anger simmered and he was tense, his innards feeling as though they'd been tied over and over again into a pile of knots. Somehow he needed to relax. He would have to change his attitude before he spoke with Christine. With her other senses so attuned she would be overly perceptive to his demeanour. After driving into his garage he sat for a few minutes, just staring through the window at the brick wall, trying to calm tense nerves by concentrating on separate sections of his body and forcing them to relax. He began with his toes, letting them flop, then worked his way upwards until he felt the day's tension ease off. With a deep sigh he opened the door and strode down the passage, tossing his jacket into his bedroom as he passed the doorway. His eyes softened when he spied her standing waiting for him. It felt so damn right having her here. He spotted Felicity seated in a chair in his re-arranged lounge area.

'I can see you two have been busy and I smell something fabulous. How was your day?' Grasping Christine's hands he lifted them, intending to kiss her fingers but thought twice. He needed to keep a step back so dropped her hands and stepped away with a sigh.

Christine couldn't hide her shiver. Was it one of delight or distaste? He didn't want to know.

'We had a great day. Exhausting, but great. Dinner is in the oven. It needs another half hour. How was your day?'

'I'll discuss that later. Felicity, how did things go?'

'Not too bad. We started with Chrissie's room and sorted her clothes. There are Braille labels on drawers and shelves. They'll only stay until she learns where everything is. Then we moved things in here so there is a clear path to walk from one room to another. We tried not to make too many changes. She learned to walk from her room to the kitchen by turning at the correct angle then counting steps. Tomorrow we work on the kitchen. You won't mind a few labels for a while will you?'

'Not at all, I'm just pleased to see a happy smile on her face.' His arm found its own way to drape around Christine's waist where he kept it while they walked Felicity to the front gate to see her off. He knew he was being presumptuous but unless Christine said anything he'd keep pushing his luck. But no kissing, he vowed.

She seemed proud while showing Ben her room and the changes they'd made, insisting she walk alone to prove she could find her own way around with ease. He noted her keyboard had been set up in her room and wondered if she would keep her practise for when he wasn't around, feeling bitter disappointment at the idea. She then led the way into the kitchen where the bench had been set for the evening meal. Moving over to the oven he inched the door open to see what was cooking.

'My, that smells so good. Would you like a glass of wine before dinner?' At her nod of agreement, Ben slid two delicate cut-crystal wine glasses from an overhead cupboard, removed the cork from a bottle of red wine then seated Christine in a lounge chair before handing her a glass. He turned on a CD and took a few sips of his wine. 'Do I have time for a shower and change into more comfortable clothes.'

'Of course, I expected you would want to change, that's how we planned the dinner.'

He wasted no time with his ablutions, all the while thinking about how he was going to approach the subject of Christine facing Casey. In the end he decided to wait until they had finished eating. No need to spoil what was going to be a pleasant meal.

He shoved the last morsel of food in his mouth, chewed and swallowed then took a couple of deep breaths for courage. 'Christine, I need to ask you to do something but say no, if you feel it will be too difficult.'

She cocked her head to one side. Frown lines creased her brow.

'You know we have one of your attackers in custody.'

She nodded.

'We spent most of today interviewing him. He has confessed to most of the crimes he has been charged with but I'm certain he's holding vital information back. We need you to positively identify him.' He searched her face for a reaction and held his breath when there was an instant closing off. Her jaw clenched, eyes dropped and fear replaced the frown.

'He claims that because you are blind, you won't be able to identify him. I would really like to show the scumbag how wrong he is. Your statement was about his breath and rough hands. In normal circumstances we would do a line-up where you would be in a closed room and he wouldn't be able to see you. We can't do that with you. You would have to confront him, smell his breath, listen to his voice and touch his hands. We'll put him under a bright spotlight if you think you can see enough to make a positive identification. I realise this is an enormous ask.' Pausing, he waited for some kind of response then worried when the silence intensified. She was statue still.

'Would you be there with me?' There was a tremor to her subdued voice as she tried to tug her hands free.

To give her encouragement he tightened his grip. 'I will be watching from the observation room next door. John will stand right next to you for support. We can't afford the chance of Casey recognising me and making an association between me and Jaye. Even though he is in custody, he could still get a message out if he really wanted to. Don't give me an answer yet, think about it.'

'When would you want me to do this?' Her voice was almost inaudible, indicating her reluctance. That, he could understand.

'Tomorrow or the day after. I'll drive you in then bring you back. Felicity can come for support, but she wouldn't be allowed in the room. I want to put this guy away for life.'

'I'll think about it.' A harder tug and she managed to yank her hands free then slid from the bar stool and headed for her room. 'Goodnight, Ben.'

While she moved across the floor, Ben watched. She was disturbed, which concerned him. Sometimes she was so hard to read and was a master at internalising thoughts and feelings. While he cleared away the dishes he heard her shower then silence. Maybe she'd retired for the night even though it was still early: too early for him. He switched on the TV, surfed through a few channels but watched the flickering screen without absorbing the programme. There was a snick of the lock on her door then muffled music. Switching off the television, he lay back on the sofa to listen then cursed under his breath at the melancholy tune. She had been in such a happy frame of mind when he had arrived home and now she sounded troubled and it was his fault. This entire mess was his fault. After switching off the lights he stayed on the sofa in the darkness, listening. He was still there when he woke in the morning.

Breakfast was ready when Christine emerged dressed in bright colours. 'I'll come with you, Ben. I don't want to, but deep down I know I have to face him.'

Noting her tremble, Ben hurried around the bench and gripped her shoulders. 'You can pull out any time you want. Just let John know. It is important for our case, but Christine, you are far, far more important.'

She jerked at the gentle kiss on her head. Cursing himself for forgetting his own vow, Ben pulled away but noticed how she shivered. Then a tiny smile tugged at the corners of her mouth. So she enjoyed his kiss but he bet his life she would never admit it.

'Breakfast is ready. Felicity will be here soon.'

A look of confusion swept over her face followed by determination as she took the few hesitant steps to the bar and pulled out a stool. The silence was heavy. Ben watched her sweep the cereal around and around the bowl. Very little went into her mouth. Hearing Felicity's voice through the intercom, he let the aide in the front gate, explaining what was happening before they stepped inside.

Felicity grasped his hand as Ben reached for the door handle. 'You have done so much for Chrissie already but you can't make her decisions for her. She's still an intelligent adult with a brilliant mind. If she's agreed then it's because she knows it's what needs to be done.'

Filled with remorse, Ben turned to Felicity. 'But it's because of me and my job that she is even in this pickle.'

'It's called life. Chrissie is losing her sight for no reason other than what life has dealt out to her. She's accepted her fate with grace and dignity, has worked like a Trojan to overcome her disability as much as one can in her situation. You two met, a quirk of fate, which is probably one of the best things to happen to her in the past couple of years. She likes you more than she is willing to admit and I know from all the phone calls you've made to me over the past few days that you are more than enamoured with her.' She grinned at Ben's startled expression. 'I hear it in your voice; something working with sight-impaired people has taught me; to use all my senses to pick up cues.'

'Yes, well, there's something about her that has me wanting to get closer.'

'Her disability doesn't deter you? It puts most people off, especially men.'

'Of course not! Who among us is perfect? Look at me. I'm a workaholic and hate sitting idle for more than a few minutes. Not being able to see doesn't alter the person she is. Christine is beautiful, intelligent and amazingly talented. What's not to like? Hell, I didn't even realise she couldn't see until I met her dog.'

Felicity laughed. 'Believe me, there are not many around who can see beyond the disability. In fact many presume that because a person is impaired in one facet it means that they are complete morons - and treat them that way. It's astonishing how many members of the public shout at vision impaired people.

'Shout. Why would they shout?'

'They assume that because the person can't see then they also can't hear, or talk or have a brain.'

Ben shook his head in disbelief. 'Surely not.'

'Believe me it happens all the time. Now let's see if we can't bolster up our girl's mood. Just treat her as a normal adult and she will shine.'

Ben knew they had their work cut out for them when he heard the quiet greeting from Christine. Felicity shot him a questioning glance.

Taking Felicity's advice, Ben immediately moved to begin cleaning up and figured following Felicity's suggestion was probably a good idea. He started chatting to Felicity, joking about how she would have to teach him where to find everything in his own house by the end of the week. He hoped to elicit a smile from Christine but failed miserably. Knowing his words were having little effect, he gave up and changed tack. Head on might be better so he took her hands and drew her off the barstool.

'You don't have to do this you know. You have no idea how much I wish there was some other way.' He enveloped her in an embrace, easing her as close as he thought she'd accept without it appearing to be intimate. He had to fight to not make it more. He couldn't believe how quickly he'd become enamoured with this particular woman. Why Christine and why now? Especially when he'd never had such a reaction before and there'd been plenty of different women over the years.

'It's okay. I'm fine. Let's go and get it over with and then I can spend the rest of the day mucking up your house and plastering signs all over the place. Signs you can't read.' She grinned, which was a relief. 'I could have some fun. I could write you secret messages in Braille and you'll never know. Let's see, what can I put on your bedroom door? Hmm, I can think of one thing that might be appropriate.'

'And what might that be?' Ben asked as he released her, glad she had sparked up. Now was not the time to inform her that he was learning Braille. Maybe he should. No, it would spoil the fun. He was keen to read what she would write.

'You'll just have to wait and see. Give me a minute and I'll be ready to go.' As she returned to her room Ben was certain her outward confidence was far greater than what she was feeling inside.

The same confidence and spark had completely disappeared when John Markham stood outside the interview room with one arm supporting their star witness. Ben noticed her shiver of apprehension before he entered the observation room then paced up and down while Felicity stood in the middle of the one-sided window staring at the man who had beaten Angel to death and bashed Christine so callously.

The moment he noticed the door at the back of the interview room begin to open Ben stopped pacing, but his heart didn't cease hammering in his chest. Of their own accord, his fists clenched in a tight ball by his sides and a tight muscle twitched for release at the side of his locked jaw. He stared at the woman in the bright, multi-coloured dress, wondering if she had worn it on purpose to show she wasn't going to allow the scumbag to think he had gotten the better of her. Or did she even know what colour it was? He had no idea how she managed to always be colour co-ordinated but she never wore mismatched clothes.

Christine straightened her back then lifted her head a notch higher. As her chin jutted out a fraction he noted the steely determination on her face but knew she would be feeling as nervous as he was on the inside. And his nerves were tighter than a piano string – ready to ping apart.

John kept his hand on Christine's back as he guided her into the room, switching on the recording unit as he passed it. A second uniformed officer followed them in and stood leant up against the wall near the door. His stance looked casual but he was alert with one hand casually draped next to his hip-holster for the slightest untoward movement from their prisoner. It was all for show. The fire-arm would never be drawn unless it was essential. Ben couldn't recall it ever happening in his time with the force.

Christine had asked John not to lead her by the hand, but to make it look as though she was walking under her own steam. To do this, his splayed fingers applied pressure in the small of her back to let her know which way to walk. Ben wondered if the bright spotlight aimed on Casey was allowing Christine to see the man.

Casey took one look at Christine and smirked. 'Told you she was a whore. She's even got you under her spell,' he blurted in a snide tone.

Ben baulked. He hadn't told Christine what Casey had called her. He hadn't thought it necessary and certainly hadn't expected Casey to repeat his allegations in front of her.

'Shut it, Casey!' hissed John.

Christine stiffened. 'What did you call me?' she asked in a voice that was like icicle shards.

'Everyone knows that the only way people like you can earn a living, is by selling their bodies, whore!'

'I said shut it, Casey!' John cut in much louder as he took a step towards the man.

Christine held up a hand to stop John. To Ben's surprise, the action stalled Casey. It must have looked as though Christine had seen John move forward. Maybe she had. Sweat broke out on Casey's brow as he took a step backwards. Maybe this was actually going to work. Ben held his breath as he glanced at Felicity, who had a look of admiration on her face.

'She can see enough,' said Felicity. 'Chrissie is a very determined person and once she has made up her mind to do something she will move mountains to achieve it. I have a feeling Chrissie will come out the victor here.'

There was a feminine snort. Both swung their eyes back towards the window.

'For your information, I earn my living by teaching young children. I'm also a concert pianist and earn quite a considerable sum of money by playing on stage. Although, through your cowardly act in killing my guide dog, I might have to resort to selling my body until I can get a new dog. Without her, I can't teach. I pity you. You are nothing more than a coward and bully. The only thing you can have power over is working dog and a defenceless blind woman. Legally blind that is.' She paused after emphasising the four words then took a step closer and moved her head from side-to-side and up and down.

'I can still see enough to know that it was you who attacked me. Hold your hands out.'

The sweat on Casey's face was freely flowing and his eyes held a look of panic.

With deep admiration welling up for the incredible strong person he was watching, Ben started breathing again. He caught Felicity's knowing smile.

John stepped a few centimetres away from Christine and grabbed Casey's wrists, forcing him to hold them out by heading them towards Christine's outstretched hands. The look of absolute fear in Casey's face was something to behold. He looked terrified and then the gentle touch of soft fingers really threw him into a panic. As she felt the tips of his fingers, his khaki prison trousers turned a darker shade from his crotch down. Glancing towards the mirror John grinned.

Christine's nose twitched then her face looked mystified as she dropped the hands then turned to face John. 'I can say with one hundred percent certainty that this is the man who held my arms when I was dragged through the bushes.

This is the animal that belted me twice over my mouth. He held my mouth closed with his left hand and I bit him.' She ran her fingers over Casey's hand. 'Here is the bite mark on his middle finger.'

There was a slight movement as Casey automatically felt the healing injury. His hand shook before he whipped it behind his back.

'He is also the animal who lifted my T-shirt and put his filthy dirty fingers on my breasts. He kicked me twice in the head. I hope he rots in hell.'

Casey jolted. His face paled.

'Can I go now please?' Christine turned with her head still held high as she walked away from the lizard. John chased after her, returning his hand against the small of her back.

Ben flew out of the observation room to see Christine had collapsed against John. He eased her away and supported her weight as he headed her towards his office, Felicity hot on his tail. Felicity sank into one of the two chairs on the other side of the desk and watched – not saying a word but with a smug grin on her face.

'Are you okay?' Ben asked as he gripped each of Christine's shoulders.

'I'm fine, just a little unnerved.'

'You were incredible,' Ben brushed stray tendrils from her face. 'You are such a strong woman. You did more than John was able to do in a whole day of intense questioning. He wasn't able to get the animal to wet himself like you did.' Ben couldn't hold back his grin when she jerked back.

'What did you say?'

'The moment you touched Casey he lost control of his bladder. I think he thought you were going to belt him. Are you sure you don't want to become a detective? I could use you every time we wanted to get the truth out of someone. You'd better spill the beans or I'll bring Madame Lash in.' Hoots of laughter echoed around the room.

'I thought there were rules around this place about fraternising.'

Caught giving Christine a hug, Ben glanced up at John then grinned. 'Brilliance deserves a reward.' Embarrassed at being caught, he set Christine away. 'I've just offered Christine a job as Madame Lash, to interview all our tough customers.'

'Yeah, I've told him he only gets one set of prison greens per week. He's blubbering like a baby and spilling a whole heap more info to Mac. Unfortunately he's not going to live long enough to get his just desserts. Doc Williams sent in his report. You were right. Casey has stage four stomach cancer and won't last more than a few months. Do I get to reward our star witness the same way?' John moved towards Christine with a devilish glint in his eye.

'Not unless you want me to tell your wife.' Ben shunted between the two, a sudden stab of searing jealousy hitting him in his solar plexus. What in the blazes was this woman doing to him?

John grinned. 'Sorry, Chris, but my boss is throwing his weight around. I'll catch up with you all soon. Thanks a million, Chris, you did a great job.' The door was closed after him with an echoing snick.

'Oh, I'm disappointed,' Christine said with a hint of cheek. 'It's so rare that I get so close to a man and hugs from two different men in one day would have been a record for me. Can't we call him back?'

Ben forced his face into an inscrutable mask as he stared at her, but Felicity was sitting back in her seat, grinning. With the mere thought of another man even touching

Christine, Ben was swift in his reaction. 'I'm taking you two home before all my men start lining up for a hug. We have crimes to solve and I want them concentrating on their job. I would prefer you two ladies create mayhem in my house rather than my office.'

Create mayhem, they did. When Ben arrived home early evening his kitchen cupboards had been re-organised with little coloured labels in Braille all over the place, including one on his door. The thought of what was written was intriguing but apart from a glance, he ignored the sign until he was alone.

After seeing Felicity off, Christine returned to the kitchen, setting places for their dinner whilst Ben hurried to shower. He paused at his door, studied the label. 'What does this say, Christine?'

'Ben's Bedroom!'

Not trusting the tone of her voice he studied the label and grinned. Having taken on the task to learn Braille without letting on to Christine, he had memorised two letters of the Braille alphabet each day. To start with, this label did not begin with a *B*. The second letter was definitely an *E*. He moved to the second word. *B* followed by an *E* had his deductive skills assuming the second word was *Ben's,* which made the first word begin with an *S*. So as to not arouse suspicions he left it alone while he showered but before he dressed he crept back to the door label and pulled out the Braille alphabet Felicity had given him. While he dragged on a pair of well-worn jeans he searched for the matching set of dots to the third letter. His eyebrows rose when he found what he was searching for at the end of the page and he didn't have to go any further to understand exactly what the label said. *Sexy Ben's* was all he needed. The last word was obvious. Grinning to himself he wondered about the best way to respond. The mere fact that she thought him to be sexy gave him a lot of hope where Christine was concerned.

Chapter Twenty-Two

True to Ben's word, Christine returned to work at the piano bar with a plain-clothes detective. Even though she couldn't see him, Ben waved as they left. With a fairly good description of Gerard, the guard was to call Ben if anyone even remotely fitting the description visited the bar. The biggest concern was that they had no idea what other members of the gang looked like. Any of them could be waiting for an opportunity to abduct, or even worse, attack Christine. One well-aimed shot and she'd be dead. Ben shuddered at the thought but he wasn't overly concerned. Christine was no good to them dead or harmed. They wanted her alive for ransom. Intense questioning of Casey had yielded a big fat nothing about any other gang members. It appeared that both Bobby and Casey only dealt with Gerard, but was he the head honcho? Ben didn't think so and he was also concerned about the woman who had posed as a nurse. Somewhere on the scene there was a female of whom they had only a vague description: medium height and build for a woman, with dark shoulder length hair fitted at least twenty percent of the local female population and who could say whether or not the woman was wearing some sort of disguise?

With Christine out of the house it gave Ben a chance to retaliate for the label on his door. Enlisting Felicity's help, he wrote out an invitation, which Felicity printed on a Braille machine. Wanting to be around when he saw her face, he stuck it across Christine's cereal bowl with adhesive tape.

Even though Christine had a key to bypass the electronic gate, Ben's instincts had him awake not long before she was due home. Dragging on his favourite lay-about jeans that had been washed to a sensuous softness, he waited until he heard the unmarked squad car pull up before opening the gate. He had the passenger door open before her minder had a chance to alight.

'How was your night?' he asked as he grasped Christine's hand and placed it in the crook of his elbow. 'Any problems, Simon?' Peering over the roof of the car he acknowledged the officer assigned to Christine's safety.

'No, nothing out of the ordinary. I wish all our assignments were in such luxurious surroundings and with such terrific company. It beats being cramped in a car hour after hour. Give me this job anytime, boss. Goodnight, Chrissie.'

'Goodnight, Simon and thank you.' She waved farewell then turned to Ben. 'What are you doing up?' They headed up the short brick pathway, a gibbous moon lighting the way.

'I woke a few minutes ago, how was your night?'

'It was great being back at work. I really enjoyed it but right now I'm looking forward to my bed. I still have a few muscles that ache and I wish I could sleep in tomorrow. Goodnight, Ben.' Tugging her fingers free, she headed in the direction of her room.

'Sweet dreams, Christine.' Perturbed by her hasty and pointed get away, he watched her retreating figure before turning into his room where he set his alarm to go off earlier than normal.

He hated waking her when it was obvious she was tired after a late night but with Felicity arriving soon for her last day, he had little choice so tapped on the door. 'Christine!'

'Go away,' came back.

He couldn't help but laugh. 'Felicity will be here soon and breakfast is ready,' he called through the closed door. A muttered oath shot back at him.

On tenterhooks, he paced around until Christine emerged then he watched with apprehension while she perched on her stool and reached out with one hand for her bowl. It was difficult to suppress his glee as her fingers felt the attached letter. While her fingers ran expertly across the rows of raised dots, a range of expressions raced across her face. He felt awed by the speed in which she read - *Christine Mears is cordially invited to dinner and dancing on Monday night. She will be picked up at seven. Sexy Ben.*

When her cheeks filled with colour, Ben was fighting back the urge to let fly with laughter.

'I'll kill Felicity!' she cried out.

'Why Felicity? It took me a whole two minutes to work out what your label said. I didn't need Felicity to read it to me. I've been teaching myself Braille ever since you agreed to come here. I hadn't got as far as the *X*. I had to look that one up. Oh, and what a delightful surprise I received.'

'You can get that smile off your face, Ben Somers,' Christine retorted, trying to hide her embarrassment by placing her hands over cheeks that were turning bright red.

'Not likely! I've been grinning like the proverbial Cheshire cat since I figured out the *X*. Are you going to respond to the invitation? Does sexy Ben get to take out the beautiful Christine to dinner on Monday?' Still grinning he reached over the bench, pulled her hand from one side of her face then ran his fingers down her hot cheek. 'And you look even more beautiful when you blush.'

Looking mortified, she took a swipe at Ben's hand, her cheeks reddening even more but before she was able to retaliate, the gate intercom sounded. Still laughing, Ben went to let Felicity in.

'I should say no,' Christine yelled.

'Should say no to what?' asked Felicity as she entered.

'Christine has been asked out on a date with someone whom *she* regards as sexy. Convince her that she should go. *He* promises to not practise what *she* preaches. Well, not unless she wants it. I'm off. I'll see you both tonight. Have a terrific day.' By ducking, Ben avoided the spoon tossed in his direction but he laughed until his car left the garage and was still grinning when he reached work.

***

Furious and mortified, Chrissie turned on Felicity. 'Why didn't you tell me he was learning Braille?'

'What, and miss all this fun? He cares about you Chrissie – a great deal. Tell me you don't enjoy his company.'

With her cheeks searing from the inside Chrissie couldn't for the life of her, answer. She loved his company and, much to her chagrin, the way he made her feel. But nothing could ever come of it. He'll tire of her disability and leave.

'Are you going out with him on this date?'

Chrissie could tell Felicity was laughing by the tone of her voice. It took some time before she could formulate an answer. 'Yes, it's only a date and I sure don't get many of those these days. I do enjoy his company; he treats me as though I'm a normal person and not as though I'm some complete freak. I'm going to remove that label.' With one hand trailing along the wall to guide her, she made her way down the passage to Ben's room then felt around for the label only to find that it had disappeared. Darn man. She itched to go and search for it but didn't dare. It could be hidden anywhere and not having been in his room before it would take forever to search. Besides it just wasn't right.

An even bigger surprise was that her protector for her next two nights at work was Ben. He sat in the back of the lounge while she played then perched on a bar stool next to her chatting during her breaks. During the second break she felt him tense then there was a tell-tale sucked in breath followed by silence, all which told her something was wrong.

'What is it?' she asked as she sought out his arm.

He didn't answer but twisted around, the almost imperceptible shush of clothes and a shift in sound waves giving her the clues she needed.

'Ben?'

He turned back. 'I don't know, just a feeling. A couple just entered and their presence sent a shiver of unease through me but I don't recognise either person. The man seemed to be searching the room then his eyes settled on you a bit too long for comfort.'

'Maybe he was looking for me since I'm not playing at the moment. For all I know he could be a regular.'

'Maybe,' Ben murmured, the fading voice telling her that he'd turned away again.

'Where are they now?' She wasn't really concerned. So many people came in, many of them on a regular basis and who would be stupid enough to attempt any sort of misdeed with all these people around.

'They've sat together in a bench seat along the side wall. He has his arm around the woman and his back to me so I can't make out his features.'

A sudden warm breath on the skin of her cheek told her that Ben had leant towards her. 'The woman seems familiar but even after wracking my brain, I can't place her. The man isn't Gerard. He's too lean and no-where near tall enough.'

'Then let's not worry and I need to get back to entertaining them.' She returned to the piano, deciding to play a more upbeat selection for the next hour to alter the atmosphere a bit. She heard the shuffles of dancing feet along with murmurs of light conversation and from the side, suppressed laughter from one particular group; all sounds of contented patrons.

More than usual, Chrissie enjoyed the remainder of the night, playing until three in the morning, in particular - the breaks. Having Ben to chat to made the night far more interesting, less lonely and helped the time to fly.

Chapter Twenty-Three

It was early Monday morning and Chrissie had just been introduced to John's wife, Mary Markham. It felt ridiculous when early hesitancy felt uncomfortable for Chrissie had always been self-confident when meeting new people. She couldn't figure out why she felt so shy all of a sudden. Especially when Mary bubbled with vibrant chatter, to which Chrissie couldn't help but laugh; something that had been missing from her life since her sight loss had got to the stage where old associates felt uncomfortable and began pulling away. But thank goodness her disability didn't seem to affect Mary – or not yet. How long before she would find it all too hard to hang around?

Without meaning to, Chrissie let slip in the middle of a conversation about men, that she was going out that night.

Tears welled when Mary offered to do something special with Chrissie's hair.

'I was a hairdresser until a couple of years ago. How about we create something different to knock Ben's socks off? Are you all right by yourself for a while? I need to go home to pick up my hairdressing kit. I'll ring Ben to let him know.'

'Don't bother Ben. I'll be fine. I can practise a few pieces. Can you cut my hair at the same time – it certainly needs it?' She patted her head then tugged at a strand to confirm how long it had grown. There were probably split ends as well but that was something she could no longer see. For a moment a wave of self-pity swamped her before she shivered to shake it away. She was going blind. Fact of life. She couldn't alter it so there was no point in moping about it.

'If I don't ring Ben I'll be in more trouble than you can imagine. I'll call him and wait in the car until a squad car arrives.'

Mary's voice broke Chrissie's reverie. She shook away her introspection and forced a smile, something she'd become a master at doing over the past year. Deep down she was more than glad Mary had insisted on the guard. Even though she knew she was safe locked inside, not having the clear sight to see danger coming, now unnerved her, especially after being mugged. It had never bothered her before and thoughts of the 'what if's' and 'maybe's' centred in her mind while she tinkered at the keyboard waiting for Mary's return.

The sense of relief when Mary was back in less than hour shook Chrissie so much that she became determined to whisk away all negativity for the rest of the day. She forced a smile then was overwhelmed when laughter continued as Mary cut Chrissie's hair in a style she would be able to manage without a lot of fuss, teaching her how to brush it and feel the end result. Mary used a blow dryer to create a special effect for the night out.

When Ben arrived home, Chrissie refused to come out of her room until her date arrived to pick her up, saying her goodbyes to Mary in her room. She had already showered and changed, helped by Mary who ensured everything was perfect, including make-up that covered the remnants of bruises she could never have seen. How ridiculous she must have looked since going back to work but nobody had told her that her face looked like a rainbow until Mary suggested some cover-up.

Her nerves tense, Chrissie sat at her keyboard practising a couple of new pieces until she heard a gentle knock at her door, precisely at seven according to her watch.

Feeling more than nervous Chrissie opened the door.

'You look exquisite,' Ben gasped. 'Turn around and let me see it all.'

With her heart jammed somewhere it shouldn't be Chrissie obliged, turning in a slow circle. Too fast and she'd lose her sense of balance.

'Your hair suits you like that. I liked it long as well but that looks great. Phew, I'm going to be fighting off all the guys tonight.'

All of a sudden she felt his lips brush against her mouth. It was warm, sensual and way too brief but enough to awaken long dead hormones. With her heart hammering, Chrissie reached out to run her hands down Ben's clothes, desperate for a few moments to calm her racing heart. 'Describe what you are wearing, the colours in particular.'

'Light grey suit, black cotton shirt and mid-blue silk tie with fine black and silver diagonal lines.'

She sniffed. 'And my favourite aftershave. And I bet all the women in the restaurant tonight will agree with my label. What happened to it?'

Ben laughed. 'Don't look so innocent, young lady. I bet you are itching to know what I've done with it which tells me you tried to remove it. I thought you might so I put it in a safe place. Come on gorgeous, the dance floor is waiting for us and I'm sure looking forward to being on it with you.'

As though it were natural and part of normal conversation, Ben described the features of the dining room as they were ushered to their table, his thoughtfulness overwhelming her. According to Ben the room was dimly lit with candlelight embellishing every table and subdued lighting around the edges. Ben described it as romantic but to Chrissie it was dark and forbidding. Needing bright lights to be able to discern any shapes, she could see almost nothing in this dimness apart from vague flickering of candles if she held her head in the right position and she bet she looked real dandy cocking her head from side-to-side like the pendulum of a clock.

'Our table is against the wall,' said Ben as he assisted Chrissie to sit by sliding the chair out then back in as she lowered her backside. 'I chose this position so I'll have a clear view of everyone entering and leaving.' He leant forwards. 'It's also not so far from the amenities so you can have easy access without feeling embarrassed having a man guide you.'

That's all very well and good, thought Chrissie but she felt like she was entombed.

They spent a considerable time making their choices for a meal, with Ben making fun of the descriptions once again. These modern day menus sure had some weird ingredients.

Silken carrot puree! Why couldn't they just call it mashed carrot? It was pleasant dancing while they waited for the first course. The music was a little too loud, destroying the ambience the owners were trying to create, but Chrissie still lapped up the pleasure of being held in Ben's arms, using the volume of the music as an excuse to keep her head close to his so they could talk. She felt her body tingle every time his warm breath brushed against her cheek, sensations she enjoyed at the same time as being afraid as to why she was taking so much pleasure in his presence.

They were halfway through their entrée of fresh salmon topped with a spear of char-grilled asparagus when Chrissie heard voices near-by. She stopped eating, her fork in mid-air. It must have unnerved Ben for she heard his cutlery clatter on his plate seconds before her hand was grasped.

'What's the problem, Christine? Are you all right?' The fork was taken from fingers she knew were shaking. 'Are you ill? Is something wrong with your meal?'

Still concentrating hard on the voices, she ignored Ben.

'Talk to…' Ben said at the same time as Chrissie held up a hand to silence him.

Just to be certain, she listened until the three-way conversation ceased. 'Those people behind me who have just been shown to their table, two of them I think. I heard three different voices, a man and two women. One woman was the same waitress who showed us to our table. But the man - I recognise his voice. That's the other man who attacked me. I swear it.' She grasped her hands together, her fingers twisting into a tight knot as flashes from her mugging shot through her mind.

***

Glancing over Christine's shoulder, Ben noticed a tall man had just sat with his back to them. His partner was a scrawny woman with white blonde hair that could only have come from a bottle. She looked vampish with over the top make-up and gaudy jewellery hanging from her ears, neck and wrists. One other occupied table stood between them. His muscles tensed. He had no recollection of ever having seen the woman before, but the shape of the man's head had his brain cells working overtime trying to recall some hidden piece of information, bringing forward aspects of the drunk to see if they fitted and trying to remember the thousands of people he had studied over the past week or so. This man had greying short hair whilst the drunkard's hair was darker, longer and scraggly. It could have been a wig. Scrutinizing the hair, he searched for evidence it was a wig. Too close cut, too short. Height was hard to compare although the man was tall. The drunk had been bent over and this man was sitting – just how long were his legs? Hell, why hadn't he noticed them come in? Wasn't that the whole idea of sitting here? He glanced at his companion. There sat the reason his mind wasn't on the job. She was too darn beautiful and he was acting like a besotted teenager.

To keep his voice low, he leant across the table. 'Are you absolutely certain? He is tall but I can't see his hands.'

'I'm almost one hundred percent certain.'

'Almost isn't good enough.'

'Describe him to me.'

'He's a big man, broad but not fat. His back is to me and he's seated so I can't see his face. Damn it, I wish I could see his face. He wouldn't have recognised you from the back because it is quite dark in here and you have altered your hairstyle. Hang on a minute – he's moving his hands. Heavens, they are huge. We need to keep a low profile here. It will be better if you don't speak or keep your voice very low. Try to relax. Eat your fish. Now are you certain it's him?'

'I will never forget that voice. I heard him speak to the waitress. It was the same accent, the same tone. I'm absolutely positive.' Feeling around with her hand, Christine searched for the fork Ben had taken from her trembling fingers. He placed it back into her hand.

'I have to be certain, now are you sure it's him?'

'Ben, I don't know how to explain this but when a person loses their sight, nature seems to teach the body to compensate for the loss of one of the senses by enhancing the others. I pick up and remember so many cues from around me that I was never even aware of before I lost my sight. That man's voice is imprinted in my brain.'

'Okay, I trust your judgement. Look, I'm not going to use your name again and I'm going to ring my men with a coded message you probably won't understand.' Sliding his mobile phone from his shirt pocket Ben punched in a number. Under normal circumstances he would leave the room to speak, especially in a restaurant, but he couldn't risk leaving Christine alone and taking her outside past that particular table would only make her presence more obvious. He searched the room for another exit but couldn't spot one. There had to be an emergency fire door somewhere but it could be through the kitchen, out past the amenities or tucked behind some corner. But it sure wasn't in sight.

While he waited for his call to be answered he wondered at the probability of Christine and this man being in the same place at the same time. It was too much of a co-incidence. Something didn't add up and his stomach began its customary churning to tell him things were not right. How the hell did Gerard, if it was Gerard, know they were here? But she was certain it was the same man and somehow he trusted her instincts and her well-honed abilities.

His hand began searching pockets for a small electronic device he knew wasn't there since these particular clothes hadn't left his house for months. Had they somehow planted a tracking device on Christine? He glanced at her as he wondered what these hoodlums had planned. The dress was one he'd not seen before – not even at the piano bar so there was no way they could have had access to it. Where else could they have planted a homing device? He knew of tiny devices that could be attached to the skin. Worried, he roamed all the skin on Christine that he could see, searching for some miniscule splotch. Without completely undressing her, he'd never know. But then how could they have had access to her? No one was allowed near her at work and that was the only place she'd been. He dismissed the possibility. The nurse? Had she attached one? Christine would never be able to see it but surely she would have felt something when she showered. But that didn't make sense either because why then would they have sent the listening device in the flower arrangement? They wouldn't have needed to if some bug had been attached to Christine.

Had they broken into her home and planted a device? But it would have to be in her clothes and nobody would know what she was going to wear? Was another member of the gang sitting somewhere in the room? His eyes darted around the restaurant but no one was looking in their direction. As if they'd be staring at him in any case. Who was the woman? Mac's voice interrupted his thoughts.

Ben gave a standard type coded message: one his department had made up and could be used when one of them needed assistance and there was a possibility that they could be overheard. 'Dad,' the word for help, 'what happened to you?' or rather, I need your assistance. 'We were expecting a table for six, but there is only seating for two.' There are two of us here and I need four more. 'Are we in the right place – the York Hotel? You're on your PC?' – Plain clothes are needed. 'What poor target are you chasing now?' The target we are chasing is right here. 'Yeah, she's here with me, you don't think I'd be dining with anyone else do you? Okay, we'll go ahead and eat and you can join us as soon as you can. See you soon.'

After listening to Mac relay the decoded message, Ben replaced his mobile phone then slipped his hand further inside his jacket where they curled around the handle of his police issue gun hidden in the holster under his arm. Taking care to keep it hidden by his jacket flap, he slid it down his chest then slipped it into his belt, within close reach. With his head lowered to shade his face as much as possible, his eyes flashed down to his plate every now and again, but for the majority of the time they were planted on his target, without seeming to stare.

All his instincts were screaming that he should recall where he had seen the man before but not being able to see any facial features made it almost impossible. Instead he assessed the woman. From where she sat, she seemed to be too tall to have been the woman in the hospital and he was certain the nurse had dark hair. But he had changed his appearance overnight so he wasn't dismissing the woman from being another member of the gang. Besides, wigs were easily obtainable as were hair dyes and contact lenses – he should know. She wasn't the woman who had sent unease screaming through his body at the piano bar.

When loud laughter followed by an accented comment came from the man, Christine stiffened. 'That's him – I'm more certain now,' she whispered. Both sat in silence, straining to hear the conversation above all the others in the room. There was definitely a European accent to the man's voice. While the waiter took the couple's order, Ben studied the man's profile then stiffened when he recognised the shape of the face. This man was in the bar at site five, but then his hair had been darker and longer. Turning his intense study to the clothes, he recognised the suit the man had been wearing, the wide stripes being distinctive – too distinctive. All right, Ben thought, Gerard knew I was at site five because he'd planted a bug in my pocket but how the devil did he find out about this place? He must know I'm Jaye or be expecting Jaye to turn up. Was that why the man was sitting facing the door? Damn, this has got to be another set up. Or is he following Christine? But that didn't make sense for neither the man nor the woman had paid them any attention – that he knew of. Hell. Had they studied him when they'd come in? The thought sent a wave of shivers shuddering across his shoulders.

More than a little worried, Ben kept observing and noting how Gerard kept searching the faces of the people seated in the packed venue, which gave him hope that neither he nor Christine had been spotted yet. He stiffened as Gerard stood then walked to the men's room and when he returned he was scanning the room, obviously searching. When Gerard's eyes settled briefly on him, Ben lowered his head as though he was concentrating on cutting his piece of pink salmon that had gone stone cold and taken an unappealing glutinous look. Staring under hooded eyes, he felt confident Gerard didn't recognise either of them as he continued searching the room. A sigh of relief slipped from his lips when Gerard sat again.

His mind churned. Gut instinct told him Gerard was looking for Jaye and Christine but hadn't recognised either of them because of their different hairstyles. And he was wearing far more sedate clothes minus the outlandish jewellery. So somehow, one of them must still be bugged but it didn't make any sense since Christine had been at his place since leaving the hospital and he had been transformed back to his real identity since then. So what was going on? How do they know where we are?

Knowing by a quick glance at his watch that it was almost time for his team to arrive, Ben turned to Christine. 'Listen carefully. When I see my men, I'm going to take you to the disabled amenities. I want you to lock yourself in and only open the door to me or John. Are you okay with that?'

She nodded.

'This is just in case we have any trouble. Your safety is my number one priority. Now, continue eating. He has his back to you and even though I feel sure he knows we are in here somewhere, or expecting us to turn up, I'm equally certain he is unaware of exactly where because he hasn't recognised us. Your new hairstyle is opportune. He's still searching the room.' Ben was for once gratified Christine couldn't see his face for even though he hoped Gerard was unaware of where she was sitting, he certainly wasn't sure about it - in fact he was more certain Gerard's presence was deliberate and knew damn well Christine was here or at least that she was supposed to be here.

The very moment Ben spied the first of his team enter the glass doors his gut clenched. There was going to be trouble. Mac and Simon were dressed in such a conspicuous manner that the only person who wouldn't recognise them as coppers would be Christine. It was obvious to Ben that the name of the establishment hadn't completely registered with Mac for they should be dressed more like they were going out to a classy meal than to the local pub. PC mean-

plain clothes and it was also supposed to mean plain clothes to suit the environment into which they were going.

'Damn!' Ben cursed under his breath. 'A change of plans,' he murmured to Christine. 'No matter what happens, don't move from your seat and don't dare turn around.'

As if in slow motion, Ben watched Gerard raise his eyes to stare at the two detectives who were speaking to the headwaiter. Did they have to look straight at the suspect? He noted the sudden tenseness in Gerard's body and the slow straightening in his torso when it registered that the two men, plus the other two who had just entered the door and joined them, were not diners, but policemen and since they were looking at Ben, it appeared they were also looking directly at Gerard. It was obvious by his fidgeting that Gerard was uncomfortable by the presence of the law and maybe was contemplating fleeing so Ben figured he needed to act. In a flash he withdrew his gun from the waistband of his trousers while he strode past the table behind Christine. He had the barrel of the gun pressed between Gerard's shoulder blades just as the man began to turn around at the noise. Lord only knew why he was turning but hell, he was making it obvious he had a guilty conscience.

'Going somewhere, Gerard?' Ben hissed in his ear while he held out his police identification badge in front of the man's wide-open eyeballs. He really didn't want the man to see him close-up. 'You're under arrest for the assault causing grievous bodily harm on Mrs Christine Mears.'

Ben's sudden movement brought an instant reaction from the other four detectives and within seconds Gerard and his lady friend were surrounded. When Gerard turned his head towards him, Ben stepped sideways but a flash of instant recognition assaulted Ben's mind. He was definitely the drunk in the street and the man in the bar and he had also seen him with a different woman in the piano bar. This was the person who had been following him but how did he know they were here?

Before he could ask the question, pandemonium broke out. Patrons flew in all directions in a cacophony of yells, shrieks and dragging of furniture legs. Some people cowered behind tables and chairs, others fled outside, to the toilets, into the kitchen, wherever they found a nearby exit or felt they would be safe. Glasses tinkled and smashed, liquids running in rivulets across the immaculate linen tablecloths then down onto the floor. Food from upturned plates fell in globular splats on the upholstered chairs and the highly polished floorboards. Clean napkins fluttered down more slowly, landing like huge, pristine white snowflakes amongst the detritus of food, cutlery and china.

One glance behind him told Ben that the only person who remained still was Christine. She had obeyed his instructions implicitly; not even moving or turning around, probably more out of fear than what Ben had told her.

'Could you boys have been any less subtle?' Ben asked, his voice dripping with sarcasm while Mac handcuffed Gerard. Simon did the same to his lady companion. By the look on the poor woman's face, Ben figured she had no idea what was going on. Simon narrated them their rights in a practised monotone before the four detectives left, one on each side of their prey, leaving Ben standing to face the headwaiter, who was not looking in the least bit impressed as he approached.

As he holstered his pistol he surveyed the room. In two minutes flat, a swish eating house full of elegantly clad diners had turned into what now looked more like the aftermath of a cyclone. He was really quite bemused because the few words that had been uttered hadn't been audible to many of the patrons, no shots had been fired – he hadn't even released the safety catch on his gun and his was the only gun drawn.

'Sorry folks, the fun and games are over. You can all go back to your dinner now, knowing that a dangerous criminal is now off the streets.'

Knowing his comments were inane and feeling fit to burst out in laughter, Ben moved over to the only unspoiled table in the room and grasped Christine's hand. 'I have a feeling it would be wise for us to leave now. My boys created a bit of mayhem in here.' Removing a generous amount of cash from his wallet, he left it on the table then led Christine on a zigzag course through the restaurant, avoiding the worst of the mess, while feeling the stunned eyes from staff and patrons boring into his back.

It was difficult, but Ben managed to stifle his laughter until he was sitting in the driver's seat of his car with Christine next to him.

'Would you mind explaining to me, everything that happened?' she asked when his laughter subsided a little.

'I'm not really sure. It wasn't as though we called out *bomb* or anything like that. The few words I uttered weren't audible to many people but it was like a chain reaction. The only person in the room who didn't panic was you. We do have Gerard in custody. Which, I'm sorry to say, means I am going to have to go into work to interview him – which leaves me in a bit of a quandary. Even though you are safe locked up in my house, I don't like leaving you there on your own. Especially as there are at least two other people and possibly more, unaccounted for, namely the nurse who tried to abduct you and the big boss of this gang, both of whom are going to be rather peeved tonight and could try anything to get their hands on you. I have a strong suspicion they knew we were dining in this particular restaurant. How – I don't have a clue.'

'They must have followed me to my home from the hotel so they could have done it again – to your place to find out where I'm now living.'

'Possible but Gerard didn't recognise us in here tonight.'

'How do you know?'

'Because he kept searching the place, looking for either or both of us.' I'm certain he was looking for Jaye and you with longer hair. So Gerard didn't follow us here tonight or he would have recognised us.'

'But they knew we were here. How?'

'Beats me.' He turned the key and the engine rumbled to life. 'Now what am I going to do with you?'

'Ben, I'll go with you. I can wait in your office, but first, please tell me what happened?'

As he drove Ben pondered the suggestion for a few moments and was still thinking while he negotiated his way out of the car park. 'That might not be such a bad idea. I'd like you to listen to the voices of Gerard and his lady friend while we interview them. See if this lady is the nurse. Somehow I don't think she is. She's too tall and scrawny but she could still be related to any of the men or even be Gerard's partner. We'll go home first to change. I'm sorry about dinner. I'll make it up to you – I promise.' He groaned. 'It's the story of my life, ruined dinners and dates because of work.'

'Ben, it's your job. I understand. My work has revolved around nighttime engagements all my life – I truly understand. Maybe you should take your dates out to breakfast, it seems to be the most regular time you are free. And besides, if I recall correctly, it was me who started all that mayhem tonight. Now please, please, please, describe to me what happened.'

Christine laid one hand on Ben's thigh as a gesture of understanding. Her touch sent a sudden jolt through his body. He fought to regain his composure then related in detail everything that had happened, making it sound as though it was some comedy sketch. By the time he drove into his garage they were both wiping tears of laughter from their eyes.

Chapter Twenty-Four

Forcing one eye open, Ben cursed and blinked at the fierce streak of sunlight searing through the half-open slats of Venetian blinds. It was early afternoon. He'd slept heavily, unusual for him but it sure felt good. His first thoughts, before his brain started functioning properly, were that he was in some strange place for he was hearing sounds that were more unusual than a deep sleep was. Shaking his head to clear away fuzzy cobwebs, he eased out of bed and pulled on a pair of old blue jeans to cover his nakedness as he hopped across the room. Just to increase his confusion, the door was shut – something he couldn't recall ever having happened before. This was his house and living alone he never shut inside doors. Feeling as though he were in some kind of warp zone, he searched the recesses of his mind for a logical explanation.

Christine. She must have shut his door because he distinctly remembered leaving it half open as he did every night in case she called for him. Not bothering with a shirt he padded down the passage on bare feet, following the noise. His CD player was playing an unfamiliar disk but at the same time other music was coming from her room in accompaniment in a finely tuned duet. He reached for, and read, the CD cover – *Carnival of the Animals.* Replacing it, he moved panther-like to Christine's door and stood, stunned.

She was playing the piano part of the music on her keyboard. Her faultless and furious fingers flew over the keys. How in hell's name can she do that if she can't see? A niggling memory nibbled as he leant against the painted wooden doorjamb, transfixed. The interview with Casey – something she said. Wracking his brain he tried to recall all the words. When he did remember what she'd said he straightened when the word's *concert pianist* slammed into his conscious memory. She'd said she was a concert pianist. Damn, why didn't he connect the dots? She hadn't been referring to being just a lounge bar pianist – she was a real, serious concert pianist and listening to her now, he could well believe it.

Knowing how acute her sense of hearing was, Ben took care to not make any noise as he returned to the lounge room. He picked up the CD cover once again in order to study it in more detail because it wasn't one of his. His eyes popped wide when he read the name of the pianist playing on the recording – the world-renowned Miss Christine Wilson, conducted by Sir Arthur Mears. A photo of a younger Christine leaning up against a grand piano told him that both Christine's were the same person. Eager to hear more he sank into the soft leather lounge; his fingers entwined behind his head while he continued listening, fascinated as memories of the previous night ambled through his brain.

It was just on 5a.m. when they'd finished interviewing Gerard and his lady companion. It had been a frustrating night with Gerard denying any knowledge of the attack on Christine. She wasn't at all pleased when Ben had suggested that he may need her to confront Gerard as she'd done with Casey. The lady friend swore she was from an escort agency, paid to be Gerard's companion for the night. She'd been released but under surveillance because Ben couldn't afford to believe her.

The music stopped. Footsteps approached. Christine walked up to the CD player, removed the compact disk, replaced it with the one she'd taken out and then turned around to search for the cover.

'Was Sir Arthur your husband?' Ben drawled.

Squealing in fright, she dropped the CD onto the carpeted floor. 'Don't scare me like that. How long have you been listening?'

Amazed, he watched her face alter from the happy smiling pianist who had just been immersed in her playing, to the shy, withdrawn and defensive lady he was more familiar with.

'Long enough to appreciate your brilliance. Are you deliberately not answering my question?' Rising, he retrieved the CD from the floor and slipped it back in the cover before placing it into Christine's hands.

'No, he was my father-in-law and I don't want to talk about it. It's past history.' As she turned to return to her bedroom, her eyes shot daggers at him and her tone was definitely frosty.

Ouch. It didn't require genius status to figure out this was a no-go subject, but no way was she getting away so he leapt up and shot between her and the door she seemed desperate to hide behind. Soft flesh bounced into hard then she reached out, her fingers finding the bare flesh of Ben's chest, causing her to gasp as she jerked her hand away. He said nothing, smiling at her reaction, but at the same time feeling delighted with the amazing sensual sensations her touch evoked.

'Why don't we discuss your music instead? From what little I know, I understand that an electronic keyboard has a different response when the keys are played, although one wouldn't know it from the way you just attacked that piece. Am I right?' He placed his hands on the outside of her shoulders to keep her from fleeing.

'Yes.' Downcast eyes accompanied a timid reply. Why so self-conscious about her skills? Something wasn't quite right here.

'Would you prefer to have your piano to practise on?' he asked, keeping his voice soft in an attempt to ease her tension.

'It's too hard to move it and I don't want to impose any more.'

An exasperated sigh escaped as Ben gave her a gentle shake. 'It will take nothing more than a phone call and a couple of hours of our time and I thought I have already said that your being here is not any imposition. What will it take for you to believe that? I love every minute of you being here. You have a bad habit of avoiding answering sensitive questions, don't you? I can't figure out why but first things first. Would you prefer your piano to practise on?'

'Yes.' The word came out as nothing more than a humble whisper.

'Then consider it done, my beautiful girl and… it's going in here. There's to be no more hiding away.' Ben bent and dared a brief peck on her forehead. 'I want to continue this conversation later but for now, I'm going to make a few phone calls. Your piano will be here by tonight.' Sensing her bristling at his demands he added, 'you can argue all you like but it will make not one iota of difference.'

A sly smile spread across his face. 'And then I'm going to get dressed since the touch of my naked skin alarms you so much.'

'You're not n… ' Chrissie bit her tongue as a red tinge rushed up her neck.

Was he glad she couldn't see his grin. 'Naked? Why don't you feel lower and find out?' Grabbing her hands he drew them down towards his hips.

She struggled to free herself causing her head to bump against his chest. She jerked back, the suddenness of her reaction sending a spasm of hurt through Ben until he noticed her cheeks redden even more along with a sucked in breath. So, she wasn't as immune to him as she made out. Interesting.

Giving a final tug downwards, he pressed her hands against the fabric of his jeans. Her shoulders slumped – probably in relief, then he couldn't help himself but he wrapped his arms around her, drawing her close and delighting in the sensual feel of her skin against his. It felt like he was in heaven while Christine looked as though she was dying with embarrassment. The mixed messages she unwittingly gave were addling his brain. The way she folded into the curve of his body made it obvious she enjoyed the experience but at the same time she was putting up one hell of a fight as though she didn't dare allow herself to enjoy the feel of a man. Or maybe it was just *his* body she didn't enjoy. Damn, she didn't like being held by him.

Disappointment hit so he released her then scarpered back to his bedroom while giving himself a severe silent talking to, which continued all the time he stood under a another cold shower. 'Cool it, Benny boy. You're never going to get her to fall for you like that. Just cool it. She needs time and she needs careful handling, so hands off, mate!'

***

Even though she was mortified, a strange sensation of euphoria tingled all the way up from her toes as Chrissie sped towards her room, stumbling in her haste which caused her to teeter before her outstretched hand thumped against the wall. After regaining her balance she felt around until she found the door and slammed it before leaning against the wood, the smooth coolness easing the heat of inflamed cheeks and just about every single cell in her body. Oh, my! What an idiotic fool. She never reacted that way - not even when she'd been married and she sure wasn't ever going down that track again. The heartache of rejection followed by the crippling sense of inadequacy was too hard to want to go through it a second time.

Seeking comfort from the only friend she'd had for too long she turned, took three precise steps until she brushed against the end of the bed. Sinking to the floor, she reached under her bed for the small wooden box. She ran the tips of her fingers several times over the raised dots spelling out Angel's name then as she knelt, she placed the box on the edge of her bed. Just as she had done so many times before when she needed comfort, she poured out her heart to her best friend.

'Angel, what am I going to do? I can't fall in love with Ben – nothing can come of it. I know I'll just get hurt again. But Angel, it feels so good in his arms. They are so strong, so warm, so wonderful. The way he kissed me – I know he feels for me but… oh, Angel, I can't let it happen. Ben needs someone who can see, someone who can give him everything he deserves. I have nothing to offer him. I have to be stronger, Angel.' Anguished she wrapped her arms around the box, holding it against her chest and allowed her tears to fall unchecked.

More determined than ever to not allow Ben to break down her barriers Chrissie presented a more subdued persona when they drove to her house so she could supervise the loading of her beloved piano; a gift from her now dead parents on her eighteenth birthday. It had replaced a battered old model passed down through several generations when her talent had gained her a scholarship into the Australian Conservatorium of Music.

It took a lot of persuasion on Ben's part before Chrissie agreed to the piano being set in the lounge-room, backed against her bedroom wall so she had easy access. This required a second re-arrangement of furniture after which Ben guided her several times over the route from her bedroom door to various points in the room until she felt confident about finding her way around. At Ben's suggestion, they ordered a home delivery of pizza for dinner, eating it perched on the kitchen bar stools while washing it down with icy cold sparkling Shiraz. They seemed to have reached an amiable truce but Chrissie felt more determined than ever to remain aloof as far as her emotions went. She had to be strong.

***

After the meal, Ben was treated to a concert, albeit after a second round of pleading on his part but Christine played a few solo concert pieces while he sat back listening, overawed by her talent and skill. Her piano-bar playing was excellent but it didn't hold a patch on how she was performing for him now. The emotion she managed to wreak out of those pieces of wood and ivory was mind-blowing. When her fingers tired, she closed the lid then sat in the sudden silence with her hands clasped demurely in her lap. It worried him how unsure of herself she was. Time to give her morale a boost, so he crossed the floor and stood beside her.

'I am constantly drawn to the piano bar to listen to you play. You have a magic touch, bringing those keys alive. Thank you. Come and sit on the sofa to rest while I make us a nightcap.' Drawing her up from the stool, he settled her against the soft cushions on the lounge, joining her a short while later with two mugs of steaming hot chocolate.

'How many recordings have you made?'

She paused so long Ben wondered if she would open up. 'About a dozen.'

'I'd like to listen to them, do you have copies?'

'Most of them. I'll leave them out if you like.'

'I would love to hear them. Do you still play at the concert level?'

'No!' At the loud and emphatic response Ben stared at Christine. Oh, wow! Such a reaction.

'Is there any particular reason?' Even though he felt as though he was treading on dangerous ground after such a curt reply he wanted to know more, to find the reason she was holding back her emotions so staunchly. Even though he'd already talked himself into taking a step back and to try to contain his feelings for her, he knew it was going to be beyond difficult. His innards seemed to churn in turmoil every time he so much as saw her and he would like nothing better than to show her how much he felt about her. He'd never felt this way about a woman before. He wasn't sure if it was love because he didn't even know what true love felt like, but the effect she had on him was something he'd never experienced before. Somehow he felt it important to find out what had happened in her past that had caused such a steel clad cage to be built up around her emotions. He felt certain it wasn't just because her husband had left because she was losing her sight. It had to be something more. His well honed detective skills and gut feeling told him that much.

'One, I can't see the conductor. Two, I can't see the music to learn new pieces and there is a third reason which I don't wish to discuss.'

The first two didn't make sense since she managed so well in the piano bar, leaving Ben to figure they were just excuses she used to cover the real reason. It was the, "*I don't wish to discuss it*" bit that he was more interested in. 'Would you need a conductor if you played as a soloist without an orchestra? You just entranced me for over an hour. Why couldn't you do it in the public arena?'

He winced when her lips tightened into a thin line. She was clamming up so he couldn't see the harm in playing devil's advocate. Might as well push her a bit further for things couldn't get any tenser.

'Christine, you are so talented. You make those keys speak to a person's soul. I feel it is such a pity you no longer share your gift with the world. And I don't understand about learning new pieces. You learn pieces for the piano bar at the hotel.'

'They are my own arrangements and interpretations. For concert pieces, you need to play what the composer has written and to have my own concerts I would have to be always extending my repertoire. I can't play the same pieces all the time. Can we cease this discussion? It just isn't going to happen. Ever!'

Sensing Christine slamming down the shutters he figured a change in topic was needed. 'I'm afraid we are going to need you to confront Gerard to see if you can break him. Would you be prepared to come in? I know I'm asking a lot from you but it would help convict him. How about doing it for Angel?' Settling one arm around her shoulders and drawing her closer he knew he was being unfair by using Angel but what the hell - things weren't going so hunky dory in any case.

It really surprised him that after an initial tensioning of almost every muscle in her body, Christine relaxed then dropped her head onto his shoulder while she thought. Step one to me, he thought until an inordinately long silence followed before she sighed.

'For Angel, I'll do it.' She paused again. 'I'm sure it was him who beat her up because Des Casey was holding me down on the ground when it happened.'

His heart twisted at the sad, soulful voice. Another pause was broken by a sniff. Was she crying? He didn't dare move to have a look.

'I miss her so much. She was more that my eyes - much, much more. Angel was my best friend. No make that my only friend.' Her voice had changed to one of deep despair. 'Losing her was much worse than my marriage breaking up.'

Even though he couldn't see her face he heard the catch in her voice and figured she needed quiet companionship, so he reached out for the remote control of the sound system, tightened his arm back around her shoulder and they sat wrapped up in their own thoughts, comforted by the silent presence of each other while the background music played. A strange sensation of contentment surrounded him. This felt so darn right but he didn't dare say a thing lest Christine became distraught again and leave in a huff. He'd take every single scrap of harmony and friendship and do his utmost to build a relationship. One brick at a time and if a brick became dislodged he'd just cement it back in place before adding another brick.

Chapter Twenty-Five

Two sets of footsteps echoed down the uncarpeted, concrete passageway. Chrissie could hear and feel the thundering through her temples as her heart pounded in fear. She'd already met Detective Robyn Mitchell from the drug squad, who was waiting in the observation room and watching through the glass. Detective John Markham was waiting in the room ahead, the same room where she'd confronted Des Casey. This other man, Gerard, was in there as well. She heard a mumble of voices but the wall was too thick for her to make out the words. Then there was silence

'Are you okay?' Ben asked, his fingers pressing a bit harder into her back.

'Terrified!'

Ben paused and her arm was grasped, tugging her to a halt. 'You can pull out.'

For a moment she felt desperate to turn around and ask someone to take her away. But this man, no, man was too good a word to describe the animalistic attack on her. This lunatic, this thug, deserved to be punished for what he did to her and more importantly, to Angel. So she stiffened her spine and shoved her shoulders back. 'No, I can't. I need to do this.'

'Christine, are you sure you can handle this?' he asked, his warm breath wafting against her cheek.

No, no, no, screamed through her brain but she nodded, sucked in a deep breath and did her best to plaster a smile on her face. It didn't work – she was still petrified.

***

Outside the heavy metal door, Ben stopped then turned to Christine. Her face was ashen and looked petrified. She wasn't anywhere near the confident witness they needed. He had to do something, fast, and there was only one thing he could think of. It might make her mad but that was better than the visible fear. Sucking in a breath of courage he snaked an arm around her waist, drew her closer, bent his head and gave her a scorching kiss, deepening further and further until he felt a twinge of response. He continued the onslaught until he felt Christine relax and mould her body against him, her fervour matching his. Only then did he lift his head, eye the softened features on her face and satisfied, shoved open the door to the interview room. He felt like a heel using these tactics but how else was he supposed to get the woman to relax? He smiled as he added one more brick to his still tiny wall. She'd kissed him back.

Similar to what had happened at her previous identification session, Ben planted the splayed fingers of one hand in the small of her back, directing her into the room using pressure. Having no time to recover from his kiss, her face showed a bewildered calmness that hadn't been there moments before. Success! Since he still didn't want to be seen by Gerard, John was waiting and took over, guiding Christine inside. Ben shut the door and scooted into the observation room.

Gerard's seat was a hard, wooden, spindle-backed chair, the front legs a few millimetres shorter than the back so that he kept slowly sliding forwards causing discomfort and forcing him to keep edging his way backwards into the back of the chair. It was a method used to keep the criminal from being able to relax. Ben smiled at the twitches of tense muscles along Gerard's jaw. The man looked as though he was beginning to unravel. Things were looking up. To keep the man unaware of what was happening so he couldn't be prepared for Christine's appearance, Gerard had been led to believe they were simply waiting for the essential second police officer that was a legal requirement at all interviews.

An armed, uniformed officer stepped in behind John then stood motionless inside the doorway, one hand never far away from his holstered pistol that would never be used but its presence was effective in preventing suspects from making a break for it or losing their cool. Gerard was a huge man. If he wanted to lash out, Christine wouldn't stand a chance. He had to be twice her weight.

He must have heard something for Gerard twisted his head. A sudden pallor replaced the stoic frown when he spied Christine. John switched on the recording unit and recorded the relevant details of time and who was present.

'Good morning, Gerard, I believe you already know Mrs Christine Mears. Mrs Mears, is this the man who assaulted you in the park?' asked John in an authoritative tone.

She nodded. 'Yes,' she said much stronger than he'd expected.

Gerard blanched even further then straightened his back after screwing his eyes in concentration. 'You're lying. You're blind. You can't possibly recognise me or anyone else.'

That, thought Ben as he spied Christine tense then shove her shoulders back and her chin high, is as good as an admission of guilt.

'Yes, I am classed as legally blind but that doesn't mean I have no sight at all. I still have some vision, especially under the spot light.' She pointed upwards to the light, an action that stiffened Gerard's spine a little more.

Ben smiled inwardly.

'Then why do you use a guide dog, you bitch?' Gerard called out. Sweat broke out on his brow. Ben suspected the man realised what he'd let slip. Christine's responsive laugh was scoffing which seemed to unnerve Gerard even more. There was a visible tremor that snaked across his shoulders.

'If it wasn't you in the park, then how do you know I use a dog?'

Gerard swore under his breath, further admitting his guilt.

'Hold your hands out please?' Christine stared straight at Gerard's face then smiled. With one finger she pointed to his jaw. 'You have a scar, right there.' The man flinched as she brushed the tip of her finger directly on the spot.

Way to go girl, thought Ben as he sent up a prayer of thanks that the lighting set up especially worked. Christine could see enough. An unbidden thought flashed back to her close scrutiny of him at the beach, causing a particular part of his anatomy to spring to attention. He shifted his feet to find a more comfortable stance and to ensure that particular area wasn't in any one's line of sight. He was so distracted it took a few seconds before he became fully aware of what was happening right in front of his eyes.

'Hold out your hands!' The stern bark from John jerked Ben's attention back. Gerard refused to move. John stepped around the table, grabbed the man's hands and plonked them onto Christine's outstretched fingers. Her soft touch as she felt all along Gerard's hands seemed to unnerve him further. He blanched, quivered then a second wave of cold sweat exuded from his pores.

'This is definitely the man who beat Angel to death while the other man held me down. I am certain this is the man who carried my legs and pulled down my track pants and shorts, then sexually abused me. As I said in my previous interview, he was tall and had uncommonly large hands and fingers. His voice, I would recognise anywhere, especially with that distinctive accent. The snatches of vision I had whilst being jostled along match what I've seen today. I am one hundred percent certain this is the man.'

Christine seemed to be unnerved for a shiver swept down from her head to the end of her toes moments before she jerked her hands away and dropped them to her side. She spun around to face John.

'Please, Detective, I can't stand looking at this creep any longer. His very presence makes me feel ill.'

She collapsed against John's chest, which gave him the excuse to escort her out of the room with an arm around her shoulder. To any onlookers, Christine could see perfectly well and only required assistance to leave the room because she was so distraught. The moment the door closed behind them she leant against John's body, trembling. Already out of the observation room, Ben took over. He drew her into his arms to prevent her from sinking to the floor when her body turned liquid. Damn but she shouldn't have had to go through this but there was no other way. Once her tremors had ceased and she found her balance, Ben directed her back to his office where he had a policewoman remain with her while he returned to observe the happenings in the interview room. John was relentless in his questioning of Gerard until, at last, the man broke and began giving more information.

***

The moment he opened his office door, Ben noticed Christine stand then turned so accurately to face him that he felt sure she could see him. 'Detective Somers, I have a bone to pick with you – in private.'

Ben smiled at the female constable. 'I think I can handle Mrs Mears alone. Thank you for your help.' He took his time in ushering the constable to the door, quietly closing it behind her then stood right in front of Christine. 'You have a problem?' he asked smugly, knowing full well what she was going to have words with him about.

'Why did you kiss me like that?' She tried to sound cross but it didn't quite come out that way. Her voice was husky and sounded downright sexy.

'Like what?' he asked as he stepped closer, a grin he had no control over spread across his face.

'You know what I am talking about, Ben Somers,' she retorted.

'You mean like this?' Ben planted his mouth on hers again, resisting her struggle to escape. It didn't take very much searching before her lips softened and moulded to his and all her resistance faded away.

He lifted his head, just a fraction, keeping her held tight. 'Because it was the only way I could think of to wipe away the terrified look on your face and calm your shot nerves.' He gave her another gentle peck. 'Plus, I enjoy kissing you – a great deal – and even more I love the way you kiss me back.' Ben chuckled as he smothered her protest with yet another kiss. Satisfied, he stood back just out of her reach. 'Plus, much as you might deny it to yourself, you enjoy it just as much as I do. Now, John and I are taking you out for a late lunch with Mary then she will be spending the rest of the day with you, at their place. We still have at least two other people who, we suspect, would love to get their hands on you, and I'm not about to let that happen.'

'I get no say?' she asked, her defiance rising, but it didn't dissipate the rosy glow of her cheeks.

'Not where you safety is concerned – no! It was a police operation that got you involved in this mess and the Department will do their utmost to protect you until this little gang is caught and we are satisfied you are in no more danger. Gerard van der Berg has started talking, thanks to you. We now hope we can obtain some more answers very soon. In the meantime you are under my personal protection. Oh what a hideous job!' He laughed as he grasped a firm hold on her hand, placed it in the crook of his elbow and led her to collect John.

Mary met them at a nearby café where they enjoyed a pleasant light lunch. Ben then drove them to Mary and John's house, ensuring the two women were safely locked in before he and John returned to work, satisfied the house would be kept under discreet police surveillance for the rest of the day.

***

Chrissie was kept busy for the rest of the week with a different person keeping her company each day. At first she found it difficult making friends with Jenny Gallati, Mary Markham, a couple of other officer's partners and the regular housekeeper, all who spent a full or half day with her while Ben worked. After initial unease each day, she found the women's company a godsend. She hadn't had so many different people to chat with for what seemed like forever. The easy camaraderie with each was something that had been sadly lacking in her life before. Simon was her minder at work on Thursday night while Ben kept watch on Friday and Saturday despite the fact that she knew he must be exhausted for he kept long hours.

A wonderful aroma woke Chrissie late on Sunday morning. Hearing Ben working in the kitchen she knew he must have opened her door because the sounds were not muffled and the smell of cooked bacon was strong, making her mouth water. She wandered into the kitchen, a robe wrapped around and tied firmly at her waist. Her hair was un-brushed and there was still sleep in her eyes. She was startled when a sudden nearby whisper of sound was immediately followed by warm lips brushing against her cheek.

'Good morning.' The warmth of his breath caused her senses to inflame in an instant along with heat on her cheeks. Then, remembering her resolve to not allow her emotions a free rein, she took a step back and planted what she hoped was a mask of indifference on her face.

'Brunch is ready when you are. Would you do me the honour of accompanying me to dinner tonight? I promised I would make up for our last disastrous night out. I'm hopeful we won't be interrupted this time and to make sure, I've asked John to take any urgent call-outs. He owes me a few. I know of a nice quiet place up near the National Park in the hills, which has an open fire, great food and live music. Neat casual dress is the norm. How about it?'

Lord, no. No more romantic outings. But coming up with a feasible excuse was almost impossible. She was living in his house, for goodness sake. She couldn't use the excuse of housework or ironing or anything. What choice did she have? 'Sounds good to me. Thank you. I would enjoy it.' And hate it at the same time.

Chapter Twenty Six

During the day a late winter storm had sprung up. Leaden clouds rolled in from the coast, accompanied by gale force winds and blinding rain. Ben drove with caution, especially when they travelled along the winding roads through the hills.

'Tell me, Christine, how does this type of weather affect… jeeze, I would just like to know…'

'How a blind person copes with wintry weather?' Christine laughed. 'Don't be afraid to ask. It's when people beat around the bush and get all embarrassed about wanting to know these things that disabled people get all antsy. We just want to be treated like normal human beings.'

'Sorry, I didn't mean to sound condescending.'

'You have nothing to be sorry about. In fact, apart from the people at the association, you are the only person I've met, since… well since being diagnosed, that has treated me as though I don't have some deadly contagious disease.'

'Really? I find that hard to believe.'

'Truly, and to answer your question, I love stormy weather and don't mind in the least if I become wet through getting caught in a shower. Right now I love the sound of the squish of the tyres spurting water from the bitumen and the thrum, thrum of the wipers while they sweep the steady stream of water from the windscreen. You probably aren't aware of the sounds and most likely don't appreciate them. I know I never did before.'

'You make me want to close my eyes and just listen, but since I'm driving…'

'Oh, please don't!' she called as she reached out a hand and with unerring accuracy, placed it on his arm.

'We're here and my eyes are wide open.' Finding a space in the car park near the entrance was impossible since the earlier patrons had filled the area closest to the restaurant, so he parked on the far side then removed his leather jacket to hold over their heads while they dashed for the door, his arm tight around Christine's waist to guide her. He lifted her over the worst of the puddles and kerbing, setting her down under the cover of the portico.

Keeping in the shadows, Ben shook the water from his jacket then slipped his arms into the sleeves, needing its protective cover to keep his holstered pistol hidden. Then, as if it was already a habit, he placed Christine's fingers inside his elbow then paused before escorting her inside. 'Just so you know - I find you no different from any other woman I've taken out. You are beautiful, incredibly talented, smart, maybe a little too reserved but I understand why, and a pure delight to be with.'

Christine's mouth opened but no sound came out then a pink blush suffused her cheeks. She blinked as her mouth closed again then she finally found her voice. 'Thank you, that's probably the nicest thing anyone's ever said to me.'

'You're more than welcome. Now let's go inside so I can enjoy more of your company.'

When he shoved the door open they were met by a waitress wearing standard black and white. Once seated, Ben scanned the room, noting the people already dining. After being caught out so many times by not keeping his mind on possible dangers he was intent on being on the alert but wasn't expecting anyone from the gang to be there since nobody knew where they would be. Their table, booked under a false name only he knew about, was not far from the warmth of an open fire but far enough away they wouldn't be on the menu as roasted meat. Ben sat with his back to the wall, examining in detail the patronage and mentally assessing each person. A quick sweep of the room and his gut instinct told him they were an innocuous lot and no threat. He wished he had some clue as to who was the leader of the drug ring. It was one thing none of their suspects had been forthcoming with – neither name nor a description. He eyed all the women present a second time, to see if there was any recognition, any hint that one of them looked even remotely like the nurse who had drugged Christine. But, heck it was difficult since he'd seen the woman's features for no more than a second before she'd turned her back on him and sped away like a maniac.

Satisfied the nurse wasn't here, Ben kept his voice low as he read the menu. After placing their orders he sat back relaxing while they listened to the folk duo, a man and woman. The tall, slim man with an untidy greying ponytail sat on a chair strumming chords on a guitar while his younger female companion perched on a slightly higher stool, the two singing together in harmony and creating a pleasant atmosphere.

While they ate, Ben kept his eye on the doorway, noting each person as they entered and his eyes followed them until they were seated. He was thankful Christine couldn't see his face, because all the while he kept up a light-hearted conversation, his eyes were forever roaming around the room. To a sighted person his eye contact would have been non-existent and considered rude. It wasn't until they'd ordered coffee that for some perverse reason his nerves began to rattle him. He had been feeling more and more uneasy as the evening wore on but now the unease had strengthened to something replicating the sound of a jumbo jet taking off. He noted those people leaving then listened intently for the cars to drive away, recalling if the patrons had been there before them or had come in after. Christine must have felt his tension, because moments after their coffee was served she asked him why he seemed to be so on edge.

'Sorry, Christine, but I have this uncanny feeling something is wrong. Do you mind if we go as soon as we drink the coffee?'

At her nod of assent he called for his bill so that he was paid up before he made a move to leave. A couple of women left, pausing at the desk to pay before going outside. One was tall with long hair tied at the back, the other average height with reddish curly hair. They were closely followed by another group of four. The two couples were obviously together and had been raucous during the evening: probably due to too much alcohol by the number of empty wine bottles on the table. Ben only felt satisfied when he heard two cars start up and detected two sets of lights sweep across the windows as they turned out of the car park, the engines humming away into the distance.

When Christine pushed her coffee cup to the centre of the table Ben stood, eager to depart, his own coffee untouched and unwanted. With as much gentleness as he could muster with his nerves feeling as though they were about to snap apart, he grasped her hand as soon as she'd scooped up her tiny evening purse and tucked it into the pocket of her sleek black slacks. Assisting her away from the table then out the door, his stomach twisted in a tight knot of apprehension. The way to his car on the other side of the car park was well lit by powerful lights for the first half of the distance, then the light faded to the extent his car was only just discernable through the light fog that had settled and was swirling close to the ground. He decided on a circuitous route around the darkened edge so they wouldn't be highlighted. Not that he was overly concerned for he'd ticked off a car leaving with each group of patrons.

They had covered barely half the distance when a shot whistled past his head.

'What was that?' Christine whispered at the same time as Ben rasped, 'Stay beside me and run!' Since the car was still fifty metres away he headed towards the nearest cover - the bush, one arm gripping her in a firm hold around her waist, his other hand withdrawing his firearm from its holster.

She obeyed without question, and flung one arm around his waist. She had no choice but to stay tied to him as he tugged her along. The smell of gunpowder was just strong enough to detect. For a moment her feet didn't move so he hoisted her higher so they wouldn't drag on the ground.

'Move your feet,' he huffed as he twisted to change direction. She obliged but her feet were moving in mid-air as Ben gripped his arm tighter, lifted her even higher and super-glued her against his body. He felt her heart thump mercilessly against his rib cage, mirroring his own frantic heartbeat.

His gut tightened. It was his fault again that Christine's life had been threatened. She was under his protection and he had let his guard slip. That first niggle of unease was when he should have acted. Sure, he had scanned the restaurant repeatedly, but not knowing the identity of the people he was searching for made it damn near impossible. A chunk of ice formed in his stomach.

Ben dragged her forward through the waist-long underbrush. Prickles pierced his clothing, scratching his legs while unseen branches whipped wet leaves against his face. He felt Christine tuck her head down and press it against his shoulder for protection from the stinging leaves. There was little he could do about it since both his arms were occupied.

A second bullet whizzed past his right ear and lodged in a nearby tree with a dull thud. Slivers of bark sprang out and fell. There was no way the other diners would hear the gunshots as a silencer was being used. At the whirring sound, Christine jerked and whimpered. As they barrelled through the bushes, Ben wondered if her lack of sight sent her sense of balance awry. If so she wasn't going to have a clue which way was up or down.

'Two!' Christine gasped.

'Two what?' Ben panted.

'Two people following. I hear their footsteps and the rush of bodies whipping through the dampened undergrowth quite a way behind us. Definitely two.'

Damn but she was good. He'd guessed a lone shooter. Another shot pierced the dense gloom, but here the fog was thicker. The shot was not so close for there wasn't such a loud whiz, but any flying projectile fired wildly, was far too close.

Pushing forward, Ben zigzagged through trees to avoid being an easy target – searching for the densest and highest bushes to keep them hidden. He never slowed, running hard despite the body plastered to his side. He veered to his left, his lungs burning, desperate for oxygen. He had to hide Christine. He couldn't outrun their pursuers carrying her like this even though she was of such slight build and barely half his weight. A large fallen tree loomed into his peripheral vision. He twisted to the right and headed for it.

Ben swung his head around and plastered his mouth on Christine's ear. 'I'm going to hide you then take off to lead them away from you. Stay put. Don't move or make a sound until I come back for you.'

Not giving her a chance to answer he flung Christine onto the ground behind the log. 'Sorry,' he said at the whoomp of air whooshing from her lungs as she landed with a thud. He ripped off his leather coat and tossed it over her head and back to hide her light coloured top. Then he dragged a fallen branch over the top of her. A quick glance at her lying in the shadow of the massive old tree told him she was hidden well enough. She blended in with the shadows with his dark coat and her black slacks hiding her well and the mist smudged the outline making her appear to be no more than an extension of the log.

He was more than thankful for the dark storm clouds that kept moonlight to a minimum and the steaming mist now hovering up to a metre from the ground while he crept away from her, making as little sound as possible. Then he took Christine's earlier advice, and attuned his ears for sounds. To his left there was a rustle and snap that sounded like their pursuers searching for them in the distance.

Stooping, Ben fumbled through the undergrowth until his fingers found a fist sized rock then hurled it as far as he could at a ninety-degree angle, away from Christine and close to the direction he intended going. Silence was followed by a shot then footsteps heading in the direction of the fallen stone. That's four shots with two more in the chamber. But with two people? How many weapons did they have? Ben turned forty-five degrees, halfway between Christine and the rock, glanced towards the faint light of the restaurant to ascertain where he was going then crept about fifty metres away from Christine before racing off at full speed, not caring about any noise. To give the impression she was still with him, he whispered harshly as though talking to someone else. Come on, guys, follow me.

Pistol in hand and safety catch off, Ben ducked and dodged through the dense bush, wet branches whipping at his body. The rain had ceased but the ground underfoot was sodden and in a very short space of time, his shirt, damp from the soaked leaves and his perspiration, was plastered to his body. His shoes were splattered with wet grime and had taken on a distinct squelching sound. He was thankful he had chosen a dark blue shirt to wear. It made it a lot harder to distinguish. The tie! It was lighter so he ripped it off, balled it up and flung it to his left without faltering his stride.

Finding himself in a clearing all of a sudden, he stopped abruptly then backed up. He needed to remain under the cover of the bushes. Dark clouds still kept the moonlight hidden, but he couldn't afford to be out in the open and an easy target.

When a massive hollowed out tree stump came into view he shouldered his way into the gap, stood and listened. All he could hear was his own heaving breaths and despite searching for other sounds he couldn't hear any following footsteps. Damn, where are you? Please don't find Christine.

Realising now was a good time to make a phone call he peeled his mobile phone from the sodden fabric of his shirt pocket. How wet does a phone need to be before it stops working? He swept his hand over the front, which was a useless exercise since it left as much moisture as it took away. Praying to the heavens he opened it out and sighed at the site of the lit up face. GPS. He stared at the monitor and racked a brain that felt like it was spinning in a tumble drier, for the instructions on how to activate the GPS. After pressing several buttons and hoping for the best he scrolled down to the first number in his call up list, his office. Casting his eyes around while keeping his ears alert he waited for his call to be answered. There was no choice about the risk of being overheard. At least if they were close enough to hear him, then Christine would be safe.

A click was followed by a familiar voice. 'Simon - Ben here. I'm under fire in dense bush area behind the Caspian Restaurant. I'm about three hundred metres due west. Two armed assailants using a silencer were waiting when I exited the restaurant. I need the chopper and armed men Night scopes would be good. Christine Mears is with me. I think I've activated my GPS.' As he hung up as soon as his message was repeated back to him, he noticed an unusual character blinking on the screen. He smiled. The GPS was working. All he could do then was wait and pray.

With his brain beginning to compute facts he came to several conclusions. First, he was well hidden as far away from Christine as he dared. He couldn't afford to get lost.

He was also sure he had been followed but the absence of human sounds now, had him more than a little concerned. Had the ploy of speaking as though Christine was with him, worked? The next fifteen minutes felt like forever while his concern changed to real fear when he still couldn't hear any one following him. His fear for Christine intensified every agonising long minute.

Chapter Twenty-Seven

Too petrified to move, Chrissie stayed stretched out behind the log, her face buried in the mouldy damp undergrowth. The pungent smells of rotting leaves stung her acutely aware nostrils. Cold moisture seeped from the ground into her clothes, the only warmth being from Ben's jacket draped along her back. A sharp twig pressed into her cheek and there was a solid lumpiness of a rock under her hipbone. Alerted to a new noise she listened then held her breath at the sound of footsteps not far away. When they moved closer, Chrissie surrendered herself to the thought that she was going to be found, shot, and left to die. Absolute terror gripped her innards into a tight ball, while wondering how much a bullet hurt when it penetrated. She hoped it would be mercifully quick.

She heard the mumbling of voices and had to restrain herself from moving. All she wanted to do was get up and run but her run would be nothing more than a staggering around with her hands outstretched.

Footsteps neared. She was startled to hear two female voices. When the splish of steps stopped she realised the two women were close enough she could clearly make out the whispered words.

'They can't get far. She can't see where they are going. We have to find her; she's our only hope. The tracker indicates she's somewhere nearby and he has to be with her. Kill him, but not her. I want her alive. You go that way and we'll circle around to the car park. Make sure they don't get back to the car.'

The voices stopped then one set of footsteps moved away to the left, through the bushes behind her. The other set advanced closer and closer. They moved around to her side of the log.

She held her breath.

Something crawled over her hand, up her wrist then onto her lower arm. She swallowed the scream she felt welling up from her stomach. Soft feathery legs - lots of them, rippled along her bare skin.

Centipede.

She just knew it was a centipede and it was gigantic. The animal made a rapid journey up her arm, onto the sleeve of her top. Her skin prickled in its wake. She waited, petrified, desperate to shake the thing off.

The woman's steps moved away a few metres then stopped again.

The centipede finished its journey up her sleeve. It paused. She visualised it lifting its head with those fierce looking hooks at the front seeking another foothold. Then it dropped down from the collar of her blouse onto her neck. A cold sweat broke out. She squeezed her eyes shut. Her body convulsed and she jammed her throat shut to swallow a scream.

The steps started again then stopped. Chrissie heard the woman turn around. Had she really screamed, made a sound or gasped? Did the woman hear the centipede? Could she feel Chrissie's fear? Bile rose up her throat, the acidic taste settling in her gullet for she was too scared to swallow lest she be heard. Desperation made her want to scream out for Ben and tear the animal from her neck. Her skin crawled.

The centipede left her neck and found moist, damp leaf mould. Chrissie had visions of it finding the cleft between her breasts and wished she had buttoned her blouse right to the collar. She gritted her teeth and her hands clenched tight, waiting, but she didn't move.

The woman turned away and receding steps crunched on wet leaves and fallen twigs: squiffy, squelching sounds through the mud and puddles, gradually fading until there was blessed silence.

Slow, long and silent, Chrissie expelled the breath she had been holding for what had felt like an inordinate amount of time. She released her stiff fingers from the tense grip she had held in the slimy leaf mould and eased her cheek from the sharp stick. Very slow, she lifted her hip and curled her body around the protruding stone, always waiting for the return of the hundreds of tiny feet creeping along her skin. She feared that more than she feared a bullet.

Her ears on full alert, Chrissie budged her body to find a more comfortable position. Inching around, she was able to turn on her side and draw her legs up a little to ease the tension in over-stretched muscles. Then she tucked her arms into her chest, freeing one hand to brush away any further invasions from cruel creepy crawlies. Ever so thankful for the warmth of Ben's jacket Chrissie drew in a deep breath, savouring in the masculine aroma that was exclusively Ben. It was the one pleasant thing holding her sanity together.

Realisation hit. She was there for the long haul. Ben wouldn't come back until he was sure it was safe. If he didn't get shot in the process. She snorted silently. She had no hope of finding her own way out of the bush without sight. She could blunder her way around for hours, never knowing which way she was going. With the National Park being so vast, she had only one hope; that Ben survived and came back for her.

Just to make her night even more perfect, it started to rain again: heavy, steady plops. The dead branch afforded little protection to her legs and within minutes she was soaked from her hips down and an intense cold penetrated.

Chapter Twenty-Eight

Ben swore under his breath when rain began tumbling again. He was fairly well protected from the worst of it, hidden in the hollow tree although an incessant drip managed to reach him, no matter which way he wriggled. The drip soon turned into a steady rivulet running down his back and continuing down his leg, but his thoughts were with Christine. She only had his leather coat. It would keep the top half of her dry for a while but not forever. His heart ached for the misery and terror she would be enduring, but he knew he couldn't return to her yet. To keep her relatively safe he had to stay away. He waited - on full alert.

The intense silence was broken by the *thwack, thwack* of helicopter rotors tracking his GPS signal, the blessed sound telling Ben that help was on the way. He hadn't heard any sirens yet but guessed they wouldn't be far behind for the local area police would have been called. Reaching into his pocket, he removed his mobile phone to call John, knowing his second in command would have been the first person notified of his predicament. He was relieved to hear John's voice telling Ben he was in the chopper and, daring to stick his head out from his hiding place, Ben was able to guide the chopper to his position. Two armed men shinnied down wire ropes to his side. They were dressed in full battle fatigues and wearing night vision goggles. Logic told him his pursuers would attempt to escape so he sent the helicopter to the restaurant car park. He was going back to rescue Christine.

The three men moved as one. Forming a triangle they drifted through the bush like a giant globule of mercury. Around bushes and trees, over rocks, back-to-back, their eyes scanning the misty gloom, each one covering the others in case of attack. Ben's only words were to inform the elite squad that there were two armed assailants and he had left Christine hidden. He had been handed a flak jacket and immediately slipped it over his head, thankful for the minimal warmth the heavy garment afforded him. With utmost caution, they made their way back in the direction Ben had run. He wasn't a hundred percent sure exactly where Christine was, but he had measured a rough distance while fleeing, so had a rough idea.

The rain was gnawingly persistent. It dripped from the trees in cold heavy drops running from Ben's sodden hair, down his nose, then melding with the already wet cotton of his shirt, plastering it to his body to ensure his skin remained icy cold despite the warmth emanating from within.

At a sudden thud then scrape, they stopped, backing into each other in a tighter knot. Fleeing footsteps then a shot fired towards them zinged past Ben's head.

'I see movement.' The man on his left said seconds before he fired. There was a yelp of pain then a heavy thump accompanied by slides, slurps and snaps. The triangle altered direction, heading towards the squeal. Ben heard increasingly loud moaning, then an all-encompassing silence. They reached the fallen body. The man next to him reached out feeling along the torso for a pulse. 'She's dead.'

Ben jolted. Surely Christine hadn't left her spot. A lump of lead settled in his gut. 'I have to see her. I have to make sure it isn't Christine. What other woman would be out here?'

Breaking ranks from the little group Ben turned to his side. He knelt on the ground and his knee sank into the thick squishy mire sending up a whiff of rotting leaf mould. With barely enough light to make out anything other than a fallen form, Ben had a sudden awareness of the difficulties Christine had. Her whole life was like this.

Not having the advantage of wearing night goggles like his two friends, he reached down, petrified, his heart forgetting how to beat for a moment. His long fingers felt along the body, grasped long thick hair that had been plaited then he expelled a long, loud sigh of relief. Unusual scratchiness spread across his eyes before his heart kick started again and he blinked away the unbidden moisture.

'It's not her.' And Christine wouldn't have had a fire-arm, he suddenly realised.

He continued his exploration until he found a handgun clutched in the stilled fingers. Removing it, he tucked the firearm into the back of his soaked trousers. The three men regrouped then continued on their way. The body would be retrieved later.

It took longer than Ben liked to find Christine. He wanted to call out to her but knew it could be a death sentence if he did. Seeking a large fallen log they found several before the correct one loomed in front of the crouching trio. Ben recognised the branch, reached down and whispered, 'Christine,' seconds before he felt for her body.

She didn't move, didn't reply.

Cold fear stabbed. He slipped his hand under the waterlogged leather of his jacket and felt blessed warmth. His hand reached further and rested on the sweet mound of one breast where he felt the soft rise and fall of her chest. His held breath gushed out as the same salty moisture washed across his eyes again. She was alive. He called again.

'I can't believe it – she's asleep,' he whispered. Gently he shook her, all the time repeating her name over and over so as to not startle her.

It felt like forever before she stirred. He pressed down his hand over her mouth to stifle her scream.

'Christine, it's me. You must keep quiet.'

She leapt to a half sitting position, dislodging the branch then plastered her dripping wet body against him - her chest flat against his, the sudden movement knocking him off balance and pushing him to the ground with a frantic Christine on top of him. Her arms curled around his neck as she clung to him in relieved desperation, hot salty tears brushing against his face.

When a soft male chuckle intruded, Christine jerked. Half upright, she paused.

'Don't mind us, we'll just turn our backs and keep guard, but for Christ sakes, hurry up,' drawled the quiet and very deep masculine voice from the other side.

She squealed and peeled herself away from Ben's arms and scrambled upright. 'What's...?' was as far as she got before a different deep voice whispered.

'You must keep quiet. There is still another armed person out there. We're not safe yet.'

Pulling himself out of the mire Ben brushed the worst of the detritus and slime from his arms and legs. He picked up his fallen leather coat and placed it around Christine's shoulder, ensuring she slipped her arms into the sleeves before zipping it up.

'I'm going to carry Christine. She has very little vision and can't see the ground or bushes,' Ben whispered. He then wrapped one arm around her waist and the other behind her knees then hoisted her off the ground, overwhelmed by the sudden sense of protectiveness he felt for this woman. She tucked her head against his chest and whimpered. He didn't know if it was in relief at being found or if she was as frozen as he felt.

Ben kept his gun in one hand. The other two men went either side of him and sidled sideways while he headed towards the twinkle of lights from the restaurant. He smiled when Christine nestled her head against his shoulder, then her frozen lips found the warmth of his pulse along his neck. He tightened his grip when he felt the gentle, warm kiss against his skin. Despite them both being frozen to the core, he felt a sudden glow of warmth spread from deep within.

As they neared the restaurant they slowed to assess the situation. Flashing red and blue lights indicated the presence of squad cars but how safe were they? Could they break cover without being shot at by a hidden sniper? Ben dropped Christine's legs to the ground and the three men regrouped once again. Christine was held, cocooned in Ben's arms. He walked behind her, gun ready, while the other two shielded her front and sides, Ben's soft voice at her ear guiding her and telling her what was in the way. He stepped over the kerbing, eyes flashing in all directions, ever alert for a sudden movement or sound.

It wasn't until Christine was sitting in the security of the helicopter wrapped in a warm blanket, an armed man on each side of the machine that Ben relaxed.

Chapter Twenty-Nine

Wrapped in blankets, Ben ushered Christine inside then pulled her into his arms. An overwhelming sense of relief swept over him. His blanket slid to the floor revealing saturated, ruined clothing and allowing dollops of mud, water and remnants from the bush to plop to the floor. At first she struggled to get away, but then relaxed and moulded against him as her arms slipped around his neck and drew him down further, her grip tightening then her lips found his mouth.

Stunned at her kiss, he sent a silent message heavenwards and mouthed, 'Thank you,' then hearing her soft whimper sanity returned to his brain. He paused then lifted his head

'Sweet Christine,' he said, 'go and have a hot shower shampoo your hair thoroughly to remove half the bush from it then change into warm clothes.' He picked a mouldy leaf from her hair. 'Leave your clothes on the shower floor and I'll bring a bucket in to carry them to the laundry later. You wouldn't believe the amount of gunge we both have on us.' As he spoke he pulled more twigs and leaves from her hair. 'Then we'll talk.' Turning her around, he gave her a gentle shove in the direction of her room then sucked in a breath. Sweet mercy, she had kissed him. An entire row of already mortared bricks flew through the air and set firm into his wall.

***

Still reeling from the effects of the searing kiss, Chrissie's nose twitched as she peeled sodden items of clothing from her body. The stench from rotting plant matter and thick, slimy mud was beginning to register. She had to sit on the shower floor to divest her legs of the clinging fabric of her slacks and was almost at the stage of having to call Ben in to help when her persistence finally paid off with the legs parting company from her skin with such a force she shot back against the tiles and knocked her shoulder. Another bruise, she thought as she piled her clothes in the corner of the shower then struggled up to turn the taps.

Sighing in blessed relief she allowed the needles of hot water to cascade over her body, thawing out frozen flesh. Her fingers massaged rich lather into her scalp and felt for the foreign items, pulling them out one by one and dropping them onto the floor. For once she was glad she couldn't see. Her thoughts went to the centipede and her body trembled in response. She lathered soap over every centimetre of her skin to ensure the critter wasn't still clinging to her then rinsed several times until she was certain every skerrick of mud had disappeared. She pulled on a warm tracksuit before returning to the lounge room.

***

Ben had been quicker and had cleaned up the mud and puddles on the tiled floor before Christine came out. He stood in silence, watching her from the moment she opened her bedroom door, revelling in the fact that she was still alive – no make that both of them. He didn't like to recall the number of times he had felt his heart stutter from the dread that she had died during the night. He loved her. There was no doubt now.

'You don't know just how beautiful you look to me right now,' he murmured softly as he strode over and took her hands in his. He didn't trust himself to kiss her again. Once he started he wouldn't be able to stop, so instead he tugged out a bar stool for her and set about preparing a hot drink.

'Tell me all that happened,' said Christine. 'After you left me there was silence for quite a while. I heard you disappearing and footsteps following you and then the footsteps coming back towards me. At first I thought it was you. Then all of a sudden two women were talking. They were standing almost right next to me – just on the other side of the log. They wanted to kill you, but not me. Why?'

Ben sucked in his breath and the intense feeling of dread returned. 'I think they want to use you as ransom to get their hands on the drugs that don't exist. Are you sure they were both women?'

'Absolutely, why? And I'm sure one of them was the nurse who drugged me.'

Then it registered. The dead woman had a long braid. The two women who left after he'd paid his bill. He'd thought they'd driven away. The group of four must have had two cars. 'We got one of them. Once I moved a long way from you, I hid and called John for help. They sent the chopper with two elite marksmen who joined me. One of the women was shot. She's dead.' He looked up at the hiss of a drawn in breath. Chrissie was frowning.

'Sorry, but there's no way of telling the facts without being honest. When the woman shot at us, one of the men shot back. Those boys don't miss their target. As soon as I had assistance we came back for you. I can't believe you were asleep under that log, but I guess I'm glad you were. When I found you and you didn't move or answer me, I... I thought the worst. Do you have any idea what that did to me? Was I relieved when you woke? The rest you know. It just took such an interminable long time and I had no idea how you were faring. I've never been so afraid in all my life. Not afraid for me – but for you.' Reaching over he placed his hand on her shoulder and squeezed gently before returning to his task of spooning the ingredients for hot chocolate into two large china mugs.

'The scariest part for me was the centipede.'

'Centipede?' Startled, Ben held the teaspoon in mid-air.

'While those two women were standing there talking, a huge centipede crawled on my hand then up my arm and dropped onto my neck. I couldn't move, couldn't scream. All those little legs, one after another sent my skin quivering. Then it dropped onto the ground and all I could think of was it moving down between my... well you know.' She flushed.

'Christine, you are so delightful. We are both nearly killed by flying bullets, have a terrifying rampage through the bush, drown in a torrential downpour, get covered in stinking sticky mud, my heart stops beating through abject terror that you have been killed and your greatest fear was a harmless little centipede?' Ben burst out laughing then planted a soft kiss on Christine's damp hair.

'It was huge and they bite.'

'Weren't you afraid any of the other times?' Ben asked as he set her steaming mug of chocolate down in front of her then wrapped her still icy fingers around the outside.

'Of course I was. I was petrified. I thought those two women were sure to see me and I wondered how much it hurt when a bullet penetrated your skin. I was just hoping it would be quick and I didn't have to suffer very long.' She sniffed at the rising steam. 'Then when they said they wanted you dead and me kept alive – yeah, I was very afraid. I thought I was going to die just from the terrible feeling of dread I had inside me – then that flaming centipede crawled on my hand. I was just wishing they would get it over and done with and shoot me.'

Two large tears welled then plopped before Christine dropped her head as though embarrassed at such weakness. Ben grabbed her chocolate just in time to prevent it from sloshing as she began to weep loud, wracking sobs. 'Oh, Ben, I was so afraid I'd never see you again.'

He couldn't stand keeping away any longer. Delayed shock had set in. Placing the two mugs on the kitchen bench, he gathered her up in his arms and carried her to a lounge chair, settling her in his lap. He so much wanted to declare his love for her but that ever-persistent gut feeling of his slammed it into his brain that the time was not right. Both of them had been through a traumatic ordeal, with emotions swinging from highs to the very depths of despair. Instead he remained silent while cradling her head against his shoulder to give her the caring and comfort she so desperately needed. They sat like that for nearly an hour, each occasionally murmuring recalled memories as they talked about the events of the night, their fears coming out into the open. Ben saw it as a healing process. Christine had almost fallen asleep when she jolted upright.

'What is it?'

'Tracking device.'

'Pardon?'

'One of the women, the nurse, I think, said that the tracking device indicated I was nearby.'

Ben shot up out of the seat and stumbled at the awkwardness of still having Christine in his arms. Regaining his balance, he settled her feet onto the ground.

'Ben, what?'

Those clothes you were wearing tonight, have you worn them to the piano bar recently?'

'The slacks, yes, but…'

'How recent?'

'Last week. I wear them almost every week with different tops. Why?'

'Stay here.' Muttering under his breath about his crass stupidity, Ben flew into Christine's bathroom and flung back the glass shower-recess door. Squatting, he yanked the pile of sodden clothes from the floor and dumped them into the hand basin.

'Ben what's going on?' came from right behind him.

'I think that, somehow, some-one has managed to plant a tracking device on you while you were at work.' He tugged the black pants from the tangled pile and shoved fingers into one pocket and felt around. Nothing. To make sure, he yanked the pocket inside out. The other pocket held nothing more than her tiny evening purse: a purse, he now recalled, she took with her to the hotel every darn night.

'This bag, where do you leave it while you are playing?'

'On the end corner of the bar. Mick keeps an eye on it but there's nothing much in there.'

'May I open it?'

'Of course.'

His fingers shook as he unsnapped the tiny catch and emptied the contents onto the vanity bench. Out tumbled a sodden tissue, still neatly folded, a twenty dollar note folded even smaller and a lip gloss.

'Damn,' hissed from his mouth when he lifted the tissue.

'What is it?'

'There's a small tracking device inside. This is how they knew you were at both restaurants. It makes sense now. They were following you. I suspected something like this but not that they'd got into your purse.'

'But how could they?' She was standing brushed up against his side.

'Christine, you wouldn't be able to see anyone near your purse while you work. It would be easy to sit at the bar, drinking then wait for Mick to clear tables so they could slip this into your purse. Here, feel how tiny it is.' Grasping her hand, he lifted it and dropped the small circle into her palm. 'I presume you don't use the bag very often.'

'I never open it, or hardly ever. It's just a couple of emergency items plus I slip my house key in the top each night.'

Ben snorted. 'One mystery solved. Now go to bed. I'm exhausted. I'll deal with this in the morning.'

'But can't they still track me?'

'It doesn't matter for they must know where you are but it's obvious they can't get to you in here so they've been waiting until you leave. You've been under police guard at the hotel, which has made you unattainable. They were hoping to snatch you tonight. In the morning I'm going to put this some place so they think you've left here. Right now, both of us need rest.'

Before seeking the warmth of his own bed, he rang John to inform him he would be at work after he'd managed a few hours sleep and not to call under any circumstances until then. He'd had enough drama for one night.

***

After a scant four hours of sleep they went into the office together where Christine related everything she could recall to a couple of officers while Ben studied all relevant evidence. The dead woman had yet to be positively identified but a photo of her ensured Ben it was not the fake nurse from the hospital. The dead woman was far too tall and too well built and the thick braid of hair would never have fitted under a wig. Which meant the other woman was the nurse since Christine had recognised her voice. As he tried to recall her description he jotted down details, but he'd not seen much of her. Her red curly hair had been the only thing that stood out. It worried him that there was still another woman on the loose with at least another man. Each day the case became more and more complicated but they were reeling in the suspects one by one. Yet each time they arrested someone, it meant there were still more to be apprehended. Just how big was this band of criminals? Were they just reeling in the small fry with the big fish safely hidden away? With his concerns mounting about how desperate these people were to find Christine he knew he had to do something more to end her nightmare. He spent a considerable time on the phone to organise a joint meeting between the two investigating departments and slipped the tracking device into a squad car. Let them trace that.

One phone call he received brightened his day and solved one of his most immediate problems – how to keep Christine safe. Replacing the receiver, he went in search of her, watching through a glass panel in the door while she completed her interview. He was waiting outside the room when she emerged. Grasping her fingers he led her into his office. 'Can you arrange two weeks away from work?' he asked as he settled her in a chair.

'If it is important, why?' She looked mystified but her face still wore drawn and haggard lines from her long ordeal and lack of sleep.

'Honey is ready for you to meet and become acquainted. They'd like you over East on Monday morning for two weeks training together. But I guess you already know the routine.' Seeing her eyes light up he felt delighted for her but at the same time knew he was going to miss her a great deal. He prayed she would miss him just as much.

'For that, I can take time off – no problem. I'm so looking forward to meeting her.' She wrapped her arms around her torso unable to suppress the excited grin on her face.

'I guess it has come at an opportune time. We can send you away under a false name and you will at least be safe while we hunt down the rest of this gang, but I'm going to miss having you around. What if I organise a flight for Sunday?'

She nodded her agreement just as a knock was heard on the door. Ben stood and opened it to find Jenny Gallati standing there.

'Hi, Ben, Chrissie. Are you ready?'

'Ready for what?' asked Christine.

'Jenny is your companion for the rest of the day.'

When Christine's lips tightened, Ben glanced at Jenny who must have read the same message from the body language for she immediately hooked her arm around Christine's elbow. 'I need your help today. I'm going shopping for nursery gear and I need someone to prevent me from buying the entire shop or my husband is going to throw a major hissy fit.'

'Fat lot of good I'll be then,' Christine retorted.

'You'll be perfect for I'll describe everything to you then because you can't see I can slip a few extras into the trolley.'

When Christine laughed Ben felt relieved. He had no problem in leaving her in the care of Jenny – after all she was a trained officer and knew to be alert and Christine was minus a tracking device. He saw the two women off then gathered his notes relating to the case before leaving for his meeting with the two departments.

The meeting was long. They discussed everything they knew, studied interviews, tossed around ideas and came up with a possible solution. Ben hated the idea but was outvoted unanimously. He was going back undercover. Jaye was returning with another stash of cocaine. Vince was to put the word out. Before he agreed, Ben insisted on one thing. 'We wait until Christine leaves the state before I go under cover and the minute she returns, Jaye leaves. I don't care if we don't have a result.'

'You can't leave us in limbo if we haven't made an arrest.' Greg was adamant.

'Unless you agree to my terms I won't be going back undercover. We have two weeks in which to wrap up the case. Take it or leave it.' Ben strode towards the door.

He grinned when he was called back. They had little choice but to agree. He returned to his seat so they could finalise plans.

Chapter Thirty

A sense of heavy emptiness filled Chrissie as she stood next to Ben in the small private room. Feeling uncomfortable with the tension in the room, she wasn't sure how to act. Determined to keep a tight rein on her emotions she fought back the desire to lean closer. Then she heard the nearing footsteps of a third person. It could only be the man posing as her husband for this journey across the country so she drew away from Ben with her eyes itching with held back moisture. A strong sense of relief engulfed her as she turned away from Ben so he couldn't see her face. She refused to admit how much she was going to miss him. Well, she could admit it but the result would be the same. She could never let him know how she felt about him.

She held out her arm as though seeking his elbow. There was a pause before her fingers were taken and Ben led her to the door of the private room at the airport. With her departure being kept under wraps they couldn't be seen together in public. They had arrived in separate vehicles then met in this room. Travelling under an assumed name, Chrissie was being accompanied on her flight by an officer posing as her husband. The plane was loaded, ready for take-off and waiting for these last two passengers to climb the steps.

'Let's go.' She tugged her hand free only to find it being grasped again but this time the fingers were different; shorter, leaner and colder than Ben's. 'Take care, Ben,' was all she could get out before her throat jammed up. It was ridiculous feeling so choked up since she was only going away for two weeks. She took a couple of steps, tugging at her minder's elbow. With tears threatening to fall she had to get away.

'You too,' she heard Ben mutter as she continued walking. She was more than glad of the stranger's assistance for without his guidance she wouldn't have been able to find her way to the plane – not because of her disability but because her eyes were awash with the tears she could no longer hold back. I love him, she thought then knew the pain was not going to go away because loving a man she could never have was not going to be easy. After all, she was almost blind and men didn't stick to women with a physical disability. She'd learned that lesson and once was more than enough.

***

Ben had done his best to keep his emotions in check but was finding it difficult to maintain an aura of calm. Leaving her in the care of another man was difficult enough but as he watched Christine's departing back until she was out of sight, his innards clamped tight.

Hell, man, she's only going away for two weeks. And she'll be out of harm's way. Get a grip. Straightening, he shoved his shoulders back then stalked towards a second door that led to a separate plane for a flight that was officially taking him away for two weeks on a special investigation up north. In reality he would be back first thing in the morning as Jaye Hammond. His first meeting with a prospective buyer had already been set up. Word had already gone around that he would be back with a large stash of cocaine, but Vince had no idea whether the buyer was the person they were after. He didn't think so, were his words but all leads had to be followed.

After being flown to various airports in the north, Ben was given a different identity on each flight and somewhere along the line his appearance changed back to the blond headed, grey eyed professional surfie with a bag of surf boards in tow. When they landed for the final time, he felt bone weary. He'd had very little sleep over the past twenty-four hours, being one of those who found sleep on an aeroplane almost impossible. He envied those who could relax cramped up in a plane seat but being a large framed man, he found it uncomfortable even sitting in the small seats, let alone trying to sleep. Impatience showed in his restlessness while waiting at the carousel for his luggage. He huffed in relief when his two bags came off in the first minutes. A private taxi was waiting outside the airport doors when he ambled out. He was driven to the same unit he had used before. Once inside he didn't bother with the food set out for him but instead stripped off, showered, fell into bed and was asleep in an instant.

When he awoke it was with a start. A loud noise had him jerking upright. Twisting his head in all directions since the fug of sleep had him completely confused as to where he was, his eyes finally settled on a man leaning against the doorjamb. Greg Williams.

'Hell man, what time is it?'

Greg smiled. 'You've been asleep almost twelve hours.'

'Why did I let you people talk me into this? Go away,' Ben grumbled then turned back over, drawing the pillow over his head.

Footsteps neared then Greg yanked the pillow away, laughing. 'Come on, Sunshine, we've got work to do. You've had more than enough beauty sleep and let me tell you, it isn't working. We have drug thugs to catch.'

It was only the thought of Christine's safety that drew Ben to full consciousness. He sat up, dragging the quilt over his nakedness just before it slipped to the floor.

'How about letting a man dress in privacy then? You go and find me something to eat. A hot coffee would go down well for starters.' He waited until the door closed behind Greg's retreating back before collecting a change of clothes and moving to the en-suite bathroom. When he emerged, Greg had coffee ready and was doing his best to put together a meal of sorts for them both. It became apparent that cooking was not Greg's greatest strength when Ben tasted the barely edible meal, but hunger forced him to eat while they discussed plans for the following evening.

***

Eighteen hours later Ben wasn't so sure he liked the gnawing feeling that was developing in his gut. He hoped it was the half raw, half burnt offerings Greg had concocted, that were giving him the pain and not the sensation of impending doom.

Not wanting their foe to pre-arrange a welcoming party, they had selected a new meeting place. Vince was picking up his contact. Once again Ben ensured he was early, driving a burgundy sedan with a fake hire car sticker. This car was scanned with utmost precision for an electronic tailing device, despite the fact that it was impossible for anyone to have got to it, before he drove around the large coastal town sussing out the layout and searching for a suitable place to park. The location didn't sit well with him. With long stretches of freeway where he couldn't pull off, he wouldn't be able to shake off pursuers easily and he wasn't one for high-speed getaways. Finding secluded parking spaces non-existent he opted for street parking, pulling into a bay close to a driveway.

To ensure he had a safe escape route, he took some time ambling around the streets, noting sheds, backyards, fences and other places where he could disappear if needed. In particular, he watched out for dogs and chickens. He had learnt to his detriment that both made a lot of noise when a large man lobbed into their yard. The chickens he could handle but large dogs protecting their properties he wasn't so keen about.

When he entered the premises his stomach churned. He had a desperate desire to turn around and walk straight back out. With all the tables in one big room and by the way the place was decorated, he figured it wasn't the classiest place in town. Plastic tablecloths, ancient artificial flowers in vases that hadn't been dusted for months, mismatched chairs that had seen better days and gaudy cheap light fittings were telltale signs. There were a few small alcoves with plastic bead curtains partitioning them off, but no-where near the privacy they'd had before. Despite the early hour quite a few seats were taken so he was hoping that maybe the food was a draw-card. A female waitress moved up to him, eyed him with speculation then handed him a menu.

'This way sir, we have a table reserved for you.'

Following the curvaceous brunette he hoped she was the police officer who he had been assured, would be looking after them. After settling into the corner seat in the furthest reaches of the restaurant he glanced around, noting that he was partially hidden from the main room but he certainly wasn't happy with the lack of privacy. To make a bad situation a tad better he pushed the table out as far as he could so that he had easy access then settled back into the uncomfortable chair that wasn't built for a large man, ensuring he had positioned himself so he could see the front door. Only then did he browse through the menu.

Ben prayed the food was better than the menu indicated, especially after having to stomach the concoction Greg Williams had created the previous night. His prayers went unanswered as he eyed with trepidation, the greasy dish served to him. He lifted his fork and searched for something on the plate that wasn't going to give him another bout of severe indigestion. After tasting each item on the plate, he gave up and called the waitress over.

'I can't eat this junk. Are the sweets any better?'

'Sorry, sir, apparently the regular chef who is supposed to be a genius with food, called in sick. The owner is cook for the night and yours isn't the first complaint. How about plain ice cream? They can't possibly get that wrong.'

'One would hope not. Okay, plus a very hot white coffee. See if they can't put some music on and turn it up a bit. You'd better get me a glass of house red as well.'

While he waited, Ben eyed the customers for a while then moved out of his seat and followed the signs to the public conveniences to see if there was a back entry. When he returned to his seat his ice cream was waiting, along with a glass of red wine. He sipped the wine, knowing full well just by looking at it what it was going to taste like. An establishment serving such terrible food wasn't going to have good wine available. His worst fears were confirmed when he shuddered as the acidic vinegar went down his throat and he began to wonder just which side was trying to kill him – the law was winning the race so far. He should have opted for a labelled wine instead of the house variety.

The coffee was a pleasant surprise, being better than good and he was on his third cup when he noticed Vince entering the door, followed by a woman. His fingers froze on the handle of his coffee mug - they hadn't told him the contact was a woman. His stomach recoiled and the contents bounced. Recognition stabbed.

The nurse. Hell.

Picturing a wig and glasses, Ben could now see the likeness to one of the two women who had left the restaurant after he had paid his bill. 'Damn,' he hissed under his breath then added a few more colourful imprecations for good measure. What the devil was he supposed to do now? There was every chance she would recognise his voice the moment he opened his mouth and after what Christine had told him, he was one hundred percent positive she was the other woman who had stalked them through the bush.

All options disappeared the moment Vince ushered the woman behind the beaded curtain, the two standing less than a metre in front of him. Scrambling for ideas, Ben nodded to indicate the two were to sit. Once they had settled, Ben sat in silence for a few moments, eyeing the two of them while his brain frantically tried to figure out what the hell he could do. There were two options - he was going to have to either wing it, or get up and walk straight out without saying a word. From the corner of his eye he noticed the anxious look Vince sent him.

'What's going on here, Vinnie?' Ben drawled. The startled look from the woman told him instantly that she knew who he was. While trying to maintain a look of nonchalance, his fingers edged closer to the gun he had placed on the seat next to him. It was under the jacket he had arranged with such precision over the top. And now it felt as though it was a mile away.

'Cindy, here, is interested in your product, Jaye.'

There was a slight movement of the woman's hand. His eyes followed a line to where he noticed the bulk under the lower part of her loose, flowing jacket, which was unbuttoned. Damn, she was armed. Just dandy - the night was getting better and better. The small beads of sweat on her brow indicated she was more than nervous - a very dangerous combination. And he was just as uptight. A quick glance at Vinnie by the woman and Ben wondered if she had guessed that he too, was a copper. While he maintained eye contact in an unblinking stare, his fingers grasped the handle of his gun and curled around the cold metal. He aimed at her under the table. He didn't want to kill her, just brush her side.

'You know I don't deal with women,' Ben ground out, his eyes still staring, unblinking towards Cindy. 'Especially women who come in here armed.'

Out of the corner of his eye he spied the alarm on Vince's face. 'I particularly don't deal with women who drug and abduct innocent blind people.'

At the drawn in hiss from Vince, Cindy's fingers moved a fraction closer to her gun while a drop of sweat puddled on the end of her nose, then dripped onto her lap. Now that she knew she had been set up, he figured there was only one way she was going to escape this standoff. Things were going to get more than nasty. She was waiting for Ben to shift his unmoving stare and he knew it.

'Nor women who fire at random in public places such as restaurants in the hills then chase that same blind woman through dense bush.'

There was another hiss from Vince's direction while Ben watched Cindy's arm moving ever so slightly, millimetre by millimetre. The muscle in Cindy's tight jaw tensed a fraction. She was like a cat ready to pounce on its prey; with Ben being the prey and sitting pretty. She couldn't miss. Even Christine wouldn't miss this close.

'Go for it, sweetheart, because it will be the last chance you have of killing me. That's what you wanted to do wasn't it? Kill me but keep Christine alive because she was your only hope?'

Eyes widened and a look of shock swept over the woman's face, Ben allowed a cynical smile to turn up the corners of his mouth as his words hit home. It had dawned on the woman opposite him, that she had been overheard in the bush.

'You can kill me now, but it will be the last thing you do and you will never find Christine. She's gone, out of harm's way. Without her to use as ransom, you can't get the cocaine. Would you like to know how close you were to her?' Ben smiled and leant forward just a fraction to make a point, but his heart was doing a great job of trying to escape from his chest. It was thumping so hard and every ounce of adrenaline in his body was flooding through his veins.

'About as close as we are now. You almost trod on her and she heard every word you said to your female accomplice. There's something maybe you don't know about blind people. Their other four senses become highly attuned, especially their senses of smell and hearing. Vision impaired people absorb and remember a lot more than a normal sighted person does. She even knew what sort of perfume you were wearing. These are the sorts of things she recalls. She knows when I change the brand of soap I use. She can detect it even under my aftershave.' Ben paused.

'Now what are we going to do here? Vinnie, do you have any ideas? I suggest your female friend here allows you to remove the gun she has hidden in the waistband of her slacks. Her fingers are edging closer and closer. But what she doesn't realise is…'

He got no further. With the sudden movement from Cindy, Ben had no choice but to fire. It was either him or her. The woman was cornered and desperation swallowed any rationality she might have had. Ben's gun blasted one shot a split second before she managed to pull the trigger on hers. Not wanting to kill the woman, his unsighted aim was not all that brilliant with the bullet lodging in her abdomen instead of brushing against her side where he had intended but she had moved too far, too fast. Without having time to aim and with Ben's bullet piercing through her skin and jolting her, Cindy's shot went wild but slammed into Ben's shoulder. The force jerked him backwards and from the sudden pain he knew the bullet was embedded against a bone and hadn't gone clean through.

He managed to duck the second shot, agony wracking his shoulder as he dived below the table. By the time Cindy was about to pull the trigger a third time, Vince had knocked the gun from her hand. It clattered on the table then slid over the edge, landing on Ben as he rose. Vince had his own gun drawn, pressed up against the woman's temple. The entire scene took about two seconds.

'Christ almighty, Ben, did you have to?' Vince called out above the loud rumpus that had ensued from the restaurant behind them.

'Sorry, mate, I knew who she was the minute she walked in that door but I couldn't let you know. She recognised my voice the moment I opened my mouth. She knew damn well I was a copper and that she was cornered. If we'd let her go the game would have been up in any case. This way, I get to arrest her and I'm going to enjoy interrogating her. Christine has a few grudges against this lady and I will be delighted in paying her back for all the trauma she has meted out to an innocent bystander.'

Searching the table with his eyes, Ben pulled a paper napkin from the pile crammed into a silver holder and, hoping it was a lot cleaner than the rest of the establishment, eased it under his shirt and pressed it up against the steady flow of blood pouring from his shoulder, turning the bright yellow paper crimson in an instant.

'Where's that damn waitress?' he yelled while keeping the pressure on his wound at the same time as he did his best to ignore the nauseating agony. His face tensed and his mouth drew back in a thin line.

'Probably trying to calm a room full of terrified patrons,' Vince muttered as he frisked Cindy to make sure she had no other weapons. He then pushed her roughly against the back of the chair from her slumped position and inspected the wound. Ben's aim hadn't gone as wild as he thought. There was a large flesh would in the side of the woman's waist. He didn't think it had gone through any major organs. Removing a clean handkerchief from his pocket Vince pressed it tight against the bloodied hole then told the woman to keep pressure on it. 'I'll call for backup.' Vince drew out his mobile phone and was about to dial when the waitress and two plainclothes officers shot into the gap, guns drawn.

'One wouldn't want you guys in an emergency. What took you so long?' The deep sarcasm from Ben was interspersed with a groan as he attempted to stand. Flopping back into the chair, he gasped in pain. 'See to her first and call an ambulance – no make that two. Leave me in an ambulance with her and she won't arrive at her destination alive. Better still, you can drive me, Vince. You owe me that much.'

By pushing hard with his legs Ben managed to get himself upright, swallowing a gasp of agony as he swayed on unsteady legs. Thinking about the diners he had to walk through, he insisted on Vince helping him put on his jacket so as to not alarm the patrons with the blood seeping through his shirt. Damn, but it hurt! After tucking his pistol in his pocket since there was no way he could lift the arm to use the holster, Ben strode out through the opening, across the floor of the restaurant and straight out the door as though nothing had happened, Vince by his side.

Ben's stride wasn't so strong and confident when he walked through the doors of the emergency hospital back in the city. He had spent the long drive telling Vince exactly what he thought of undercover work and the drug squad, being particularly expressive about what he thought of Vince for suggesting the idea in the first place. His language was just as colourful when the young doctor who examined him wanted to call the police, as per regulations whenever a gunshot victim was brought in. Being undercover, Ben didn't have his badge on him. He knew he was causing grief to the poor young intern until Vince was dragged into the examination room. Vince not having his badge either didn't help matters, his disclosure causing another wrathful outburst from Ben, but hell, he was mad. Mad at himself mainly for numerous reasons and he hated not being in control of a situation. Even more, he hated being ill and was probably the worst patient on this earth.

'Just get this flaming bullet out of my shoulder and by the time it is out I'll have the whole flaming police force down here to vouch for me. Vince, go get some authority. Call John and tell him I want him here pronto with the picture on my office wall of me in uniform, not that that is going to help with my hair looking like a freak show.'

Turning to the hapless young intern, he continued venting his spleen. 'By the way, if you are going to operate, you need to remove the contact lenses that are a part of my undercover disguise. Hell, that woman we just arrested knew I was a cop.'

It took a while but Ben gradually calmed, the anaesthetic shutting him up completely for a time, while the surgeon probed for the bullet and repaired the damage to Ben's shoulder muscles. When Ben came around, he immediately wished he was still out to it when he saw John's grinning face watching him from the drawn up chair by his bed.

'I hear you have been causing a bit of mayhem around here.' There was no disguising the grin on John's face. He was taking a great deal of pleasure enjoying Ben's discomfiture.

'God, give me strength. I'm glad none of these people work for me. What a farce.' Ben's frustration hadn't eased a bit.

'Can I take that as a backhanded compliment? I'll pass it on to the rest of our department,' chuckled John.

'Take it any way you like but just get me out of this place. I'd rather die at home in my own bed.' Determined to leave, he attempted to sit up but a serious wave of dizziness beset him and with his arm bound across his bare chest, immobile, he lost his balance and flopped back onto the bed.

'I'll go and see the surgeon. You stay put for a few minutes.' John was back almost as soon as he left, with the doctor in tow.

'Detective, I hear you want to leave. I have one young intern who will be glad to see the back of you. We removed the bullet that was lodged in the muscle tissue against your shoulder joint. You are going to have to keep it immobile until the tissue heals if you want full function. The binding stays on for at least a week, when I want to see you again to remove the stitches. Then your arm will be in a sling until I say it can be removed. I'll release you after my rounds in the morning but only if you have someone to care for you full time. You can't drive or lift anything until I say so.' As the news was getting bleaker and bleaker John grinned wider and wider.

'The man finally has to take a holiday.' John said with a chuckle. 'You can stay with us. Mary will love to keep you pinned down and there is no way in this world she will let you disobey doctor's orders. Take it from one who knows. I'll have her here first thing in the morning. See you later, Ben. Are you going to call Chrissie or will I?'

'Don't you dare! I'll phone her later to let her know we have caught the nurse. Go and leave me in peace and make sure you bring me a full report when you come in.'

With the anaesthetic in his system making him drowsy, Ben settled down then slept for what remained of the night.

He was shaken awake, none too pleased to see John still grinning as was the damned doctor. His wound was inspected then Mary was shown how to dress it and given instructions on what to look for if the wound became infected. When the doctor commented that Ben was not to remove the bandage binding his arm against his chest, the words came out as more of an order, causing John's glee while Ben growled in frustration. The list of things that Ben could or could not do was too damned extensive and Mary wrote every single one down, much to Ben's disgust. He hated being incapacitated and was proving how poor a patient he was. He sighed. The week was going to be torturous with mother hen watching his every move and him being able to do a big fat nothing. He was going to be stir crazy.

By the time he was settled into Mary's sofa, Ben was glad to swallow a couple of prescribed painkillers. The incessant ache in his shoulder kept him quiet and resting for a couple of days. After that he became bored and restless. Then he discovered the ache had moved a few inches lower, settling into the region of his heart. Missing Christine more than he ever thought he could miss a woman he finally rang her Saturday morning, his heart leaping about in his chest when he heard her voice.

'Christine? How are things going? How is it with Honey?'

'Oh, Ben, she is gorgeous. I'm told she gets her name from her colour. I love her to pieces and she is so smart. I've missed you. What have you been up to?'

There was a long pause before Ben could find the words to answer. That she'd missed him sent a warm glow through his body, rendering him speechless for a moment. Things were looking up. But there was no way he was going to tell her that he had discovered how much it hurt when a bullet entered your body. 'I went undercover again and we managed to catch your delightful nurse. A real charming piece of work she is. I'll tell you all about it when you return. We still have some interrogation to do. The other woman was Bobby's wife and had been blackmailed into the gang to pay off Bobby's debts since we had arrested him. I miss you heaps, Christine. Ring me on my mobile any time and I'll be at the airport when you return. You take care.' Hanging up before she could ask any further questions he felt better for having heard her voice but the lump in his heart hadn't moved at all.

Ben insisted on returning to work Monday morning. No way could he stand sitting idle another second. He could read reports one-handed and promised Mary, crossing his heart as well as lifting two fingers in a Scouts salute of honour, he wouldn't do anything wrong. He didn't figure it would be wise to inform the woman that he'd never been a Boy Scout. When John made sure he kept his promise by carrying out his own tasks in Ben's office, Ben vented his disgust. Poor John managed to ignore all the insults thrown at him by his best friend. Tuesday morning he was driven back to the hospital for a check-up and was thankful when his arm was unstrapped from his body even though it was ensconced in a sling. At least he would be able to take a proper shower and he had a bit more freedom of movement. He'd already figured out the shoulder would stiffen and require exercises to regain full mobility and strength but he was thankful it was healing well.

Chapter Thirty-One

Deep thoughts about Christine and how much he wanted her as a part of his life on a permanent basis were constant, day and night. But he needed to find out why she had such a tight hold on her inner emotions. He figured Felicity might give him an inkling so he rang her to invite her to lunch. Still unable to drive, he walked the short distance from his office to the small eatery where he found Felicity already seated at an aluminium table in a corner. Settling into the seat opposite, he waited until they had ordered before conveying his real reason for the meeting.

'Felicity, you know Christine better than anyone. I want to have a deeper understanding of her past and why she holds her emotions so close.'

'You're in love with her aren't you?' Felicity dared to grin at him.

'Very much so, I want to marry her.'

Felicity raised her eyebrows at his bluntness but there was no point in hiding the truth.

'She vowed she would never marry again, never allow herself to fall in love again. You could have your work cut out for you. She's a determined lady and once she makes her mind up on something, it's almost impossible to get her to change it.'

'Yes, I've struck her stubborn pride and fierce determination and it's something I admire about her but I would like to understand what made her that way. My instincts tell me it is not just because her husband left her due to her failing sight. There has to be more. I don't believe he ever loved her to start with.'

'You're very astute aren't you? All of those things are true. I'm not really at liberty to tell you what happened. I can't betray Chrissie, but I could give you some hints; put you on the right track and you can discover it yourself. Don't ever let her know it was me who helped you. My role as her aide depends on trust and I'm not sure I should divulge anything. But on the other hand you would be good for her. She needs a man in her life and I know she thinks a lot of you. I even suspect she's in love with you but I doubt she would ever admit it.'

Delighted at the disclosure, Ben had little control over the grin that spread from the corners of his mouth. 'Another thing I would like to know is her concert work. She claims she could never play on stage again but I don't believe that for one minute. She has a God given talent and I'm sure she could play her own concerts without an orchestra, but she says it is never going to happen.' He paused while their meal was served then waited, toying with his food until Felicity responded, getting antsy at the lengthy silence.

'Her reasoning has to do with your first problem. They are related. Solve one and you should be able to discover the other. This is the only clue I am going to give you. You need to find a copy of a CD featuring Richard Mears playing the piano. There is only one that I know of. It's fairly recent, about a year to eighteen months old. Play it in her presence, but be prepared. She will not be happy. You may be able to break her when she's angry. The only way to get her to snap is by constant pushing. And she needs to snap because she is harbouring a very deep grudge and until she gets it out of her system she won't allow you into her heart. And that would be a great pity.'

'I take it Richard was the husband,' Ben murmured under his breath. He didn't really expect, or want an answer. He pushed his half-eaten plate away, losing all interest in food then changed the subject by talking about everyday matters while Felicity finished her meal.

'What happened to your arm?' she asked.

'Undercover job went skew-whiff and I underestimated my opponent. I collected my first bullet on the job. No permanent damage but a damned inconvenience. The important thing was that we caught the woman who tried to abduct Christine and I'm fairly certain her life isn't in any more danger.'

Ben called the waitress over to settle the bill. After Felicity had gone, he walked into the city centre and searched record stores until he found what he wanted in a shop dedicated to classical music. It was late afternoon by the time he arrived back at his office. He insisted John drive him home, collecting his gear from John's place on the way. As expected, John argued the point with him.

'Damn it, John, I'm not going to risk permanent damage to my shoulder. Give me some credit for having brains. I truly appreciate Mary's and your help, but I can manage myself from now on. Besides, Christine will be home on Saturday.'

John eyed him then grinned; a grin Ben didn't like one little bit. Then John had the nerve to laugh.

'The man has finally been caught. How are you going to pick her up? You still can't drive.'

Damn the man's astuteness. 'Ever heard of taxis?' Ben's voice dripped with sarcasm.

'Ben, tell me to mind my own business, but when are you going to stop tormenting yourself and ask Chrissie to marry you? It's obvious to everyone that you're head over heels in love with her.'

'You're right. Mind your own business. I don't recall ever interfering in your love life,' Ben retorted.

John's shout of laughter was more of a scoff. 'Then you must be suffering from amnesia, amongst other things. I can relate a whole list of times when you set me up with Mary. Thank God,' John added with a wry smile.

Ben grinned at his friend. 'Yeah, well, you needed a bit of a shove but you leave Christine to me. She has a few ghosts she needs to lay to rest and you interfering may not help the cause. In fact it could set in a huge wedge. Trust me on this one. I'm working on it. And you are right. She is the only woman I have ever loved enough to want to ask her to marry me.'

Settled back home after suffering another five minutes of John's teasing, Ben slipped the CD he had purchased into his player then sat back to listen to the recording in an attempt to figure out what Felicity was talking about. He listened intently right the way through but could glean no clues. The second time, he studied every word on the CD cover, but still couldn't discover anything out of the ordinary. After setting the recording to play a third time, he settled back on his lounge to rest. In his half-asleep state thoughts of Christine centred in his brain and he imagined her playing the pieces, visualising her in one of her stunning evening gowns poised over the keyboard, her deft fingers hitting the chords and running rapidly up and down the keyboard. His eyes shut, almost asleep, his memories of her playing the exact same piece for him on the first night her piano came to the house.

With eyes shooting open, he shot up straight. It *was* Christine playing that piece. It was Christine playing nearly all the pieces. He had doubts about three of them but he knew how she played – he'd heard her practising often enough. She spent hours at the keyboard and he spent hours listening, enjoying every minute. After his discovery, he spent most of the night at his computer, researching every detail he could find about three people – all with the surname of Mears and what he learnt made very interesting reading.

Chapter Thirty-Two

Ben was supposed to be working. He knew it and to any one who looked in he was studying the open files spread out on his desk. A closer look would reveal a mass of jottings: ideas on what to do about the love of his life. Most of them had dark scratches through them. He weighed each up, tossed around the pros and cons and came up with him losing Christine altogether. A dark line scrubbed out the idea. Felicity wouldn't give him any more help and he respected her reasons. By Friday night, he was back to his original idea, the one Felicity had said all along – play the recording when Christine was around and face the consequences head on. Not wanting to ruin their first night together he decided to wait for the right opportunity.

Glancing at his watch, Ben knew that the plane had already landed when the taxi reached the airport. He felt beyond frustrated, unable to believe how many calls it had taken for a taxi to finally arrive. At one stage he had been tempted to toss his sling away and drive. Running into the terminal, he scanned the arrivals list and found the correct door, just as the first passengers came through. Needing assistance from the cabin crew, Christine would either be one of the first or last. She was last, which only increased his anxiety. He was hopping around like an excited young child until he saw her on the arm of a male crewman – a very good-looking crewman. Jealousy stabbed when he saw the two laughing together and Christine's fingers on the man's elbow. They drew closer. His eyes softened when he took a couple of steps and stood in front of them.

'I'll take over now.' He grasped her free hand.

'Ben! It's so good to see you.'

Oh, wow, with that greeting a brick landed. He bent his head to brush her mouth, savouring the taste of her soft lips. Immediately she pulled away. The new brick dropped to the ground. She wasn't interested. He could only watch as she thanked her minder with such enthusiasm or was it a deliberate ploy to keep Ben at bay?

When she turned back there was a broad grin on her face and she reached out and gave him a hug. Elation hit until she paused when she felt the sling on his arm, her face swinging from joy to consternation while she felt all the way along his arm and up his neck.

'What happened? You didn't tell me. You told me you were fine.'

'It's nothing - an injury in the line of duty. I have to keep it in a sling with no driving and no lifting until the muscle heals. It's on the mend now. We need to catch a taxi home. I've missed you so much.' Not wanting to explain finer details he flung his good arm around her shoulders and drew her close in a hug before leading her to the luggage carousel with her hand inside his bent elbow.

On the way home, Christine chatted incessantly about Honey. They were walking in the front door when he asked when Honey was arriving.

'In two weeks. She only needs her final training and then she comes over with her trainer and they train her to my needs over here.'

Ben fell silent while he carried the bags into her room, one at a time. He only had two weeks. She would want to go back to her place unless he could convince her otherwise. He already knew Honey would be trained to suit her local environment. His gut began churning. It was nowhere near enough time.

They hadn't been home long before Christine drifted over to her piano. It was like a magnet the way she was drawn to the instrument. But then it had been part of her life for so many years. She often put on one of her own recordings and played along with it so that she kept her own concert pieces up to scratch. She didn't need to see the conductor and knew the pieces off by heart although on the odd occasion she lost her way when she missed a key through not being able to see the keyboard, but in the main, she played by instinct and played extremely well. He'd learnt her sneaky little secret on how she managed to find the right keys. Tiny Braille labels in a see-through plastic had been stuck to every *C* and *G* on the keyboard.

To keep her close Ben sought her help to prepare dinner. He was her eyes while she was his hands, a situation that had them working in harmony and with quite a few laughs. Things were looking up. After the meal, Ben wanted to maintain the mood so didn't dare bring up what he most wanted to ask. He had discovered how much she enjoyed films and videos even though she couldn't see them. She explained that it was a bit like reading a book; you use your imagination and visualise the scenes in your head. He'd learnt to explain long scenes containing few words. After setting a new DVD going they spent a quiet evening together. Ben dared to edge his arm around Christine's shoulders. There was an initial tensioning from Christine then she relaxed so he kept it there but restrained himself from any heavy romance. He wasn't that brave. One brick at a time and he had two weeks.

The film finished. Ben flicked the machine off then leant over and brushed his mouth over hers in a chaste goodnight kiss but knew he had done the wrong thing when she stiffened at his touch. Damn, he'd ruined it. Disheartened, he pulled away.

'Goodnight, sleep well,' he said as he rose, hoping she would think it had only been a friendly goodnight peck. But damn, by her stoic features his slow building of that wall of trust seemed to have lost a few too many bricks.

***

Enjoying the hot needles of water pounding on her skin, Chrissie stilled at the strains of music. Disbelieving of what she thought she heard, she swung the shower door open so she could hear better. Deep anger tore through her. Grabbing a towel, she wrapped it around her body and tucked the end in before charging through her bedroom then straight towards the CD player, not bothering to think about what she looked like or how wet she was. Water didn't matter in the least but that darn CD needed to be binned or incinerated. Incineration wasn't even good enough.

'Where the hell did you get that?' she gasped, despite having no idea if Ben was actually there and was more talking to herself than any person as she felt along the panel and pressed the button to cease the playing then removed the CD and tried to snap it in half.

Ben reached over her shoulder and tugged the offensive CD out of her hands.

'I was listening to that. I bought it. I found two others of you playing as well; two you didn't have in your collection. I thought I would compare the styles between you and your husband's playing.'

Too angry to utter a word Chrissie stood still, making a puddle on the floor as the water ran down her limbs.

'Talk to me, Christine. What's your problem with this particular recording? Apart from the fact that it has the name of the pianist on it as your ex-husband.'

'That is the problem,' Chrissie yelled. 'Give it to me!' Reaching out she felt along Ben's arm until she found his hand. Not finding the disc in his good hand she traced along his sling until she found his other fingers. They were empty. 'Where is it Ben? Please give it to me?'

'What, so you can wreck it. I happen to like the playing and it is my CD. You want it so badly then you come and get it. It's on my body.'

Stomping forward she reached out, her hands none too gentle as she felt around for the disk, fury churning through her. Her inability to locate it made her even angrier. Sidling around the back of him she felt down his back, her fingers slipping into the waistband of his slacks, down over his butt, then his legs until she reached his bare feet. No CD. She stood again.

'Ben, give it to me.' she cried out.

'I'm not moving it. If you find it, you can have it.' His voice was quiet but steely.

Starting with his head she worked her way down the front of his body.

'The third piece on the disc – you played that same piece for me.'

Her fingers reached his shoulder where she felt all along the top, pausing when he drew in a breath of pain as she probed his injury.

'I very much enjoyed the way it was played.'

This resulted in a hard poke to his ribs while her hands explored all the way around his chest.

'The last piece was particularly good, such dexterity with the fingers.'

Chrissie thumped him on his chest, her eyes spitting shards of ice at him even though she could barely make out his shape.

'The first piece, such feeling.'

She dug her hands into the waist of his pants and paused.

'I promise you, it's not there,' Ben whispered, 'but I don't mind if you want to find out for yourself.'

She swiped at his head but felt the sudden shift in air pressure as he ducked.

'Such emotion in the first piece. It reminded me of the first time I saw you playing in the piano bar. How you drew me in, how you always draw me in.'

Unbidden tears began falling. To hide her chagrin she crouched down and felt down the front of Ben's legs.

'Where is it Ben? Please?' Her words broke on a sob.

'Higher.'

She stood. Her hands went back to his arms and she began probing in the only place it could be, between his body and the sling.

'I was lying on the lounge, half asleep, listening, with visions of you in your gorgeous green evening gown. You looked so beautiful. I was imagining it was you on the stage playing those pieces.'

Her fingers closed in on the disk.

'Suddenly, it seemed so right that it was you playing: now why would that be?'

There was a sharp snap as a superhuman effort, spurred on by intense anger, gave Chrissie the strength to break the disk.

'Because it was me!' she screamed as she hurled the two pieces across the room. They ricocheted onto the kitchen bench then back up to the ceiling, one piece tinkling in the sink and the other landed on top of something else hard by the sound of it. Ben's arms went around her as he gathered her into his chest, her still soapy, wet hair resting under his chin.

'Tell me what happened. Why is your husband's name on that CD and not yours? Even I could tell it was you playing.' Despite struggling to get away he tugged her closer to his body.

'He never made it in the concert world. He was never good enough even though he believed he was. I had begun making a recording before I was diagnosed with my eye problem. I was losing my vision then and just thought I had an illness or needed glasses. After extensive tests, I was diagnosed.' She was so mad words just tumbled out. She had no control. 'I struggled to learn the pieces but managed to get most recorded. Then he left me, just walked out one day when I wasn't home. The only things he left me were my clothes and my piano. No furniture, nothing. I came home to an empty house and an empty bank account. I haven't seen him since. All contact was through a lawyer. He sold the house from under me by forging my signature on the sale papers. Because I couldn't finish the last few pieces on the CD, I thought nothing more of it. He published it under his name. Three pieces are his. He gets all the royalties and it got him a soloist job with an international orchestra. I have no idea where he is now. His father told me that if I went to the authorities, he would blacklist me in the music world. I think he did that in any case. I've tried to get bookings for my own concerts. No-one wants to know me. Oh, God, I can't believe I just told you that.' She struggled to free herself but he tightened his hold.

'Maybe it's about time you did let it all out. How did you find out about the CD?'

'I heard a piece being played on the classical radio station. I knew it was my playing and I knew it was one I had recorded. I rang up as an interested listener. I think he only married me so he could climb up the concert ladder and gain social status. He was incredibly jealous of both his father and me. I learnt that the hard way.'

'You know that what he's done is illegal. You can still have him charged. Those royalties belong to you as well as a portion of your savings and the money from your house. I know where he is. Once I figured out it was you playing, I wondered why your name wasn't on the cover. I did a bit of research via the Internet.'

Chrissie yanked away. 'Then why did we just go through all that? Why didn't you just ask me?'

A snort of laughter escaped through his nose. 'Would you have told me the truth? I doubt it. You have a habit of clamming up about anything that might rock your emotional stability and create a crack in that armour you've built up around yourself.'

She felt his lips brush against her brow and tried to move further away but his arms tightened, holding her pressed against him.

'I needed to find a small chink in your armour. I bet I can tell you which three are not yours - the three before the last piece. They had me puzzled. They sound so mechanical with very little emotion. Not at all like you and now I know why.'

She felt him pull away but he kept his hands on her shoulder.

'Now my beautiful Christine, much as I am thoroughly enjoying holding you in my arms with you having nothing more than a damp towel around you, I'm not so pleased with the soap bubbles squelching into my face. Go and finish your shower and sad for me, I guess you'll come out dressed in something that is not quite so revealing and tempting to my male hormones.' She was drawn so close that she could feel against her abdomen, the effect she was having on him. Then he kissed her with enough passion so she knew exactly how his hormones had been fired up. Heat surged up her neck and cheeks as she tugged free and scurried away while chastising herself under her breath. She'd vowed to keep well away from Ben and look how long that had lasted. Stupid woman.

Chapter Thirty-Three

As Christine regained her equilibrium, Ben saw the shutters coming down. She shunned any close contact or personal conversation making him feel as though he was back at square one. His brick wall was crumbling away. Every time they happened to touch, she sidled away. While she assisted in the preparation of dinner she asked about what was happening with all the people who had caused so much grief. Ben grimaced. It was a safe topic for her and she had a right to know.

'Casey has spilled the beans. He isn't expected to live more than a few weeks and will die in jail. He has confessed to all he has been charged with. Bobby, his real name being Robert Daniels, arrived from the East where he had gotten himself into financial difficulties after borrowing from the leader of the gang at an exorbitant rate of interest, much as Casey had. They were blackmailed into doing the dirty work but after so many bungles and then finally getting caught, the other members of the gang began to take a more active role in the skulduggery. Bobby's wife was also blackmailed under the threat of death of her three children. She was the one killed in the bush. Gerard dealt in drugs in Europe and had come to this country looking for richer pickings. The drugs he tried to bring into the country were found by customs, which left him with little financial resources. He borrowed from the same Shylock. When he heard about Jaye Hammond on the grapevine, he hatched a plan with his lender to get them all out of the financial bog hole they were in.

'You were seen with Jaye Hammond and this gave them the idea of using you as bait to get their hands on the drugs without paying for them. One by one, they were either arrested or taken down and that left them with only the woman who tried to abduct you. She was the leader. Greed was her only motive. She had lost her source of income and quite a substantial amount of capital from the loans she had given, so using a number of different disguises she and Gerard had followed either you or me around. She knew you were living here and was waiting for the opportunity to grab you again.'

'What happened while I was away?'

'When our lady friend heard Jaye was returning with another cache of drugs, she was at the desperate stage. I'm certain she didn't know I was the Ben Somers you'd been staying with but she recognised my voice when we met. Since she was cornered she attempted to just shoot her way out. As though I would be carting around that much cocaine.'

'Shoot? Is that what happened to you? You were shot weren't you? Why didn't you tell me? You lied to me!' Chrissie waved her fork around in the air.

Ben grabbed hold of the steel missile when it flew too close to his face. 'I didn't lie. You think about my words. I said that I was injured in the line of duty. Well I was. I just didn't say how I was injured and you never asked.'

Christine finished chewing then swallowed. 'That's tantamount to lying.'

'I didn't want to alarm you. If you'd asked the right question I would have answered it honestly. I've always been honest with you. It was the first time I'd taken a bullet and I can answer a question for you. It hurts like hell when a bullet enters your body.'

Christine shivered. 'So, you've been in hospital. That's why you didn't ring me that first week. Ben! I'm so sorry. All this is my fault.' She searched around the bench for her fork.

He placed it in her fingers. 'So you did miss me. That's good to hear. Why is it your fault? You did nothing wrong except seduce me with your brilliant playing. I couldn't keep away from you. It was because of that association you got tangled up in this mess.'

'Seduce you!' She spluttered, almost choking as she swallowed her mouthful of food and slammed the fork down on the plate.

Ben laughed at the look on her face. 'Do you want to hear the rest or not?'

'Yes please,' she said. 'I did not seduce you,' she added under her breath.

'I could see she had a gun and also that she had recognised my voice. She knew the moment she heard me exactly who I was and that I was a copper, so I tried stringing her along. I was about to tell her that I had a gun aimed at her chest when she suddenly moved and drew out her gun. I fired first causing her aim to be wild. Her second shot missed.' Ben leant towards her, 'Yes you did seduce me. I was under your spell,' he whispered.

'Second shot! How many times did you get hit?'

'Only the once but she got her just desserts. My shot found its target. She's still in hospital, under armed guard. I would have liked to have done a lot more to her for putting you through so much. Now finish your dinner.'

His appetite gone, Ben pushed his plate away. Then he waited until Christine had finished eating before stacking the dishes into the dishwasher while she moved to the lounge and began playing her piano; moody pieces he'd not heard before.

Suddenly, she stopped playing, closed the lid to her piano. 'Ben, does this mean I'm not in any danger now?'

Oh, hell. Ben stilled. He thought he had two weeks, not two days. His stomach recoiled.

'That's what we believe, why?'

'Which means I can go home as soon as Honey comes over.' Standing she pushed the piano stool out of the way then moved over to a single lounge chair where she sat and slung her legs over the arm, her hands folded in her lap.

His fear mounting, Ben followed every single movement with his eyes. 'You don't have to go, ever. Stay here.'

'I can't do that, Ben, it wouldn't be right.'

'We could make it right. Marry me, Christine.' Ben swallowed his fear.

'Marry you?' Her laugh sounded scornful, which sent his nerves shuddering in fear. 'You have to be joking! I'll never be stupid enough to get married again.'

Staring, Ben stood, his heart turned into razor sharp icicle shards with every single one stabbing him to the core. 'You don't have to make it sound as though it would be such an abomination to be married to me.' He had to get out. 'I'm going out for a run. Don't wait up for me.' Fighting down the intense desolation he felt, he fled down the passage and left via the garage. Checking his runners were in the car he drove off, ignoring his sling and squealing tyres after he had reversed out then turned into the street. He drove with a numb brain and with his chest region feeling as though every single brick in his wall was being hurled at him. He pulled into a nearby park, dragged on a pair of musty socks he had found wedged in the toes of his runners and laced up the shoes. He ran and ran and ran until he was too exhausted to feel or to care.

***

Appalled at how her outburst must have sounded for Ben to have taken off so rapidly, Chrissie sat unmoving. The words had slipped out without thinking and she certainly didn't mean them the way they were taken. Oh, Ben I'm sorry. What an idiot. She knew he'd had feelings for her but marriage? She never figured he had been thinking of marriage. How was she supposed to know something like that? Why would anyone ever want to marry her? She wasn't worthy any longer. She couldn't see, could barely cook and as for cleaning house? She laughed: a self-deprecating snort. While she sat, she recalled the things they had done together – all the bad times and all the wonderful times. Something inside her shifted. Something tumbled and she became aware. She loved Ben and he must have feelings for her, otherwise why would he propose? And she had just done the unforgivable.

She was still sitting in the same chair when she heard Ben arrive home. He said nothing and she could tell by the distance of his footsteps that he was headed straight for his room. Give me strength, she thought then called out. 'Ben I'm sorry. I didn't mean that the way it came out.' She hoped her apology would lead to a discussion.

'Christine. I told you not to wait up for me. Go to bed.' His voice sounded thick and husky.

She heard him take a few steps into the lounge room.

'Just let me know when you want to move out and I will arrange it. Good night, Christine.' He slammed his bedroom door.

She was stunned. All of a sudden everything that had happened to her in her past seemed so insignificant. She realised she had been harbouring grudges for no more reason than her own stubborn pride. She tried to recall the old adage about pride but couldn't quite get the words right, but the meaning sure hit home. But now it was too late. She'd lost her one opportunity. Her one chance of a complete and happy life had gone, all because of a few careless words. He wanted her gone. So she would go.

Even though it was late, she rang Felicity. She needed help.

After a restless night, Chrissie stumbled from bed and started breakfast, even though it was way too early. When the food was ready she knocked on Ben's door to let him know. She had no idea what she was going to say to him. Sorry sounded so inane and inappropriate and yet she couldn't think of a better word. Maybe he would give her a chance to explain. After waiting and calling several times she hesitated before opening his door. The room felt empty.

Standing in the doorway, she listened but couldn't detect any soft breathing. She had never been in his room before so moved tentatively with outstretched arms as she felt her way over to the bed. The bed was unmade, empty and cold. In pulling the covers straight she accidentally brushed her hand against the headboard when she plumped up the pillows. Her fingers ran across the tag with the raised dots. 'Sexy Ben's Room.'

Underneath it Ben had added another tag in Braille. 'One day, my beautiful Christine, the love of my life, will join me in here. I live for that day.' Chrissie dissolved in a flood of tears clasping Ben's pillow to her heart.

Chapter Thirty-Four

B en couldn't help himself. Like a magnet, he was drawn to the lounge bar. He now understood what it felt like to live in hell. He's been there for the past week. He studied the reason he felt like death. Christine looked pale and haggard. She'd lost weight and looked the way he felt with half-moon bruises under her eyes. After the first break he moved from his back seat to the one next to Christine's. Without even tasting it he sipped on his regular glass of Cabernet Merlot.

All of a sudden she switched from her regular type of soft arpeggios for background music and began thumping out chords from one of her classical concert pieces. Stunned, he eyed her, wondering what the heck was going on. Tears simmered across her eyes while the audience went quiet. Even though there was no background murmur of voices,

Christine didn't stop, going from one well-known classic to another. At the same time, the piano bar filled. Where the crowd came from, Ben didn't have a clue.

Christine brought her piece to an end and had only managed a few notes of her next piece when there was a loud thump, thump as Mick pounded his fist on the wooden bar.

The music ceased in the middle of a bar. A hush descended and all eyes turned to the piano to see Christine close the lid of the piano, stand then turn around, facing the bar.

'Ben Somers,' she called out at the top of her voice. 'I love you. I'm sorry you took my words the wrong way. What I meant was that you had to be joking because,' her voiced caught then softened. 'I'm not worthy of you. You deserve much better, someone who can see, someone you don't have to care for. I'm so sorry – I miss you so much. I know you will probably never forgive me and I don't blame you but I do truly love you, Ben.' The last few words came out as a sob before she sank back onto the seat with her head so low the tears plopped onto clenched fists in her lap.

The snapping of the stem of a wine glass broke the intense silence. Ben looked down at his hand and the broken pieces of glass, his wine spilling onto the bar towel. How did that happen?

Looking so darn sad and forlorn and so out of her comfort zone, Christine waited in the silence. 'Mick, … I can't do this… please help me?' Her voice broke on a choking sob.

There was not a single sound from the audience. They seemed to be as stunned as Ben felt. He could feel the tension as they waited; could feel the pressure of eyes boring into the back of his head. With his heart doing its best to beat from his chest, he stood and approached the piano. 'How come you can ask other people to help you, but you can't ask me?' Even though he felt he was forcing the words they came out in a husky whisper. He coughed to clear the blockage in his throat as he stood beside her, slipped his arm out of its restraining sling then reached down to her hands, grasping them and then drawing her up from the stool.

'Ben?' The rest of her words were stifled when his mouth covered hers. It stayed there a long time, searching, seeking, giving, caressing. His lips moved to her eyes where he kissed away her tears before settling his lips back on her soft, warm mouth. An arm slipped behind her shoulders, another under her legs then she was airborne but held close.

Pausing in the open doorway, Ben turned, lifted his head and called out to the crowded room. 'Sorry folks, but I'm taking my woman home, where she belongs. Then I'm taking her to my bed, where she belongs and I'm not letting her go until she relents and agrees to marry me. If I'm lucky, she will be back tomorrow night to continue her concert. If not, then you know where she will be. The only way you are going to know which it is, is to be back tomorrow night.'

Turning his back on the stunned but smiling room of people he carried her down the stairs, through the foyer and out to his car, grinning at the loud cheering and yells of, 'Say yes,' that followed them all the way out.

During the drive home, every time Christine attempted to say anything, Ben reached over and planted a finger on her lips to hush her. 'Don't say a thing, Darling Heart. I'm still trying to absorb all your words. I especially like the first five and the last six. Now hush.'

Once home he shoved the door open with his hip. 'Now you can talk, Darling Heart, because right now is the time to say no'

'Say no to what, Ben?' she whispered back but wouldn't look up.

'Say no to me opening the door to Sexy Ben's Room, say no to me seducing you, say no to me making love to you. I'm not into raping women, sweetheart.' As he stood waiting with a hand on each side of her shoulders he fought the strong desire to kiss her senseless. She had to want him as much as he wanted her.

She finally lifted her eyes. The damn wench was grinning. 'Ben, if I didn't want this, I would have said no back at the hotel. Yes, Ben, I love you. Yes Ben, tonight is the night your Christine will join you in Sexy Ben's Room.'

He stood back, more than surprised. 'You've been in my room,' he muttered as he tugged her close.

'Only the once. The morning I left, I didn't know you had gone and went searching for you when you didn't come out for breakfast. I felt your bed to see if you were all right and my hand found the labels. I cried my heart out on your bed because I had come to realise that I loved you, hurt you and lost you.'

Her mouth was silenced as Ben covered it with his, teasing her lips until he felt her complete submission. He slid his tongue inside and did to her mouth what he intended to do with the rest of her body. She melted against him as her arms reached around his neck, drawing him down closer, harder. He spread his hands out along her back and kicked the door shut.

www.ingramcontent.com/pod-product-compliance
Lightning Source LLC
Chambersburg PA
CBHW061010120726
47910CB00006B/1859